"Once we have a war there is only one thing to do. It must be won. For defeat brings worse things than any that can ever happen in war."

Ernest Hemingway

View the author's website at www.arsenex.com

Visit the author's Facebook page at www.facebook.com/stephenarseneault10

Follow on Twitter @SteveArseneault

Ask a question or leave a comment at comments@arsenex.com

Image on cover from www.RolfMohr.com

Copyright 2016-2019 Stephen Arseneault. All Rights Reserved.

All rights reserved. No part of this book may be used, reproduced or transmitted in any form or by any means, electronic or mechanical, including photocopying, recording, or by any information storage or retrieval system, without the written permission of the publisher, except where permitted by law, or in the case of brief quotations embodied in critical articles and reviews.

This book is a work of fiction. Names, characters, businesses, organizations, places, events, and incidents either are the product of the author's imagination or are used fictitiously. Any resemblance to actual persons, living or dead, events, or locales is entirely coincidental.

Novels written by Stephen Arseneault

SODIUM Series (six novels)

Butchered, abandoned.

Dissected like lab rats.

Alien machines are stalking Humans.

Man is suddenly no longer alone in the universe. Advanced enemies plague our very existence. We have to muster all our strength, determination, and courage if we are to survive. And if those can be managed, there is a galaxy to be conquered.

This six-book saga takes Man from his first encounter with aliens back in 1957, all the way to a fight for our all-out survival in the future. If you love tales written in the style of the science fiction masters, prepare yourself for full immersion in this fantastic adventure!

AMP Series (eight novels)

In a distant galaxy, Humans are on the run.

An insane species follows.

They will not stop... ever.

Trapped on an immense station with limited resources, our only option has been to flee. Years of peace are over. War is again coming to the Grid.

This time however, it's time to stand and fight.

This exciting eight-book series chronicles the struggles of Don Grange, a simple package deliveryman, who is thrust into an unimaginable role in the fight against our enemies. Can we win peace and freedom after a thousand years of war?

Continuing as a legacy of the SODIUM series, the story picks up a thousand years into the future. Don't just sit at home scratching your head about what to do because you are bored, go on a mental rampage, travel the stars, take a risk and dive head-first into this non-stop-action saga!

OMEGA Series (eight novels)

The Alliance is crumbling.

There are rumors of war in Andromeda.

Whole colonies are being conscripted to fight.

When corruption, politics, and war threaten to throw the allied galaxies into chaos, Inspection Detective Knog Beutcher gets caught in the middle. Espionage, intrigue, political assassinations, rebellions and full-on revolutions, they are all coming to Knog Beutcher's world.

Told from the unique perspective of an alien, this thrilling eight book series is cast a thousand years into the future beyond the exciting AMP series. Prepare to be reading until the wee hours!

HADRON Series (eight novels)

Billions die.

Life on Earth is shaken to its core.

We can be our own worst enemy.

After scientists using the Large Hadron Collider discover dark matter, the world is plunged into chaos.

Massive waves of electromagnetic interference take out all grid power and forms of communication the world over. Cities go dark, food and clean-water supplies are quickly used up. Marauders rule the highways. One group of citizens takes a stand. Can they make a difference?

A benevolent species will arrive in their spaceships to rescue the Human race from themselves. Only, are they really so benevolent? Our little corner of the Milky Way may be a very hostile place.

This eight book adventure begins as a modern day, Human survival story and then morphs into an all out fight for rule of our section of the Milky Way. If you love reading apocalypse-turned-science-fiction, and reading with your mouth agape, this saga was made for you!

ARMS Series (eight novels)

Selling arms to the outer colonies.

A sweet deal.

Unless you're being used to threaten the peace.

Genetically engineered and trained for war, Harris Gruberg and Tawnish Freely, former Biomarines with the Domicile Defense Force, have been out of work since the centuries-old war with New Earth came to an end two years prior. They lack the knowledge and experience needed to live among a civilian population.

Getting involved in the illegal arms trade offers the promise of working with something they know-- weapons. When the profits from their efforts run wild, they soon find out acquiring wealth so easily comes at a high cost. Will their mistakes bring a return of the Great War? Or is what's coming far worse?

If you enjoy fighting the good fight, protecting the people and what you love, the ARMS saga will keep you ripping through pages until your fingers bleed!

FREEDOM Series (six novels)

Addicted.

Enslaved to the Empire for 500 generations.

We are bought, sold, traded, and hunted for sport, our value only measured in credits.

But a mysterious virus is sweeping through our populations, giving immunity to the addiction and making us aware of our condition. We feel the call of freedom. Our masters feel different.

If you love being dependent, confined, trapped in a great story, this unique six book saga will become an addiction of your own!

QUANTUM Series (four novels)

A lifetime lived in under a minute...
Impossible, everyone thought.
Until now.

An Opamari scientist has found a way. By cloning a subject and sending the clone back in time, the subject can live the clone's entire life in less than a minute of sleep.

But all actions have consequences. Playing with the past can be disastrous for the present.

When a ruthless tycoon steals the technology, the future of the galaxy is at risk. Will humans, after being slaughtered by the Opamari more than 50,000 years before, be resurrected by the tycoon's actions?

If you love science fiction intertwined with time travel and historical fiction, the Quantum saga will keep you burning through the pages late into the night!

Find them all at www.arsenex.com

HADRON
(Vol. 6)
Chaos

Chapter 1

Jenny rolled over on the blanket. "You've got moss all over your back."

Mace lay on his belly, hands up under his chin, eyes gazing at the rushing stream that roiled and dove over round rocks on its way down the mountain.

"Moss doesn't grow on a rolling stone."

Jenny rolled him over, pulling herself over atop him for a kiss. Several long, joyous seconds of passion were interrupted by the chime of a comm device.

Jenny sighed as she reached for it. "It's Johnny this time."

"Don't answer it."

Jenny smiled. "He looks concerned."

Mace let out a deep breath before sitting up and gesturing. "Hand it to me."

Johnny's image floated over the device. "Sorry to disturb the party, but Jasper says he's been trying to reach you for twenty minutes."

"What's he need?"

"There's been activity at the Karthian rift."

"What kind of activity?"

Johnny chuckled. "Well, I would suppose it's the bad kind. He didn't say, but he looked unhappy."

Mace nodded. "Thanks. I'll comm him."

Jane stuck her head around Johnny and grinned. "Hey, Jenny."

Jenny smiled. "Hey, Jane."

Mace closed the comm.

Jenny laughed. "They are the nosiest people."

2

Mace placed a comm to the *Rogers*.

A new face answered. "Lieutenant French. How can I assist, Mr. Hardy?"

"What happened to Clive?"

The lieutenant answered, "Clive decided to move to London, sir. I'm his replacement."

Mace stood. "When did that happen? Oh never mind. I need you to open a wormhole comm to King Collins for me."

The lieutenant replied, "He's been trying to contact you for a while now, sir."

Mace nodded. "So I hear. And please stop calling me 'sir.' Mace or Mr. Hardy is fine."

The lieutenant smiled. "Yes, Mr. Hardy. Comm is coming through now."

An image of Jasper Collins in his black battlesuit hovered in the air as Jenny brushed moss from Mace's back.

"Trouble at the rift?"

Jasper scowled. "It's those dumbass Union members. They've been busy building cruisers and nuke ships. My spies were watching, but they somehow missed the numbers they were putting together. A fleet of fifteen hundred ships just showed up at the rift. We think they're waiting for several hundred more, after which they plan to attack."

Mace winced. "In those cruisers? They'll get slaughtered."

Jasper nodded. "Exactly. I've attempted to hail their command ships, but they aren't returning my calls."

"Well, if they go in and get their asses kicked, it shouldn't affect us."

Jasper shook his head. "Not necessarily true. If the Karthians have an overwhelming victory, they might think they have a clear shot at the colonies over here. This could bring them through before I have my new fleet at any kind of decent strength."

"How's the build-up coming?"

"We'll be at sixty-eight by the end of this week. Fifty-six have been flight tested and crewed. I think they can hold their own against the Karthian ships, but not against that station and whatever that green energy wave is."

Mace said, "Well, at least they have to leave that station on the other side."

Jasper scowled. "I'm just concerned they'll figure out how to package that in something smaller that will fit through there."

"Well, we haven't seen any evidence of that yet. What exactly would you like me to do about the situation?"

Jasper leaned his head to one side. "I don't know, maybe get your fanny in gear and come out to support us? I know you're busy with the little lady and all, but I think this needs your attention."

"Fine. I'll assemble a crew and we'll head your way. You want us to meet you there or at the rift?"

"I'm at the rift. Come here directly when you're ready."

"Got it. Will probably need a few hours to call everyone in."

Jasper leaned toward the comm camera. "Do it fast. We may not have a few hours."

The comms went out to the crew of the *Rogers*. Liam Hobbs was the last to arrive, having to come by skybus from the community center in London. Mace sat in his command chair on the bridge as his senior staff took to their consoles or stood waiting.

"It seems the old Galactic Union members have assembled a sizable fleet. They're taking up position at the Karthian rift, massing for an invasion. Our problem is we don't think they will win. And with the resounding beating that will be coming their way, Jasper and I presume the Karthians may decide to come through the rift, believing they now hold the upper hand.

"The Targarians have just over five hundred ships now, including about sixty of the Collins class—not nearly as much as we want. So what are we doing with the *Rogers*, you ask? We're going to offer whatever assistance we can if the Karthians do decide to come through. If we muster enough ships, we might just dissuade them from following up with an invasion of our space.

"So I hope you've all said goodbye to your spouses and children. This could be a false alarm, or it could be all-out fighting for our survival... again."

The members of the second and third shifts left the bridge.

Mace looked around. "Good to see you all here. Wish it was under better circumstances. I hope you all remember how to work those stations. I know it's been several months for a number of you."

Hans replied, "We'll do our best, Mr. Hardy. Our lives count on it too."

Mace gave a nod. "Mr. Hobbs, jump us to the rift. Mr. Mallot, prepare for a full scan. Mr. Mueller, make sure all weapons are charged and ready to fire."

Johnny chuckled. "What about me?"

"I don't know... make sure you're ready to talk?"

Johnny grinned. "Always ready to talk."

Seconds later, the *Rogers* moved into the area of the rift. A ten minute ride had them within comm range of the *Organ Cave*.

Mace asked, "Anything different since we talked?"

Jasper shook his head. "They haven't moved. Another two hundred ships have joined up."

"Wait. I thought you took all their wormhole generators."

Jasper sighed. "I did. Looks as though someone held out. Wouldn't be the first time with this lot."

"Any scans through the rift?"

Jasper nodded. "Twelve hundred ships at least, from what we can detect."

"If they have that many ships at the ready, the Union members might have just done us a favor."

"How so?"

Mace stroked his goatee. "We now know they have at least that. They could invade with that force alone and I'm not sure we could stop them."

Jasper turned to one of his aides. "Another two hundred ships are on their way in. The others look to be moving into a formation for attack."

Johnny shook his head. "Suicide. They think they're gonna march that column right past that station? Fat chance."

Jane came onto the bridge. "When's this show getting started?"

Mace asked, "You got a cake in the oven or what?"

Jane laughed. "I might. Just wanted to report the reactors are all working at optimum. No maintenance issues to report, which is a first. As far as power goes, this ship is as ready as it could be."

Jenny came over the comm. "Drives all at 100 percent."

"Sensors are all reporting," said Humphrey. "No anomalies."

Hans finished the report. "Storage wells are all charged and circuits functional."

Mace drew a deep breath. "I just want to say that no ship could have a finer crew. And no crew could have a finer ship. If we do go into action, I'm glad you are all on my team."

Johnny said, "So you want to take us down with you when you go, is that what you're saying?"

Mace nodded as he smiled. "Well, some of you."

Jasper said, "Another hundred ships coming in. This gives them two thousand even. Hmm."

"What is it?"

"These latest ships, they don't look like any of the others. I've never seen any like them."

Humphrey pushed a visual image to the main display.

Johnny said, "What do you think that dome on the front is?"

Mace shook his head. "Haven't a clue. Jeff? Opinion?"

Jeff shrugged. "Looks like a big radar dome. Although I don't know what purpose that would serve."

Humphrey said, "The sensors are reporting strange energy readings, Mr. Hardy. It's like nothing I've seen."

Humphrey passed another image to the main display. "This is the energy profile for the space surrounding one of those ships. The gravity drives and the remainder of the ship look normal, but that dome is putting out some serious spikes."

Jeff nodded. "Some type of shield?"

Jasper said, "They're moving to the front of that column. This may be it."

Jasper turned to one of his officers. "Admiral Bellok, pass word for all ships to be ready. If anything Karthian comes through that rift, I want it taken out. If the Union pukes want to kill themselves they are welcome. We don't want the Karthians thinking we are weakened in any way, so we'll take up the fight on this side."

Humphrey said, "The dome ships are in position. The entire column is moving toward the rift. First ships will be passing through in approximately three minutes."

Gnaga came onto the bridge. "I believe I know what that is."

"Tell us," said Mace.

Gnaga zoomed the display in on one of the domes. "I had heard rumors of experiments with dark matter. To date, its only use was to be combined with gatrellium during the formation of wormholes, or in the amplifier plates of gravity drives. Since experimentation other than at Galactic Union labs was prohibited, our scientists conducted all of their work using theoretical properties and formulas. One such theory promised an energy reflector. This may be a result of that."

"Aren't the dampening fields energy reflectors?"

Gnaga shook his head. "Not at all. The inertial dampening field absorbs energy, dissipating it across the entirety of the field. If this is what I believe it to be, energy weapons—including that green monstrosity coming from the Karthian station—would be reflected back at the source."

Johnny smiled. "Now this I wanna see."

As the Union fleet approached the rift, several dozen plasma rounds shot through the opening. Bright, fierce looking bolts of lightning shot out from the domes as the plasma made contact. With part of the plasma energy annihilated, the remainder returned toward the firing ships. Without the gravitational containment that held the plasma in a tight sphere, electricity sloughed away from the receding plasma rounds, reducing their power and rendering them inert.

Johnny raised an eyebrow. "That is one spectacular lightshow."

Seconds later, the plasma rounds began to come through in a steady stream. All were reflected, and the heavens were lit with a continuous show of lightning flashes as the Union ships moved forward, the lightning itself seemingly traveling toward the edges of the rift.

As the first of the domed ships reached the opening, the green energy wave from the Karthian station ripped into the front ships. The green energy turned into bright orange lighting as the majority of the wave was reflected back. Two dozen Karthian cruisers moved forward, holding their weapons fire as they raced toward the domed ships. Hundreds of Union ships opened up at once, first overwhelming the Karthians' shields and then shredding their hulls. The attacking Karthian ships were obliterated before firing a shot.

Johnny said, "This is going a bit differently than I imagined."

Mace replied, "Give it time. The Karthians just have to figure out a way past those domes."

Fifty Karthian cruisers and a dozen dreadnoughts moved into the path of the oncoming column. A thousand small fighter craft were released at once. A gray cloud of fighters moved to intercept the Union vessels. Hundreds of Union ships fired at once, decimating the fighter assault but failing to slow it.

The fighters reached the Union column just as the second and third row of ships began passing through the rift. The fighters circled in and around the domed ships, attacking at will. Most of a minute passed before the first of the domed ships exploded. Then another set of Karthian ships advanced, releasing another tranche of the small fighter craft. Energy bolts and impact flashes burned brighter than the nearest star as the column pushed forward through the rift.

Jasper came over the comm. "No fireworks display I've ever seen could do this justice. Watching this is both thrilling and terrifying."

As the column reached a third of the way through, the Union cruisers following the domes dispersed, engaging the enemy fully. Karthian and Union ships circled each other in a relentless exchange of plasma and laser fire. Because of the close interaction, the great green energy weapon of the Karthians could not be used.

Humphrey said, "I'm detecting shuttle launches, Mr. Hardy. It seems they've adopted our boarding party technique. I count seventy-five Karthian ships already with shuttles attached."

Mace sat in awe with his mouth open. "I almost want to join in, but I have a bad feeling about what's coming. The Karthians have yet to commit all their ships."

Jasper said, "Hang tight. We're moving in for a closer look."

"I wouldn't advise that."

Jasper smiled. "Well, you aren't the King, so you don't get the final decision."

The *Organ Cave* zipped away, closing rapidly on the tail end of the Union column. Just on the other side, half the known Karthian fleet were fighting for their lives. As Jasper and his flagship flew closer, the Karthian station blasted out a green energy wave. The bright blue Collins class vessel attempted to evade but was unsuccessful. The energy wave impacted the dampening field, frying the transducers and blistering their gatrellium skin.

"Crap," said Jasper. "Admiral! Take us home!"

Mace yelled, "Mr. Hobbs! Take us in! Draw fire from that weapon! They can't take another hit!"

The *Rogers* shot forward as the *Organ Cave* came back their way.

Jasper said, "Mace, we've got a problem. Our wormhole generator took damage. We can't jump... or turn... or accelerate of decelerate. Our inertial dampening field is non-existent."

Mace said, "Just keep coming. Mr. Hobbs, slip us in behind them and open a wormhole to Divinia."

Jeff winced. "What about the green wave?"

"If it comes, we'll just have to suck it up. Have everyone move in from the outer compartments."

Jeff nodded. "On it."

"Mr. Hobbs, what's our ETA?"

Liam replied, "Twenty seconds."

Humphrey yelled, "Detecting an energy buildup! That station is about to fire!"

Mace squeezed the armrest of his command chair. "Come on! Get us there!"

An eternity seemingly passed as the ships closed. A bright green ball of energy blasted from the Karthian station on the other side of the rift. The *Rogers* spun, slowing at first, and then matching and surpassing the speed of the *Organ Cave*.

Mace yelled, "Open a wormhole to Divinia! Now!"

The generator engaged. A tiny tear in space-time opened. The Targarian flagship slipped through just as the green wave caught up to the *Rogers*. The hull jerked and rumbled, displays flashed and sparked. Power flashed on and off before restarting. The wave dissipated as it moved across the retreating ship.

Humphrey said, "We have damage reports coming in... and casualties. Gravity drives are at 30 percent. Sixty percent of our reactors are showing instabilities and are shutting down. Dampening field has held, but the wormhole generator is gone."

Mace grimaced. "Injuries? Casualties?"

"Two moderate injuries, the rest minor. Oh, and we're out of range of that weapon."

A new Targarian ship jumped into space near the *Rogers*.

Johnny grinned. "It's Jasper on the comm. He's already made a transfer to another ship."

Jasper said, "OK, the *Cave* is headed for the repair docks. I suggest you take the *Rogers* there as well. I have crews waiting. And thanks for saving my ass back there."

Mace nodded. "Open a portal for us. Ours is dead."

"You'll find a new Collins when you get there if you want to come back. Those repairs are gonna take a while."

A micro-wormhole was opened to Divinia and the *Rogers* slipped through. After they had passed, the wormhole was kept open for a sensor feed from Jasper's new ship.

The battle at the rift raged on. The Union ships appeared to be dominating. Karthian ships were being destroyed or leaving the field of battle in tatters. Because of the close proximity of the ships, the massive Karthian station remained out of the fight. Again the Karthian threat was being thwarted.

Chapter 2

The *Rogers* moved into a repair dock. The crew, excluding those who were injured, transferred to a new ship. The *Ravix* was the latest to receive a commission in the Targarian fleet. The controls on each of the new Collins class vessels were switchable between Targarian and English. The changeover was made and the crew familiarized with the new stations.

Humphrey commented, "The layout is quite similar."

Mace replied, "Check every sensor in every configuration. That goes for each of you. Spend as much time as you can learning your stations fully. It's likely we'll find ourselves without time if we join the fight like I think we will. The Karthians have yet to fully commit."

A jump back to the Karthian rift was made.

Jasper was waiting with the rest of his fleet aboard his new command ship, the *Robert E. Lee*. "I can't say I believe this. The Karthians are getting trounced. They've lost a third of their ships, and that station has been taken out of the fight. I don't understand. They have to have more ships than that. Why aren't they using them?"

"War is hard to predict. More than one battlefield commander has made an error that cost his side a war. Just look at WWII when Japan attacked Pearl Harbor. Had they continued in with troops, they could have taken the islands, completely changing the map of the war in the Pacific. Or Hitler's invasion of Russia. Had he stayed in Europe until he had it consolidated, he could have taken the British Navy out of the fight using his air force, leading to an invasion. Instead he spread himself too thin to fight on both fronts. History is littered with examples."

Jasper laughed. "You don't need to explain it to me. I was actually alive back then."

Humphrey said, "Mr. Hardy, a number of those shield ships are forming up. It looks as though that station is the target."

Jasper added, "They take down that station and I might just commit to this fight."

The Humans and Targarians watched for hours as the Karthian fleet was cut in half. The Union had lost three hundred ships to the six hundred of the Karthians. The shield ships continued to frustrate the fight by positioning themselves between the great station and the bulk of the fleet. The Karthian defense of the rift was changing for the worst.

Humphrey said, "Mr. Hardy, we have ships moving toward the station."

Fifty of the dome-fronted ships were followed by two hundred Union cruisers. They closed on the Karthian station and began and all-out assault. Defensive guns on the station were taken out and boarding parties put into use. Within minutes of the first assault ship attaching itself to the station's hull, thousands of Union troops were storming aboard. The great green energy weapon was quickly taken offline.

Jasper said, "Give me your thoughts on joining in."

Mace replied, "I'm not convinced the Karthians aren't playing some game, although it sure looks like they are getting their asses kicked."

Humphrey said, "Mr. Hardy, I show another stream of Union ships jumping in. Hundreds of ships. And I just picked up two cruisers coming back through the rift. Sir, they're flying Stark banners!"

Mace stood from his chair. "Stark? Are you sure?"

Humphrey nodded. "Undeniable. The new Union ship count has surpassed five hundred."

Mace shook his head. "Where are they getting these ships from?"

"My people had no indication that any such force existed," said Jasper.

Johnny hailed Stark's command ship.

The hail was accepted. "This is Captain Remington. Mr. Hardy, the King would like a word with you, but will not be available for another fifteen minutes. He asks for your patience."

Mace nodded. "Sure."

The comm closed. The two Stark cruisers joined with the newly arriving Union ships. The banner of Stark's command cruiser was transferred to one of the newer vessels. After a minute, a comm came through for Mace Hardy.

A dark silhouette sat in front of a back-lit screen. "Mr. Hardy, I'd like to thank you for maintaining my kingdom in my absence. I've been keeping abreast of your accomplishments. Impressive, I might add."

"Earth is a free planet, Stark. You have no kingdom."

The silhouette leaned forward. "Oh, I beg to differ with you, Mr. Hardy. If you recall, you did leave my people in charge of your new government. I should thank you for making the transition back to my kingdom so easy."

"There is no transition, Stark. The people are forming an elected body at each of the community centers and each of those will be sending representatives to a new congress."

"Yes. I do like the idea of the congress. It keeps the people involved with settling all the petty matters pertaining to governance, allowing my teams to focus on the items of critical importance. As we speak, my return is being welcomed on Earth. The battle raging here before us is being broadcast back home. I have given several prepared speeches and my media contacts ensure me they are being warmly received. The people of Earth are in need of strong leadership, Mr. Hardy. And I have returned to give it to them."

Mace scowled. "The people don't trust the Union or you anymore. Besides, other than trade, it's been abandoned and shut down. This show of force here, while impressive, won't be enough to convince the people to back you again."

Stark stood, his silhouette slowly pacing back and forth. "The people are watching this battle unfold with both fascination and pride. Their king is winning handily against the only threat they face. The Karthian menace will soon be gone. And with them any outside threat to the former members of the Union. A union by the way, which still fully exists. Excluding Mr. Collins, of course. But that will change soon enough."

"How is it you're still alive?"

Stark stopped. "We chased the Karthians through the rift. Unfortunately, we weren't able to come back once the *Moalmoth* was parked there, the *Moalmoth* being the station we are currently taking control of. Once on the other side we were able to capture several high-ranking officials. I've been working with them to cause a deep divide in the Karthian worlds. I convinced the Karthian politicians to keep nearly three quarters of their fleet out of this fight."

Mace shook his head. "That doesn't make sense. Why would they do that? And why wouldn't you just have one of your Muhathas open a wormhole for you?"

Stark returned to his chair. "The answer to your first question is simple: economics. I promised an end to the war between our peoples and a robust trade alliance with them. You see, as it turns out, the Karthians are weary of this war and its costs. They have another, bigger, threat on one of their far frontiers. Even though the Galactic Union members were the ones who started this war, the individuals I have been dealing with were willing to sacrifice this fleet to get the economic backing they require to fight on their other front."

"Wait. I thought the Karthians were the invaders."

"The Sarkesians and the Quelli discovered the rift some time ago. They sent through fleets, destroying several Karthian outposts and even a small colony. The Karthians sought vengeance by establishing colonies on this side of the rift, which my men and I wiped out. They followed with that massive attack on Harkoza. We were lucky to have pushed them back. They had victory in hand had they continued to press forward. I suppose I should thank Mr. Collins for holding back the Targarians from that fight. I believe that kept the Karthians guessing as to when they were going to commit. Anyway, they retreated and here we are."

Mace gestured toward a display. "This fight, why would they sacrifice a quarter of their fleet and that station?"

Stark sighed. "Because of the eternal game of power we all love so much to play. That fleet, and the station in particular, are controlled by their political rivals. You see, the fleet gets destroyed and our allies move in for a quick peace deal, which has tremendous potential for economic benefit. It also allows them to focus their energies on the far front. It's all a quite convoluted mess of backroom negotiations, which is something my staff and I seem to be quite good at."

"So you somehow managed a deal with the Karthians. What I don't get is how you maintained ties with the Union."

Stark leaned back in his chair, crossing one leg over the other. "Simple, really. Before passing through the rift, I gave coordinates for a point on the other side where I could be contacted, or brought home if need be. Since reaching that location, we've been in near constant contact with the Union members—excluding the Targarians, for obvious reasons."

Mace scowled. "So you're telling me you've been able to control everything, including people, from somewhere on the other side of the rift? I don't see how that's possible. Why would the Union follow your orders?"

Stark reached up, rubbing his temples. "You still lack an understanding of my abilities, Mr. Hardy. I am a power broker. I am good at convincing people to act according to my will. I lay out the potential benefits with words and they joyously follow along. I believe you would call it a gift."

"I'd call it a con. Tell me, why shouldn't we take down your fleet right now?"

Stark tilted his head to one side. "Let's contemplate that scenario for a moment. Let's say you attack and defeat my force here, including those on the other side of the rift. Doubtful, but let's play along. You would undoubtedly lose a large portion of your fleet in the process. Now... what do you think would happen to the Karthian fleets that remain? With such a weak front here, would they attack? The answer is yes, and eagerly so. You see, Mr. Hardy, you play a weak hand, a hand with which you don't have the ability to bluff."

Mace scowled. "So you expect us to just roll over and give up?"

"On the contrary," Stark replied. "I expect you and the Targarians to continue to be a force to be reckoned with. You see, it is partially your efforts that allow me to wield power with the Union. You are a plague on their existence. I offer control of that plague. It is not me that you should fear, Mr. Hardy. It's the other Union members. They view you as a nuisance, whereas I view you as a tool, sometimes to be used as a hammer, and at other times as a spoon to feed the masses."

Mace said, "You do realize we have this entire conversation recorded, right?"

Stark nodded. "And I expect you will pass it around to all those concerned, only further solidifying my position. You see, Mr. Hardy, I am one species away from having the remaining Union members uniting behind me as their king. I promise a rebound in both economic activity and military strength. And with the Karthian threat removed, the Galactic Union will once again be free to pursue expansion... which they are all again longing to do."

Mace turned. "Johnny, open a comm back to Earth. Ask Tres if anything is on the news feeds back there." He regarded the silhouette on the screen and betrayed no expression of his own.

"Well, Mr. Stark, it seems you have it all figured out. So what happens when the Union defeats the Karthians here? They sign a deal, and then decide to space their newly-proclaimed king?"

Stark moaned. "Oh, Mr. Hardy, do you think I am not three steps ahead of them? The deal with the Karthians is through me and me alone. They want nothing to do with the Union at this point. The trade deals will all be routed through Earth. This is one of the pillars of my economic foundation for man, the other being trade between the Union members themselves. Again, all routed through Earth... for a small transaction tax of course.

"And then there is the exploration of new territories and conquering of new species. You see, there will no longer be any bickering over who gets what new territory. All new territories will belong to the Stark Kingdom, with royalties paid to member species."

"And the founders are going to go for that? I thought all the species were equals now."

"They are equal with regards to rights under the kingdom laws. However, as part of the negotiated freedoms, the founders each received an extra percentage share. Founders, of whom there are now five members, will receive a 4 percent royalty on kingdom profits. Sixteen members will receive a 3 percent option. And fledgling members, those who are weak or new, will receive a 2 percent share. There are six of those."

Mace lifted an eyebrow. "And what about the Targarians and their three affiliates?"

"I'm afraid they will be left out of all trade and security deals. Offers will be extended to them to join with us. It will be their choice to do so or to remain independent."

Mace did the quick math in his head. "That takes up 80 percent of the royalties. Does that leave you with 20 percent?"

Stark shook his head. "No. That leaves Earth with 20 percent."

Mace sighed. "And what about expenses? I'm sure there will be some cost associated with determining kingdom profits. Who will be keeping track of those?"

Stark crossed his arms. "That would be Earth. You see, Mr. Hardy, an almost uncanny thing happened during the Great Starvation, as it's being called. An unusually high percentage of the accountants survived. No one knows why, although there is speculation they may have been better at planning for their survival. Whatever the cause, we will have an army of accountants to tabulate kingdom income and costs as they relate to this whole arrangement. These will be well-paying jobs with bonuses going out for both efficiency and accuracy."

"You've planned this out that far?"

"And well beyond. Oh, and I almost forgot: I would like to thank you for setting up the defense perimeter around Earth. My teams have floated many a rumor out among the Union members as to its lethality. Let's just say the founders have no interest in invading Earth space."

Stark's silhouette turned to his right as he received a message. "Mr. Hardy, you will have to excuse me. It seems the Karthian station is close to falling. I will be moving my final force in for the surrender."

Stark stood and then stopped. "Isn't it exciting when a plan comes to fruition? True, this is only the first of many parts. However, it has been accomplished with fewer complications than anticipated."

The comm closed as Stark walked out of the camera view.

Johnny said, "Jasper's been hailing you almost nonstop."

Mace nodded. "Accept. He's gotta know what just went down."

Jasper said, "Not very friendly of you to keep me waiting."

Mace shook his head. "That was Stark. I'd have joined you in on the comm but he had no interest in me doing so. I have a load to tell you, and it's not especially good. I should come over."

A short ride on a shuttle had Mace standing on the deck in front of an irritated Jasper Collins. "He's managed to somehow take control of Earth... and all the Union members."

Jasper scowled. "Impossible."

Mace frowned. "Very possible. It seems he's been in contact with the other Union members since his disappearance. That whole fight with the Karthians... that's a coup of sorts. He managed to get three quarters of the Karthians to side with him against that fleet and that station. In return, the others get full control of their empire, get peace through the rift, and a committed trading partner with Earth. And Earth will be the new hub for the prior Galactic Union. All species will be members of the Stark Kingdom, and as such will receive a royalty cut of the kingdom's earnings."

"And why would Earth follow that lunatic again?"

"Earth will be the center of the universe as far as all the species we know are concerned, excluding the UF and Hoorka of course... and your people. He hit the Earth airwaves broadcasting this fight, which is coming to a victorious close. When it's all done, there will be a peace treaty and a trade accord between Earth and the Karthians. He gets rid of a major threat and promises great wealth for all mankind.

"I almost want to join him myself. He's uniting all the Union species behind him. Except the Collins Kingdom. I suspect all your Union trading partners will no longer be interested in any deals with the Targarians. And I would expect a lot of pressure to be applied toward your overthrow. After all, the Targarians and your other species will want to be a part of this new vast kingdom and all it has to offer."

Jasper shook his head. "They love me. They won't be leaving."

Mace crossed his arms. "They love strength. You've said so yourself. And who appears to be the strongest among us now? Stark is. He arranged that fight out there. He arranged the deal with the Karthians and the other Union members. And he managed to build a twenty-five hundred ship fleet right under our noses."

Jasper waved a hand. "We were sloppy. Won't happen again."

Mace sighed. "Won't happen again because we won't likely have a chance at control like what we had. I hate to say it, but he snaked us. And he's done it with a completeness that even I have to admire."

Jasper frowned. "You aren't serious about joining him, are you?"

Mace shrugged. "I tell you, it's tempting. I could go back now and possibly enjoy a long life with Jenny as Stark takes care of all the issues. Maybe I just become the ambassador to the UF. I don't know. There's a lot to think about. His reappearance is a huge change, one I'm not certain we can overcome. He seems to be holding all the cards."

Jasper banged his fist on his chair arm. "This is unacceptable. I have a mind to order my ships in there right now. That would throw a huge wrench in his works. Might even prevent the

Karthians from signing that final deal. It would certainly leave him weakened."

"And it would leave you dead. He has two thousand ships sitting there and you have five hundred. I can't say I like those odds."

Jasper replied, "We need to make contact with his Karthian contacts."

Mace laughed. "And how would you propose we do that?"

Jasper looked at his main display. "We charge through that rift and take that station. They have to have direct contact with their home fleet."

Mace winced. "Look, suppose you make it there, and suppose you can take control and make contact, why would they join you over him? What do you have to offer? Your sixteen colonies worth of trade as opposed to over a hundred with Stark? I don't see them taking that deal."

Jasper huffed. "They have to see Stark for the snake he is."

Mace shook his head. "They'll think the same of you trying to come in to make a deal at the last minute. No, I'd say our only option right now is to take a little time to think. You have all your ships and colonies. We need a plan of attack. And that plan has to have contingencies. If we just jump right into it here, there's no telling where it ends. Most likely with all our deaths."

Jasper slowly nodded. "You're right. Just the frustration talking."

Mace said, "You know, if you gave in and joined, you could still be king of the Targarians. The members of his kingdom will have a lot of local autonomy. His rules will mostly govern interactions between species, not within them."

Jasper gestured toward the shuttle bay. "You're right. Go on back to the *Ravix*. I need to calm down and think this through for a while."

Mace turned and stopped. "You sure you're OK?"

Jasper nodded. "Yep. Fine. I'll give you a comm if I come up with anything."

Chapter 3

Mace returned to the *Ravix*. After a short walk he found himself on the bridge. The senior members of his crew were all standing around.

Johnny said, "Well?"

Mace replied, "He's upset, as you would expect, but I think he's calmed down enough to give us a little time to think."

Johnny chuckled. "He had other immediate plans?"

"His first instinct was to attack Stark's ships. His second was to try to take that station so he could make contact with the Karthians who are making the deal with Stark... so he could talk them out of it."

"What's he have to offer?"

Mace shook his head. "That's what I was wondering. He has nothing they need or want. An alliance with Earth and the other Union species is a bigger prize. I hate to say it, but this really puts Jasper in a box. The others will stop all trade and cooperation with him. And Targarian territory sits right in the middle of all those species. I wouldn't doubt Stark is already working on his overthrow."

Liam asked, "What's this mean for us?"

Mace shrugged. "Not really sure at the moment. Stark doesn't appear to be interested in our comings and goings. That could always change. Frankly, I think we may still be alive because of his fascination with how we're able not only to survive but to get things done."

"Can we go home?" asked Johnny.

"So far as I know. He didn't give me any indication of having any animosity toward us. What I do know is that we might want to start making some contingency plans. If we stay on Earth, we're likely to be asked to give up the *Rogers,* or at a minimum to disarm her. And if we leave, the question becomes, where do we go? Canto? That's now under UF protection. Maybe to Divinia? Jasper would certainly welcome us. Whatever that decision is, it's only coming after we sit and have some deep discussions about it."

Humphrey said, "Mr. Hardy, the Targarian ships are starting to move."

"What?"

Humphrey Mallot pushed the sensor image to the main display. "His fleet is moving toward the rift."

Mace waved at Johnny. "Open a comm."

Seconds later Jasper's image was on screen. "You're welcome to join the Targarians in this fight against Stark."

Mace shook his head. "What are you doing? This is suicide."

Jasper scowled. "Hardly. It's attacking the city before they can fortify the walls. If we allow this alliance with the Karthians, Stark will have what he wants: full control of Earth and the Union members. And that would include my Targarians and you."

"You must at least have some initial plan."

Jasper nodded. "We're taking the initiative. I have twenty thousand assault Marines here with me. If we can take that station, we disrupt his alliance plans. And who knows, maybe we can get that weapon operational again and teach Stark a thing or two about messing with the wrong people."

Mace looked at the floor, shaking his head. "You know... I guess we had a good run, as good as could be expected given the circumstances. Obviously I won't be talking you out of this... so I might as well offer what help I can, short of getting us all killed."

The comm closed. A hail was sent to Stark.

"Mr. Hardy, I hope our friend is not pushing his luck. I respect him for what he accomplished, but I won't hesitate to put a stop to whatever he's up to."

"He was ranting about missing out on the action. Said something about wanting to take down some of those Karthian ships before you hogged all the glory."

Stark hesitated. "Hmm, I had not anticipated this. I expected a vigorous fight from him."

Mace took a deep breath. "Maybe he thinks this is the only way for him to maintain his kingdom. I expect you'll be giving a lot of autonomy to each of the species with regards to their local governance?"

Stark's silhouette nodded. "That is the initial plan, yes."

Stark turned and gave an order to an assistant. "Mr. Hardy, please inform your friend that we will be withdrawing our ships. The remainder of the Karthian fleet will be all his to destroy. Perhaps the Targarian issue will resolve itself."

"I'll let him know."

The comm closed and a new channel was opened to Jasper Collins.

Mace said, "I may have bought you some time. The Union ships should be disengaging from the fight. You might try to strike a deal with the Karthians. Try to convince them you're double-crossing Stark and with your help they can not only keep control of the station, but mend whatever divide they have with the other Karthians."

Jasper replied, "Already in the works. So far they are refusing my hails. That may change once I attack a Union ship. We know the domed ships reflect plasma and laser energy. And whatever that green energy wave is. I'd like to know what they do with a tight microwave beam."

Jasper gave the command before Mace could reply. The microwave cannon fired upon a Union dome ship, a three-second burst that ripped into the dome and the forward decks behind it, taking the shield offline.

The Karthians quickly accepted his hail.

Within minutes, two thirds of the Union shield ships were under fire. The Karthians turned their fight to the departing Union ships as Jasper's Collins class warships shredded the domed vessels. What had been a war of attrition was suddenly turned against the aggressors.

A hail came in from Stark. "Well played, Mr. Hardy. I didn't anticipate having to defend against that weapon. You do realize this puts you in a very bad position with the kingdom, don't you?"

"Believe me, I tried to talk him out of this. I don't think you gave him any acceptable options. He understands that any sub-kingdoms will be going away as you consolidate control. The member species might fuss about this change or that, but you'll slowly whittle away their power in the name of the new kingdom. Jasper was smart enough to see that coming. And like you, he's willing to risk his life to achieve his goals."

"And what exactly are his goals?"

Mace half frowned. "To keep the Targarian people free. And that goes for Earth as well."

Stark sighed. "Freedom is such a nebulous word. What I offer is freedom as well. It's called living in a society with others. The only freedom he seeks is freedom to make the rules."

Stark's silhouette turned and gave several orders as the comm channel closed. His reserve fleet began moving toward the rift.

Johnny stood from his console. "What do we do?"

Mace slowly shook his head. "What can we do? I don't know about the rest of you, but I'd rather not take this ship into the fight unless I have to. Mr. Hobbs, how confident are you with those controls? Could you skillfully handle this ship in a fight?"

Liam replied, "I can't say I would be comfortable. I'd do what I can, but am I confident that would be enough? On the *Rogers*, yes. On this vessel... I'm not sure."

Mace glanced over at Hans Mueller. "Mr. Mueller? Weapons?"

Hans replied, "I'll make do."

"Make do. That doesn't sound like anything I'd want to take into a fight."

Johnny asked, "Well?"

Mace shrugged. "I think we have to sit this one out."

Jane stood with her hands on her hips. "So we sit and watch, huh? Can't say I like that."

Mace nodded. "I can't say I like it either. I'm not interested in sending everyone here to their deaths. I tell you what: if that fight gets down to a few hundred ships per side, we can reconsider. Until then, we watch."

The Targarian ships held up well against Stark's cruisers. In return, the microwave cannons sliced crevasse after crevasse into the hulls to the Union fleet, allowing the Karthian ships to finish the job. It was quickly apparent the Karthians had taken whatever deal Jasper had offered. Forty transports were soon latched onto the hull of the station, with troops storming aboard. Nearly three hours had passed before word came of Union troops on the station beginning to surrender. It was an outcome that Stark could not have planned for.

A comm came in for Mace. "Things not going according to plan?"

Stark replied, "I don't think your friend realizes how dangerous this move is. There is still time for an agreement between us."

Mace laughed. "An agreement? You mean like the one where you try to subvert his species and at the same time cut off all his trade with the other empires? Seems to me *you* need to make an adjustment."

Stark nodded. "Perhaps. What would you have as a suggestion? What would convince Mr. Collins to stand down?"

Mace stood and began to pace. "Well, you renouncing your claim to an Earth throne, but I don't think you're willing to entertain that idea. Next would be a treaty signed with King Collins and his Targarians that says neither you nor any of the other Union members will meddle in Targarian affairs. And that would include having any trade biases. His species would be full members in any of your agreements, giving them royalty shares, except in his mind you have no right to make laws governing everyone. Again, I don't think you would be willing to share in those responsibilities, therefore making my suggestions non-starters."

Stark took a deep breath. "What if I were to buy him out? A full 4 percent royalty to Jasper Collins himself? As well as admitting the Targarians and others into my kingdom. I would make him personally immune to all kingdom laws."

Mace laughed. "He wouldn't want any part of that deal. He's turning ninety this year. He doesn't think he'll be around all that long. So his legacy would be what he did for the Targarians that had lasting effect. And I'm not talking monetarily, I'm talking freedom. That's the one thing money can't fully buy. You may be free temporarily, but eventually someone will see to it that you aren't."

Humphrey said, "The Targarians now control two thirds of that station. His fleet is taking a beating, but dishing one out also. Out of the King's fleet, four hundred twenty were fighting ships. That number is about to fall under three hundred."

Mace asked, "And Stark's people?"

Stark replied, "I've lost nine hundred ships. Please, Mr. Hardy, I beg you for all humanity's sake, talk the man down from this fight. We are close to the tipping point where we will not be able to defend against the other Karthians should they join this fight."

Mace shook his head. "Nothing I can say to Mr. Collins is going to change his mind. You'll have to come up with something on your own."

As Mace and the crew of the *Ravix* watched, Stark ordered fifty transports carrying twenty five thousand Dellus Marines into the fight for the station. Protected by a column of Union cruisers, the Union Marines docked and boarded the station, opening a five-deck counteroffensive to the advances of the Targarians. The initial advance recaptured the five decks, but then lost a fierce battle while attempting to move up onto a new section. The fighting raged for hours before the Targarians once again gained the upper hand. Jasper Collins had come aboard personally to lead his troops.

The fighting in the heavens continued to go the Karthians' way. After nine hours of maneuvers, offensives, and defensive stands, the twenty-five-hundred ship Stark-Union force had been cut in half. The Karthian-Collins warships numbered nine hundred, but a two to one kill ratio was quickly developing. Malcolm Stark again pleaded his case and was again denied an intervention.

After repeated attempts, Jasper responded to a hail. "What is it? I'm in the middle of a war here."

Mace said, "Stark is asking that I get you to talk to him."

"He's got nothing to say that I want to hear. Give me another five hours and this station will be fully under my control. Another dozen and those Union ships will all be toast."

Mace asked, "What will the cost be to your fleet?"

As Jasper charged down a hallway he stopped, knelt and fired. "My team estimates two thirds will no longer be battle-worthy. I've started ordering those ships that are critical to jump or to be jumped back to the repair docks. I've also ordered my eight Collins ships still in flight testing to be moved forward. I don't anticipate any problems with that maneuver. Before this day is done, Malcolm Stark will be in retreat."

"You just charge ahead and don't give up, do you?"

Jasper fired off two rounds from his plasma rifle. "I gave up on things my whole life because I was satisfied with the status quo. Now that I'm ancient, I can't see giving up on anything. I don't have time to revisit it later. Stark tried to make his grand comeback and it's gonna fail. I'll see to that."

The fighting continued. The Union troops on the station were down to fifteen hundred remaining out of more than thirty thousand committed. The Targarian ratios weren't much better. Jasper commanded four thousand, the Karthian numbers were in the low hundreds.

The Union ships had fallen to less than five hundred, while the Targarians had dropped to ninety and the Karthians to three hundred. The Collins class vessels were dominating the fight, with fifty-two out of the original sixty still giving it their all.

Johnny said, "Remember your comment about possibly joining the fight when the sides had evened out? You still considering that?"

Humphrey cut in. "Mr. Hardy, I've been tracking Mr. Stark's flagship during the fight. It just docked with that station. He's going aboard and I believe his ship has a large contingent of Humans. Mr. Collins may be in for a bad turn."

Johnny asked, "Do we commit?"

Mace took a deep breath. "Those are fellow Humans. I don't want to be fighting our own, even if they are working for Stark. Open a comm to Jasper."

Mace said, "Stark has just boarded the station. He's gonna have a decent sized crew of Humans with him."

Jasper scowled. "Let them come. My boys can take it."

Johnny stepped into camera view. "Listen, these are hardened Human fighters. Real Marines. You might have several hundred Mace Hardys coming your way. Might be time to reconsider your options."

A comm came in from Stark. "Put me on a three-way. I need to talk with him."

Mace nodded to Johnny. "Make it happen."

A split screen showed on the main display. King Jasper Collins stood at a hallway corner with his troops surrounding him. King Malcolm Stark followed his fighters as they blazed a path deep into the Targarian positions.

"Mr. Collins, we should end this insanity. You are putting us all in jeopardy."

Jasper replied, "How you figure? You're the one who started all this with your attempted power grab."

Stark's voice came over a comm with no video. "We don't have time to waste here, Mr. Collins. I will back away from this station and the fighting outside if you finish off the Karthians. Believe me when I tell you the other Karthians will join in if they get word of our weakness. We don't have the ships to defeat their fleet. You're risking all of our lives with this move.

Stop now and take full possession of this station. If the Karthians are allowed to retain it, it will be used against us."

Jasper Collins scowled directly into his arm pad camera. "Look, Stark, I don't trust you or any word that comes out of your mouth. I have assurances from the Karthian commander here that he will provide whatever assistance I need to crush you. I even asked him about this station and he said I could keep it. I plan on using it to keep this rift blocked off."

Stark replied, "If the Karthians pledged that station to you the weapon aboard her must no longer be viable. They would not give her up otherwise."

Jasper grinned. "If it's broke, my scientists can fix it."

Mace said, "Mr. Stark, if you feel so strongly about the Karthians, why don't you pull back and preserve your forces?"

"If this station can be saved it gives us a huge defensive advantage. The Karthians need the rift to attack our space. Their generators are not as advanced as ours and consume larger quantities of gatrellium, which as you know has limited supply. With our depleted ship counts, this station is a must."

Mace crossed his arms. "Then let Mr. Collins have it. He doesn't want the Karthians here either. You are weakening our position just as much as he is."

Stark was silent for almost a minute.

Humphrey yelled, "Mr. Hardy! We have ships coming through wormholes on the other side of that rift! Hundreds of them!"

Mace turned to the comm. "Jasper, Mr. Stark, it looks like the other Karthians have decided to join. Ships are pouring in. I would suggest a full evacuation!"

Stark raised his voice in frustration. "This is exactly what I feared. Mr. Collins, we can't save this station, we must destroy it."

Jasper said, "Then pull your troops out. I got this."

"No, you don't. We've lost here. I suggest you finish off the Karthians around you and get back to your ships. In twenty minutes this station will be swarming with Karthian troops. Commander Frall, uncase the nukes."

Mace asked, "Wait. What'd you just say?"

Malcolm sighed. "We've lost this station. As a contingency plan, nobody gets it. Our only consolation will be that its destruction may buy us some time. They will want to ensure a solid defense of the rift before moving through. They don't yet know the strength of our reserves. When that weakness becomes apparent, they will come full force."

"You're free to go anytime," said Jasper.

Malcolm Stark banged his fist in his hand. "Collins! I'm trying to save you and your Targarians here!"

Jasper scowled. "And why would you do that?"

Stark growled, "Because I need you. We need you and your force. We will need every ship and every man we can muster. They will come through that rift with a force we cannot stop. We have to start putting our defense in order. And I... we need you and your ships to fight alongside us."

A commander made a statement to Stark.

Malcolm said, "You have approximately eighteen minutes to get your people off this station, Mr. Collins. There won't be much left when we're done. If you like the warmth of extreme gamma radiation, you are welcome to stay."

An order was given by Stark just before his comm closed. "Pull back! I want everyone off this station in ten minutes!"

The fighting in front of Jasper Collins came to a quick end.

Mace said, "If I were you, I'd be getting my butt off there!"

Jasper stood looking down the emptied hall in front of him. "Let's go! Evac! Everyone out! Admiral Tamkin, move our ships over to protect the transports. We're going home."

The seconds ticked by as the Karthian fleet approached. The two hundred forty-eight ships that remained of their original fleet of twelve hundred moved back into a defensive formation as the Union ships headed for the portal. The fifty-seven remaining Collins Kingdom vessels moved to defend their transports.

Two minutes after departure, multiple nuclear blasts obliterated more than half the station. The remainder broke into a dozen large sections. The Targarian ships moved through the rift, meeting up with the *Ravix*. With a stream of micro-wormhole jumps, what was left of the Targarian fleet returned home.

Chapter 4

Mace stood on a catwalk, looking down at the *Rogers* as her repairs continued. "What a mess. I can't believe Stark was in control that whole time."

Johnny replied, "We're gonna be paying for it. Tres said the news back home is this great deal Stark had worked out for all Humans was botched by the Targarians, and that we're now in more danger of a Karthian invasion than ever. What bugs me is that's something I can't even argue with."

Mace reached up with his hand, rubbing his forehead through his faceshield. "Up and down, up and down. Is this ride ever gonna end?"

Johnny shook his head. "At least we all came back in one piece today. Jasper's people didn't, but we did. How long before our first production ship is ready?"

Mace scowled. "We stopped it. And we had our people scrap the critical components manufacturing. We were just starting to build components, and since they're identical to Jasper's, I thought it a bad idea to produce them on Earth because Stark would have access if he wanted it."

"Stark's gonna be pissed."

"I'm having all the current components transferred to Divinia. Should be closed out before he knows what happened."

Jane joined the men on the catwalk. "There must be something we can do. Would the UF be willing to provide protection for a tax?"

Mace frowned. "Doubtful. Not that we'd want them to anyway. Their lockdown of Canto is discouraging."

Jane pointed down at the *Rogers*. "When will she be ready?"

"We should have the wormhole generator operational in a few days. After that, about a week's worth of other repairs. They're replacing one of the funnels on the gravity drives. Was cracked clean through."

Johnny winced. "I thought those things could take a beating? I know we can cut into them with the microwave cannon. Didn't know they could be cracked."

"Too bad Jasper couldn't gather some info on that weapon while he was on that station."

Jasper walked up from behind. "Who says I didn't?"

Mace turned. "If you did, please tell me. I'd want to get Jeff's team right on that."

Jasper shook his head. "So long as Jeff is on Earth, I can't risk giving him the information. This is not something we need to have Stark's people looking over."

"You do know Jeff would never turn that over, right?"

Jasper nodded. "I believe that to be true, but Stark's people don't play fair. They aren't gonna ask for it nicely. They're gonna beat it out of him, or threaten to beat Nancy unless he tells all. That's the way they work. I very much want Jeff, Gnaga, and the others to look this over. But they're gonna need to come out here. They can work in my labs with my people."

Mace crossed his arms. "I believe they would be amenable to that. When will you be ready for them?"

"As soon as you can get them here."

Mace looked at Johnny and Jane. "Ready for a quick trip home? Jane, I know you're itching to see Zax and Fina. If you want, we can drop you there. Since we're just jumping back to here it won't be critical for you to come back with us."

Jane smiled. "I'd like that."

"Well, let's get moving then. Johnny, open a comm to Jeff when we get aboard. Give him a heads up that we'd like to bring his team back, but don't give him a reason as to why. Maybe tell him we want them to go over some of the critical repairs or something. Make it sound reasonable in case anyone is somehow listening."

Johnny chuckled. "You mean somebody as in Stark?"

"Those comm devices are still based on what the Mawga gave him. The rollout of the new stuff hasn't happened yet."

"You think he can tap our comms?"

"Not on the ship, just the personal ones. You call Jeff. Jeff will call Nancy. If they're listening, we want him to have a good cover."

Twenty minutes later, the *Ravix* landed in the field by the cave. The ramp was lowered and Jeff and Gnaga hustled their entire team of scientists onto the waiting ship. Jane walked to a waiting transport where Vanessa was busy swatting and yelling at the five kids, who were jumping, climbing, and yelling continuously. Jane eagerly joined the ongoing excitement.

Jeff walked onto the bridge. "You might want to get us out of here. Two men have been snooping around the property for the last two days. I think we're being watched."

Mace asked, "Anyone tried to contact any of you yet?"

Jeff shook his head. "No, but we've detected comm intrusions. I'm guessing you don't want us to look over the ship repairs?"

Mace turned to Liam. "Mr. Hobbs, take us back to Divinia."

As the ship began to lift, Mace said, "Jasper managed to get data off that station. I thought having you and your team look it over was a good idea. We can't do that here without risking the data falling into Stark's hands."

Jeff nodded. "I would agree with that reasoning. And just so you know, I'm almost certain that none of the members of our team are Stark supporters. They aren't motivated by working for the King."

Johnny laughed. "Even though you're bringing them here to work for *the King*?"

Jeff replied "I believe they know the difference. Anyway, I expect at some point we will be returning to Earth with this knowledge, so I plan to have them divided into teams where only a single aspect—or maybe a small group of parameters—is looked at. If they don't know the whole weapon, there's less chance of Stark acquiring the knowledge of how to build one."

Mace nodded. "Good job, Doc. Thinking ahead, I like that."

Johnny turned. "Incoming hail from Stark's people."

"Patch it through."

"Mr. Hardy, under the authority of the King you are being asked to bring that vessel to a halt for an inspection."

"Sorry. Not happening. We don't operate under the authority of any king."

The officer on the comm said, "I'm authorized to use whatever means necessary to stop you, Mr. Hardy. That includes the defense grid around this planet."

Mace shook his head. "You really need to work on your bluffing skills, Mr....?"

The officer replied, "Colonel Sanders."

Johnny burst out laughing.

Mace said, "Sorry, Colonel, The King knows he needs all available persons and ships for this upcoming fight. I highly doubt you are authorized to do anything more than threaten."

Liam said, "Jump coming in ten seconds."

Mace nodded to Liam before looking back at the comm. "Have a good day, Colonel."

The comm was closed as the *Ravix* slipped through a wormhole to Divinia. Ten minutes later they were on the ground in the blue city of Yentis. The team of thirty-two scientists and engineers was guided to a lab where Jasper's Targarians were waiting. Jeff had an hour-long conference with Mace before returning to give duty assignments. The *Ravix* returned to the repair docks.

Jasper was waiting on his usual perch, the catwalk overlooking the main repair bays. "My team says it was developing some kind of quantum wave."

Mace held up a hand. "You can skip trying to explain that one."

"Anyway, I was gonna say, they think it's something we can build. The Karthians had an extensive data library on that station. We believe we can replicate their lasers as well."

"Now *that* we can understand," said Johnny.

Mace leaned on the rail. "Will this ever be over?"

Jasper said, "So long as somebody out there wants what someone else has, it won't. You have to be willing to fight to keep what you have."

"I know you don't think so, but I still have to wonder if we... you, had left Stark's plans in place, would we be looking at a new age of man? A time when peace reigned, at least for a while? Might not be bad to be on the aggressor side of things for a while. Citizens could go their whole lives without being involved in any conflict."

Jasper shook his head. "At the cost of their freedom. What happens when a war doesn't go the way it was planned? What would Stark's first orders be the first time a fight is going badly? Your easy life back home would be interrupted when you got conscripted to go off and fight his war for him. If you took away his aggressive ambition, he might be OK, but that's not who he is."

Johnny said, "Jasper's right. If we sit back and just watch, we get whatever comes our way. At least out here we can shape our futures. I'd love nothing more than to have a world where Zax and Fina can grow up without the constant threat of annihilation hanging over them."

Jasper crossed his arms. "So how is it we get rid of Stark?"

"You talking assassination?"

Jasper nodded. "If that's what it takes."

Johnny laughed. "You know, I had this guy in college that used to say about the terrorists that all we needed to do was to sit down and have a rational discussion with them over a cup of coffee. It was like he believed they could be reasoned with, that somehow this little light was gonna go off in their heads, and they would understand his peace proposal. A wonderful thought, but it has no basis in reality when you're dealing with psychos."

Mace replied, "Well, you actually could sit and have a cup of coffee with Stark, but you aren't going to convince him of anything. He would just look at it as an opportunity to pitch his position, and of course to belittle you for being opposed to his great vision for mankind."

Jasper nodded. "As I said, the man needs to be gotten rid of."

Johnny frowned. "How do you get rid of someone when you don't even know where they are? We don't even know what he looks like."

Mace said, "I don't think we want to get rid of him right now anyway. He's resourceful, and we need someone to prosecute this coming war."

Jasper invited Mace and Johnny down to his palace for a small lunch feast. A shuttle landed and the three men walked to the dining hall.

Jasper said, "Similar spread to last time you were here. Pick out what you want. My staff will eat the rest."

Johnny laughed. "You're not gonna tell us they're snail butts or gall bladders afterward, are you?"

Jasper smiled. "I guess that depends on what you choose to eat."

Johnny replied, "Here we go."

Jasper waved his hand. "They are all legit, normal foods. Except those tendrils maybe. I have to admit they're disgusting, but I can't stop eating them either."

"Sounds like a disorder to me," joked Johnny.

Jasper smiled. "I have my share."

Jeff came over the comm. "I think we might be having a breakthrough!"

"On the green wave?" asked Mace.

Jeff shook his head. "On a unified field theory. We think we might have a set of equations worked out that work with electromagnetism, gravity, and quantum theory. For a physicist, this is as exciting as it gets. The Karthian data store seems to be a treasure trove of experimentation and results. We could be studying this for quite some time."

Johnny asked, "So you can build the green energy weapon?"

Jeff frowned. "I'm afraid we are a bit away from that. There's so much here to go through, I'm about to burst with excitement."

Mace put down his eating utensils, a curved fork and a sharp edged spoon. "Jeff, sorry but I have to ask... is this discovery pertinent to the building of one of those weapons?"

Jeff tilted his head from one side to the other in thought. "I would suppose it is in some ways."

"OK, I think I see where this is going. Look, the discoveries you're talking about, if true, are fantastic for the future of the study of physics. That has to be thrilling to you and the others. However, we're at war, and we're desperate for a weapon to help us defend ourselves. So I'm going to offer this only once: please, please put the theoretical stuff to the side and focus on getting us use of this weapon. Understanding all the physical properties of the universe isn't gonna help us if we're overrun, killed, or enslaved."

Jeff let out a sigh. "I understand. I'm sorry I got so excited. You are correct. Our focus needs to be on unwrapping the secrets of that weapon so we can build one for our defense."

"Think of it this way. You give us something we can fight with, and in return we give you a peaceful existence where you can make all the grand discoveries your heart desires."

Jeff nodded. "I'll pass that instruction along."

The comm closed.

Johnny chuckled. "You just burst his bubble."

"We need that weapon. We can't fight the Karthians with a series of equations."

Johnny raised his hand. "You're preaching to the choir here."

As they delved into the delicacies of Divinia, Mace asked, "What are we at, ten warships a week now?"

Jasper nodded. "With the components that came from Earth I expect that number to increase to twelve by next weekend."

"And there's no good way to increase those numbers further?"

Jasper shook his head. "Not only would we need a new construction dock, we would need more component assemblies. I've talked with my engineers about this very subject. Our resources are strained now."

Mace twirled a ghateral noodle on his curved fork. "What if we enlisted the Union species to build components?"

Jasper scowled. "That would mean giving all our secrets away. I'm not willing to risk that yet."

"Kind of a catch-22," said Johnny. "We either don't have the resources to defend ourselves from the Karthians or we give ourselves over fully to Stark."

Jasper replied, "The Karthians haven't attacked yet."

Mace took a sip of his Targarian wine. "Maybe there's a compromise staring us in the face. What if we mapped out our ideal production schedule, one that includes the Union members, and planned out what we would build and where? What if we put everything we could in place, excluding our critical technology, so we could spin up production quickly should we decide to do so?"

Johnny added, "We could probably even trick the Union into building all this while holding back on the critical stuff until the last second. Get them all excited, and then pull the rug out from under them until we're absolutely sure we need that option."

Jasper scratched the turkey-neck under his chin. "That's a possibility."

Mace said, "Think about it. Instead of a build-out taking months, everything could be pre-staged so we only need a few days to turn it on."

Jasper nodded. "I'll have my engineers work this over after we finish here. The two of you can provide input."

Johnny smiled. "See, there's a solution to every problem."

Jasper picked up a wiggling tendril he had just dipped in butter. Johnny shook his head in disgust as he placed it in his mouth and slurped it down.

"I bet you were one of those kids that ate worms when you were a toddler, weren't you?"

Jasper grinned. "Maybe. You should give one a try. You might find that you like worms."

Johnny laughed. "No thanks. I'll stick to... whatever this thing is. And don't tell me, because I know you're just gonna lie."

Chapter 5

Ten days passed with no new activity at the Karthian rift. The *Rogers* was released from repair, and testing showed her to once again be fully operational. Mace and the others returned to Earth. The *Organ Cave* was released a day later. With the ramped-up production, the Targarian fleet had once again topped a hundred ships.

The Union members had been busy with their own fleet. Among them, forty new cruisers were coming off the line every week. The fleet of five-hundred-odd ships that had survived the battle at the rift now numbered more than six hundred. Repaired ships were adding to those totals.

Efforts to coordinate production with the Union members had fallen on deaf ears. Stark was content with his own progress, as the Karthians had shown no desire to come through the rift for the all-out war that was feared.

Mace opened a comm from the *Rogers* to check on Jeff. "How's it going? Any good news?"

"We have the components used to create that wave under construction. All except two important pieces."

"I thought that weapon was really big. That's not gonna fit on a ship, is it? We building an orbital platform for it?"

Jeff shook his head. "We scaled it down. If the tests verify that it works, we can move to a larger platform."

Mace asked, "What are the two pieces that are missing?"

"We believe one to be a dark matter generator. We have no idea yet how it produced what it did. The second is a fusion combination chamber. The dark matter is fused with diamond. The result is the crystal structure breaks apart and the particles that make up the diamond are turned into this quantum energy wave… which we still don't understand."

Mace laughed. "Sounds like a technical problem."

Jeff nodded. "It is. And we will solve it. It won't be today, though. We followed the instructions for creating these components as closely as we could. During initial tests, neither performed as desired."

"Well, just keep at it. How's the team holding up?"

"We're all energized. This is the reason most of us got into science and engineering. The trial and error evaluations, the discoveries. Although I suppose we could do without the frustrations."

"Couldn't we all. Hey, you said the weapon consumes diamond. You have all of that you need?"

Jeff frowned. "Yes and no. We have enough for these initial tests. What we don't have is a supply for use once this is operational. Our current configuration will consume a two-carat diamond with each burst. Once we scale up, that changes to six carats. Our supply is very limited."

Johnny said, "Too bad we don't still have Cancri. Some of the raw diamonds we were pulling out of there were immense."

Mace said, "We could go back through our exploration scan logs. That should identify any sources we found that might give us a good supply."

"One step ahead of you on that," said Jeff. "We only identified one of those sites with potential for large stones. Jasper has a mining team out there now. Initial results aren't all that promising. They've mined a quarter of the find and only have a dozen or so potentially usable jewels. For this to be a valid weapon, we need to be able to fire it more than a few dozen times."

Mace stroked his goatee. "I think I might know where we could find more of those diamonds."

Johnny said, "I know that look in your eye. You thinking the Hoorka?"

Mace nodded. "They cleaned out that planet. They have the diamonds. Question is, will they trade for them? And what do we have to trade back?"

Johnny shrugged. "Gatrellium? We know they make use of it as well."

Jeff shook his head. "We can't part with any. It's needed for production. If you haven't been following that issue, you would know that Stark took back the mines in the Union territories. The Targarians are down to their single mine again. And from what I've heard it's nearly depleted... mined out."

Johnny said, "What about the big asteroid we gave him?"

"We're down to our last 10 percent being unrefined. Our stockpile is still enough to build six to seven hundred ships."

Johnny crossed his arms as he leaned back in his chair. "Wait, I thought we had enough for at least twice that. What happened?"

Jeff frowned. "Reality happened. We realized the gatrellium plating blistered on the *Organ Cave* when it got hit by that green wave. We've had to double the thickness in order to prevent that from happening again. It's just as well, too, we found that every trip through a micro-wormhole strips off many of the outer molecules. The way it was, we'd be replacing that whole skin every three or four hundred jumps. For whatever reason, the thicker it is, the better it seems to stay intact. At least that's what our testing shows."

Mace sighed. "Still don't have enough of that stuff. Have the deposits we've identified been mined?"

Jeff nodded. "All but two of the smaller ones. We don't see them as worth spending the effort to recover. The jumps out and back would consume a quarter of what's there."

Mace said, "So it looks like we need to do some more exploring."

"That would be my advice. The *Rogers* is ready for it. The Karthians have yet to start an attack. And if I were you, I'd be a bit uneasy sitting there on Earth. Who knows what Stark is planning for us? If he decides he wants the *Rogers,* he also gets all her technology, which I know we don't want to share."

Mace took a deep breath as he looked over at Johnny. "Go ahead and call everyone in. And this time I mean everyone. If people want, they can bring spouses and kids. I don't want to leave anyone here where Stark has some leverage over us. Tell them all if anyone wants to stay, they can, but if something happens, we won't be making any trades or negotiations with Stark for them. We can't afford to."

Johnny turned to his console. The message soon went out. Because the situation wasn't urgent, the all-volunteer crew was given five hours to decide. Four hours into the order, Tres and Vanessa came aboard with their three girls.

Mace was standing at the rampway. "Glad you decided to bring them."

Vanessa replied, "He was the one who took convincing. I know we're all safe here. Back there you have people who might want something from you. I'd rather not give them the option to take it."

Tres said, "My only hesitation was with schoolwork for the kids. We were able to transfer enough aboard to keep them busy for a while. The restaurants have been placed in the care of others. We're all set."

Mace nodded. "Well, let's get this ramp closed. And by the way, everyone is here. That includes thirty-six spouses and twenty-eight kids. Might be a little crowded, but knowing they're safe should put everyone at ease."

Mace said into his comm, "Mr. Hobbs, close us up and get us to the first prospect."

"Coordinates are in, should be up and through a wormhole in about three minutes."

Tres said, "Tell me you got the boxes from the restaurant."

Mace nodded as they walked. "We did. They should be in the kitchen. You'll have a lot more mouths to feed this time around."

Tres replied, "Only with beverages. We're still on nutrient bars. I should have a better selection for us to drink, though."

The first twenty star systems showed a plethora of mineable minerals, without diamond or gatrellium. The twenty-first scored a twenty-ton gatrellium find spread across two planets. The fifteen systems that followed showed nothing of use.

As they came into the sixteenth system, Humphrey said, "Six planets. Third is in the habitable zone."

Mace nodded. "Mr. Hobbs, start with the first and we'll work our way out."

An hour later, with results again disappointing, a short jump was made to the second planet. "I show a highly acidic atmosphere, Mr. Hardy. At those levels, our suits would start to dissolve after a few hours."

"Log it and add that as a note. We can't leave any stone unturned out here."

When the scan run was complete, a short jump was made to the third planet.

Humphrey said, "I'm showing 12 percent larger than Earth. Density looks about the same. Magnetic fields are similar. Nitrogen and oxygen in the atmosphere. And 63 percent ocean. This is as close to an Earth match as we've seen."

"Standard setup for the scan, Mr. Hobbs."

Several minutes in, Humphrey turned. "I'm showing a lot of bios down there, Mr. Hardy. Might be worth a look to see. Hold on… I have structures."

Mace held up a hand. "Bring us to a stop. Mr. Mallot, can you zoom us in?"

Humphrey passed the image to the main display. "I'd say we have us a city down there."

Mace nodded. "That's a harbor. Those are ships. Nothing looks advanced. Maybe comparable to medieval times?"

Johnny zoomed in again on a section of roadway leading out of the small harbor town. "Wagons ho!"

Humphrey said, "Bios are bipeds. Just over a meter tall. Computer counts about fifteen thousand in and around that town."

Mace frowned. "Log it for a revisit. While this is all interesting, it's not putting gatrellium in our store. Let's move along."

As the *Rogers* began to move, Humphrey yelled, "We have wormholes opening above us! Two ships coming through!"

Mace turned. "Mr. Hobbs, take us up! If we need to jump I want to have that option!"

"The ships are closing," said Humphrey. "I'm detecting energy buildups!"

Mace said, "Mr. Mueller, take whatever actions you feel necessary."

Humphrey again yelled, "We're being fired upon! I show hull breach in section A26!"

"Return fire, Mr. Mueller!"

Two plasma rounds were followed by a half dozen microwave bursts. The attacking ships turned, avoiding the incoming fire.

Humphrey gave more status: "They're firing again! Section B26 just took a hit!"

"Mr. Hobbs? How long before we can jump?"

"Thirty seconds."

Hans fired the *Rogers'* weapons. A microwave burst hit one of the ships dead-on. It leveled off and began a downward trend. Soon, flames covered most of its hull. A spectacular explosion told of its demise. The second ship turned away, jumping through a wormhole away from the planet, ending the short raid.

Johnny said, "No way those were associated with those people down there."

Mace nodded. "I'd say we stumbled on some watchers."

Humphrey said, "Mr. Hardy, I have bad news. Our wormhole generator is offline."

"What? How?"

Humphrey pushed a damage diagram to the wall display. "Whatever they hit us with penetrated the hull, went though the deck and into section C26. That's the generator room, sir."

Mace stood. "Johnny, come with me."

Johnny followed Mace off the bridge. "I don't know squat about those generators."

Mace scowled. "Me neither. And our scientists and engineers are back on Divinia. These were supposed to be cupcake runs."

"They didn't even attempt contact. Looks like someone wants us out of here."

Mace huffed, "Then why'd they kill off our generator?"

Johnny shrugged. "Luck?"

Mace opened his comm to the bridge. "Mr. Mallot, can you tell us if the generator was targeted?"

Humphrey replied, "I don't see how. Not with the gatrellium skin we have. Unless of course they have better sensors than we do. Given the location of the first hit, I'd have to say it was a random shot."

Mace stopped at section C26. The bulkhead door wouldn't open. "Do we have anyone in C26?"

Bontu Montak replied, "Two of my men are in there, Mr. Hardy, sealing the breaches. The beams melted holes that are about two centimeters. When they're done, we'll be moving up to B26. We'll have to use the bulkhead entry boxes we built."

Mace nodded. "Forgot we had those. How long before we can get to the generator?"

Bontu replied as he walked around a corner. "Any minute now. The breaches are small and may be welded over."

Johnny asked, "Just welds? Why so long?"

"They have to remove ceiling panels to get access. The walls, ceiling, and floor of that room are heavily shielded from interference."

A flashing light over the door went off. The door opened to a slight hiss. Two Mawga workers nodded as they exited the room.

Mace turned. "Thanks, guys."

Johnny followed Mace into the room. "I can't believe we came out here without one of our technical people."

Mace looked over one end to the generator as Johnny took the other.

Johnny was the first to spot the issue.

"Got it. Burned through here and into the floor behind."

"Any idea what that box does?" Mace asked.

Johnny laughed. "You're asking the wrong guy. Now, ask me about the comms and I can give you a reasonable answer. But this? I know nada."

Jane walked in behind them, setting a toolbox on the ground. "What's the problem?"

Johnny pointed. "Their weapon burned through this box."

Jane looked it over. "You opened it up yet?"

Johnny said, "You have the tools?"

Jane smiled as she reached in, grabbing a multi-headed wrench. "Here."

Johnny laughed. "What am I supposed to do with that?"

Jane sighed. "Space has made you soft. Here, up underneath. Insert the wrench and twist."

Johnny fumbled for several seconds. Jane grabbed the wrench from his hand and began the task of removing the box cover. Johnny stepped back with a sly grin. Mace shook his head.

The lid was lifted. "Hmm. Burned through this coil."

Jane pulled up her holo-display, flipping through several pages of parts. "Grr. Don't have one."

Mace asked, "Anything we can substitute?"

Jane sighed as she looked back through the list. "This is the closest we have. Inductance is double and the ESR is half."

Johnny tilted his head. "ESR?"

Jane nodded. "The series resistance. And with both of those being off, I can't say what that would do to the rest of this gear."

"Swap it out," said Mace.

Jane looked up. "You sure you want to risk that? Could fry this whole thing, for all we know."

Mace took a deep breath. "Without it we're stuck here. I told Jasper we may be out for a few weeks. He has a list of where we were checking. But Liam and I decided to start from the bottom. No good reason why. Just one of those hunches that we might find something sooner that way. So put the coil in and let's see if she'll power up."

Jane shrugged. "You're the boss."

Johnny said, "You'll have to solder that in. You sure you know what you're doing there?"

Jane stood. "You wanna make yourself useful?"

"Yes, ma'am."

Jane pointed. "Then go back to the reactor room and have Mr. Jenkins help you get the new part. I'm sending the number to your data store. And while you're there, have him give you the coil stretcher."

Johnny chuckled. "The coil stretcher?"

Jane nodded. "Yes. It's a tool we have in the reactor room. This new coil is too short. Ask Mr. Jenkins for the stretcher."

Johnny raised his hands. "OK. I'm going."

As Johnny left, Jane pulled out a small laser and a suction tube. Four posts were unsoldered and the burned coil removed.

Johnny returned with the new coil and a smile. "Coil stretcher. You had me almost convinced."

Jane smiled as she took the part.

Mace said, "Did I miss something here?"

Johnny replied, "There is no coil stretcher. She made it up to make me look like a fool to Mr. Jenkins, so she and he could sit back in that room giggling to each other about me. Well, it didn't work. I quizzed Mr. Jenkins and my suspicions of foul play were confirmed. No coil stretcher."

Jane got to work replacing the coil. "Well, it was worth a shot. I'll have to work on my delivery for next time. I never told you, but Gnaga had me searching high and low for a bovic oscillator one day. It was almost worth hearing him snort when I came back empty-handed because there was no such thing."

Jane stood. "OK, we're in."

The lid was replaced and secured.

Jane said. "Might not be a bad idea to watch this from behind the bulkhead. I have no idea what it might do."

The three walked from the room, closing and sealing the door behind them.

Mace opened a comm to the bridge. "Mr. Hobbs, can you give us a quick test of the wormhole generator? If anything looks out of whack, shut it down immediately."

"One moment."

A full minute passed. "I'm sorry, Mr. Hardy, the parameters all look green, but we have no indication of a wormhole."

Humphrey added, "Sensors detected a power build where the hole would normally open, but no space-time fracture."

Mace sighed. "Well, that's just great."

Chapter 6

Mace sat in his command chair. "Mr. Mallot? I assume we can still scan?"

Humphrey nodded. "Sensors are fully operational."

"Mr. Hobbs, put us back in the pattern. We might as well scan this world while we're here."

Liam nodded. "On our way. Mr. Mallot, thirty seconds."

Mace asked, "How long to reach each of the next planets using gravity drives?"

Liam replied, "Four hours, nine hours, and sixteen hours."

"Sixteen hours?"

Liam pushed an image of the star system to the wall display. "This one is here, the second out here, and the last all the way back over here. Opposite sides of the star from these two."

Johnny chuckled. "Not like we have anything else to do right now."

The inhabited planet, along with the remaining three, showed quantities of standard minerals.

Mace sat with his arms crossed. "Take us back to that planet. I want to inspect where the wreckage of that ship went down. Maybe we can learn something from it."

The *Rogers* slowed as it dropped into the atmosphere. Ten minutes later, she hovered a kilometer above the crash site, an expansive desert. Sensors showed a forty-eight degree temperature.

Johnny said, "That's like one-twenty Fahrenheit. Balmy."

Mace said as he stood. "We're in our gear. Won't feel a thing. Mr. Hobbs, take us down to that largest chunk."

Mace opened a comm. "Jane, since you're our senior technical person today, round up Jenny and meet us at the ramp."

Mace turned. "Mr. Crawford, your shift starts now."

Jordan nodded. As the ramp lowered, the four Humans descended. Johnny took two big steps and jumped onto the sand. He immediately began to sink. Mace reached out a hand, pulling him back onto the base of the ramp.

Jane laughed. "What was that all about?"

Johnny grinned. "Just wanted to be the first Human on this planet. Was gonna claim it for Derwood."

Jane shook her head. "Brother... you're gonna be the first *dead* Human on this planet."

"And it's already occupied," added Mace. "No Derwood. Mr. Mallot, can you give us some ground readings for this area? Johnny sank when he stepped on the sand."

Humphrey replied, "I'm showing a pocket of low density to your right. Stay left and it should be solid enough."

The foursome walked the fifty meters to a piece of the downed alien craft.

Jane said, "Not very big, was it?"

"About the size of our shuttles," said Mace. "Which reminds me... when we get back, let's see if we can put the micro-wormhole generators on at least one of those. This is the second time we could have used it as a backup to make a jump."

Johnny said, "Excellent idea."

Jenny looked over a piece of hull, kicking it with her boot. "Definitely metallic."

She reached down, lifting the meter-long piece in her hand. "Heavy too. Suit says this piece is almost four hundred kilos."

Jane said, "I've got components over here. Looks like a whole mess of coils."

Mace walked over. "What are the chances any would work?"

Jane shook her head. "Slim to none that we'd have a match. I'll take some samples and see what they test out to be at Gnaga's workbench."

Johnny said, "I got part of a dead alien over here. At least I think that's what it is."

Jenny walked over. "Ha! That's a plant, you doofus. Here's the pot it was growing in."

Johnny scowled. "Who takes a plant with them on a fighter ship?"

Jenny looked up at the *Rogers*. "If I recall, you brought two dogs."

Johnny returned a half smile. "Noted."

Mace climbed up on a twenty-meter-long section. "Anybody think this is the barrel of the weapon they shot at us?"

Jane walked over. "Could be."

Mace opened a comm. "Mr. Crawford, have Mr. Humphrey check the data for anything toxic or radioactive. If it's clean, send the shuttle down with a grappler and let's move this stuff into the docking bay. No sense in us sitting out here exposed when we can investigate from in there."

Jordan replied, "Expect a shuttle down there in about two minutes, Mr. Hardy."

Johnny smacked Mace on the shoulder. "I like that. You're using your noggin."

Half an hour passed before the major pieces of the destroyed craft had been collected.

Mace stood in the docking bay. "Wish we could get this back to the team. I'd like to know how to shield against that weapon."

Jane said, "It melted through that gatrellium and the internal decking. Which reminds me, we're gonna have to patch the gatrellium skin before we can jump anywhere. I remember you telling me about that first test shuttle at Divinia."

Johnny nodded. "It disintegrated when it hit the wormhole. Good call."

Jane pointed. "Pick up that box of parts and follow me."

Johnny reached down. "Is that all I am to you? A delivery boy?"

Jane replied as she walked away, "More of a mule, but yes."

Johnny followed Jane with the box.

Mace made his way back to the bridge. "Mr. Mallot, find us a deep hole in that ocean. Mr. Hobbs, take us there. We're gonna sit for a while, see if those aliens that attacked us come back."

The next two days were spent at nine hundred meters below the surface. A small passive sensor array was floated above, keeping watch on the heavens. Mace took a walk to Gnaga's lab.

Jane looked up as he walked in. "I think we're ready for another try. I've tested a half dozen of the coils from that wreckage. One is close, but I'm getting some odd readings from it. Once on and fully active, a resonant wave starts to build in it. After a minute it seems to take over, changing the inductance. I'm no electronics whiz, but from what I do know it shouldn't do that."

Mace smiled. "I'm surprised you actually know any of this stuff."

Jane replied, "Gnaga was insistent on explaining everything he did. And he liked to quiz me about it afterward. I guess some of it stuck. Anyway, I'd like to swap out coils and then give the generator another try."

Mace nodded as he opened a comm. "Mr. Hobbs, take us up to where we can open a wormhole. We have another test to run."

Jane and Mace walked to the generator room as the *Rogers* surfaced and headed back to space. The coils were exchanged and the circuit box holding it again secured.

"That should do it."

Mace opened a comm. "Mr. Hobbs... give it a try."

As Mace and Jane watched on a holo-display, the sensors showed a tiny fracture in space-time taking place. High-fives were exchanged.

"Mrs. Tretcher, I promote you to chief engineer."

Jane laughed. "I think we got way lucky on this one."

Humphrey came over the comm. "Mr. Hardy, we have a problem."

"What is it, Mr. Mallot?"

Humphrey pushed the data he was looking at to Mace's display. "Normally the wormhole is opened at a fixed point a kilometer in front of the ship. For whatever reason, that point has begun to move."

"Move? What do you mean?"

"The point is bouncing from the one kilometer mark… in to only a few meters away from our hull, and then back out to maybe a thousand kilometers."

"Can you scan the other side to see what's happening there? Is the other end opening to where it should?"

Humphrey ran a quick scan. "It appears to be."

"Mr. Hobbs, open a wormhole to Divinia. Let's have Jasper send us the right part. I'd rather not chance us going through there."

A new portal was opened.

Jasper's image came up on the comm. "How goes the search?"

"Cut short. We need some assistance. We were attacked and the wormhole generator took a hit. We were able to repair it but it doesn't seem stable. Would appreciate you opening a return portal for us. I'm sending over the coordinates."

Jasper nodded. "Give me a sec and I'll have it open for you. You say you were attacked?"

Mace pushed a video stream of the short fight over the comm. "Two ships popped in and started shooting. The world we're at is inhabited, but they seem to be at the medieval stage of civilization. We think these ships were from another species who's watching them. In the video, you can see we shot one of them down. The debris from it came down in a desert. The second ship jumped through a portal to elsewhere."

Jasper said, "Wormhole should be opening near you now."

Liam came over the comm. "We have it, Mr. Hardy. Taking us home now."

As the *Rogers* slipped through to Divinia, Mace continued, "Anyway, we collected the ship debris from the desert. Jane used a part to repair our generator and here we are. And please remind me never to go out without a tech aboard who's trained at repairing things. We got lucky this time that Jane knew just enough to rescue us. Otherwise we'd have been stuck there until you came looking for us. Oh, and have Jeff meet us at the dock. We have some new stuff for him to play with. I believe we have one of the weapons they used to puncture our hull, and it looks to be intact."

Jasper laughed. "I'm not your messenger boy. Call Jeff yourself."

Mace shook his head. "Sorry. Not sure why I asked."

A comm was opened to Jeff Moskowitz. "Hey, Doc. We've got some new hardware for you to look at. It's a weapon that penetrated our hull and cut through a deck."

"I'll add it to our list of things to look at."

"Any luck with the green energy wave?"

Jeff sighed. "Five attempts and no output. We may have to do a reset and start from the beginning. Were you able to find any resources?"

Mace frowned. "Not much. We did find an inhabited planet. I'd place them at medieval on the development scale—wagons and whatnot. And we did manage to get attacked. We downed one of the two attackers and collected the debris for you to analyze. Oh, and they managed to trash our wormhole generator with a shot from their weapons. Jane replaced a coil and we made a comm to Jasper to open us another portal because ours was unstable."

"How was it unstable?"

Mace shrugged. "Not sure how to describe it other than to say once it was open it kept moving around. We didn't want to chance coming through it so we had Jasper open us another."

Jeff tilted his head. "Moving around? Explain."

Mace pulled up data from the ship's archive. "Here, see for yourself. It was oscillating, going from no more than a meter from the hull out to about nine hundred kilometers and back. We sent through a comm, but I wasn't about to take us through there."

Jeff rubbed his chin. "That shouldn't be possible. How'd this happen again?"

"Jane swapped out a coil. We didn't have one that would work, so she scavenged one from the downed wreckage. She pointed out some strange behavior to me before she installed it. But neither of us knew what we were looking at. I figured your guys might be interested in whatever the cause was."

Jeff nodded. "Very. I'll have Mr. Klept look into it. He's struggling at the moment, as so much of what we're attempting with the quantum wave technology is based on mathematical formulas and theory. Gnaga's genius is much more in the applied realm. I'll have him look over the weapon too. He'll enjoy the break."

Mace walked onto the bridge of the *Organ Cave*, where Jasper was sitting. "What'cha hanging out up here for?"

Jasper replied, "Duties on the planet have been fulfilled. Was just running replays of that fight out there on my display. Looking for any ship tactics that seemed to give an edge. I lost a quarter of my new ships in that fight, and I'd like to nail down why."

"Shouldn't your military planners be looking that over?"

Jasper closed the display. "They are. I just like to keep in the mix if I can. Tell me about your encounter."

Mace gestured toward the main holo-display. "Put the video feed up on the big board."

As the main holo-display came to life, Mace said, "This is where they came in, I'd say using wormholes, since they came out of nowhere. We took our first hit about here. And the second here. This one penetrated to the generator room and smoked a coil. Hans took one of the fighters out and the other fled. That's about it. Oh, and I passed the debris from the downed ship off to Jeff for eval. I think it has a complete gun we might be able to take apart."

Jasper stood. "Come on, let's go round up a team to work on that."

Mace laughed. "Didn't know a king could get so bored."

Jasper shrugged as they walked. "We have all these things going on, but they're mostly way beyond my ability to deal with directly. I have administrators who take care of most of my day-to-day tasks of running these species. That leaves me with time to coordinate efforts up here. Only problem is, most of the work up here is beyond what I'm capable of. I can't re-engineer a quantum wave... whatever that thing does. All I can do is stand over their shoulders and ask dumb questions."

Mace chuckled. "I have the same issue. I watched Jane test and replace that coil, and frankly, other than soldering it in place, I was lost on what she was trying to describe to me."

"That's why I've been trying to educate myself ever since I took over here. I don't like people knowing so much more than me that I look like a fool when those subjects come up. I've been trying to wrap my head around all this field theory stuff for a week now, and sometimes I feel like I know less than I knew before."

Mace patted Jasper on the shoulder as they walked into a room that held the downed ship parts. "I know exactly how you feel. This is the gun over here. At least that's what I think it is."

Jasper gave the twenty-meter section a quick look-over. "I'd say that's what it is, too. Let's get this moved down to the labs."

A comm was placed and the debris moved. Mace and Jasper hopped a shuttle down to the surface, and were soon in the same engineering complex that held Jeff and the others.

Mace followed Jasper into a room as three of his engineers joined them. "Boys, they'll be bringing some ship parts through those doors in a couple minutes. On one of the larger parts is what looks like a barrel for a weapon. I want you to take it apart and tell me what it does. Can it be recreated? Can it be scaled up? All the usual stuff."

The engineers nodded. "We'll do our best, Your Highness."

The parts came in and the Targarian engineers got to work.

Mace found a chair and sat. "I was just thinking. If this weapon works, we could use it to keep any gatrellium ships from jumping. We had to patch our hull before coming through. Thanks, by the way, for providing those kits. Montak's guys were able to get out and do that patching in short order."

Jasper took off his helmet, laying it to one side. "I lie awake some nights wondering how we made it this far."

Mace laughed. "Don't get me started on that. We've had more than one too many fights that have somehow gone our way. Take that last one. I thought you were dead meat the way you charged in there."

"What I can't figure out is why Stark didn't command his ships to go after me. Wouldn't have been that difficult. They knew which ship I was on."

"Stark plays a mysterious game, that's for sure. He's had ample opportunity to kill us both. I'm not sure why he hasn't. We've screwed up his plans several times now."

"Well... we haven't really gone after him either. Maybe he looks at us as a viable alternative to him if something were to go wrong. He knows we both care more about Earth than ourselves. I think he does, too."

One of the engineers said, "Sire, we have the compartment open."

Jasper stood. "Let's have a look at our new prize."

The engineers poked and prodded for several minutes, discussing in Targarian what it was they were seeing.

Jasper asked, "Well?"

One of the engineers replied, "I am sorry, Your Highness. It appears to be an antenna and not a weapon."

Jasper scowled. "Not the news we were looking for."

A second engineer said, "It appears to be attached to a wormhole generator."

Mace asked, "Are you sure? That's way too small for what those ships came through."

The engineer pointed. "It's a similar setup to ours. I would agree, though. It is too small for use in transport. Perhaps it's for communications?"

Jasper patted the engineer on the back. "You boys keep digging. Let me know what you find."

Jasper turned. "You hungry?"

Mace nodded. "I could eat."

Jasper gestured toward the door. "We'll come back after. It'll give them a chance to get a handle on it without us hovering over them."

The two men left the lab.

Chapter 7

A comm came in from Jasper's engineers. "Sire, we must apologize. It appears the components we were evaluating earlier were indeed part of a weapon. We believe—"

Jasper replied, "Hold on. We'll be right there."

Mace finished his beverage before rising to follow the Targarian king.

"What'd we find?"

The lead engineer said, "This section is indeed an antenna. It takes the wormhole created by this generator and broadcasts it."

Mace asked, "Wait, are you saying the damage we took was from a wormhole?"

"We reviewed the damage to the *Rogers*. It's consistent with what we believe we have here. A wormhole was generated and then pushed through your hull."

Mace turned. "This could be huge."

Jasper rubbed his chin. "If true, how would it be possible to stop such a weapon?"

Mace crossed his arms. "Maybe it's not. They form a wormhole away from a ship and then move it into it. We need to find out how that's done. It would be like having the ultimate weapon. No hull or shield or field is going to stop that."

Jasper shook his head. "Well, something stopped it. Otherwise it would've gone all the way through."

The engineer said, "Perhaps the interaction with matter is what ended the threat."

Mace asked, "Are you saying every time it hit something physical it got weaker?"

The engineer nodded. "That might be one explanation. Without proper testing we won't know."

Jasper said, "Sounds like we may be wanting to add layers to our hulls."

Mace replied, "I say we build one of these and get started with testing it out. This could be something we would also add to our microwave cannon stations."

A comm came in to Jasper. "Sire, there is ship movement on the other side of the rift."

"Any come through?"

The officer shook his head. "No, Sire. However, the number of ships has grown. We count over three thousand now."

Jasper sighed. "Thank you, Major. Keep me informed."

The comm closed.

Mace said, "Should we check it out?"

Jasper replied, "If they haven't come through, it doesn't much matter."

"Should we inform Stark?"

Jasper scowled. "That clown has his own scouts out there. He knows what we know."

Mace commed into the *Rogers*. "Mr. Crawford, how goes the repair of the wormhole generator?"

"We're all set, Mr. Hardy. Will we be heading back out for more resource hunting?"

Mace thought for a moment. "No. We make a jump to Hoorka space. I want to know if they're willing to trade diamond to us. And if so, for what."

"Let me know if I'm needed," said Jasper.

A short trip had Mace back on the bridge of the *Rogers* as she came out of the repair dock. "Mr. Hobbs, take us to Promexa."

The *Rogers* was met by two Hoorka warships. "State your purpose."

Mace said, "We would like to speak with Favia of the Higatheps of Jore."

The Hoorka replied, "I will pass on the message."

Five minutes passed before an image of Favia showed on the display. She was adorned in jewels and wearing a feathered crown, a sign of Hoorka royalty.

Mace smiled. "Wow. Glad to see you are doing so well."

Favia replied, "I can't begin to express my gratitude. Your gracious and warmhearted gesture of bringing me home has made all this and more possible. Our people are at peace. And I've somehow become the most celebrated Hoorka of our day. How could I possibly repay you?"

"Well... about that. Would it be possible for us to trade for diamond? We need stones of at least five carats."

Favia smiled. "Diamond is something I have plenty of. How many do you need?"

Mace frowned. "Unfortunately that number is probably about two thousand. You'll have to tell us what we can trade for them."

Favia shook her head. "Nonsense. Consider that your finder's fee. When do you need them by?"

Mace held up a hand. "You don't have to do that. You don't owe us for your return. It was the right thing to do."

Favia turned and spoke to an assistant before turning back. "And this is the right thing to do. I'll have those stones for you in a few hours. In the meantime, could I convince you to visit me here at the estate?"

Mace smiled. "I know several people here who would very much enjoy that. They've missed you."

Favia nodded with another smile. "I'll have you brought here on a transport. You'll have to leave the *Rogers* where she is. I have pull with just about everyone, but it only goes so far."

The transport shuttle landed on a field of blue-green grass. Topiaries lined a stone path leading up to an immense four story home that resembled a stack of pancakes. As with most worlds, architectural tastes were very different from the boxy, utilitarian shapes on Earth. A moving sidewalk whisked the guests quickly up to the third floor. A grand room, with windows pulled back, overlooked a pristine lake where various waterfowl camped on the shoreline or lazily paddled about. A friendly breeze swept through the open room as Favia descended a staircase.

Jane's grin stretched from ear to ear. "You look incredible."

Favia smiled. "Thank you. Although I sometimes wish I could slip out of this thing for some comfortable attire."

Jane asked, "You have to dress like that all the time?"

"I don't have to, but I've been heavily encouraged to. I'm constantly in the news, partly from my wealth, partly from my age, but mostly because of my donation that made the truce possible. Everyone is ever grateful that we are at peace. Funny, it was a centuries-long war that I never knew anything about. Or I should say, slept through."

Jenny looked over the jewel encrusted gown. "We used to see expensive gowns made for celebrities. Nothing like this, though. This is spectacular."

Favia frowned. "I sometimes feel like a fool walking around in something that is worth more than a thousand common laborers would make in a lifetime."

Jenny looked around. "I don't think I could complain about this place, either. Look at that view."

Favia pointed. "You can see all the way to Mount Ressat. The spires over there are from our capital, Helingras."

Mace said, "The images on the walls. Were those your family?"

Favia nodded. "They are. I keep them close, as they are also responsible for getting me here. Had it not been for their sacrifices, I would have perished on the *Telemunde* as well."

A tour of the estate turned into a boat ride across the lake. A case containing three thousand stones of five carats or larger was delivered and loaded on the shuttle. Goodbyes were said, as well as promises for a longer visit. A short ride had the Humans back aboard the *Rogers*, and a jump to Divinia had the stones in the hands of Jeff Moskowitz and the other scientists.

Jeff asked, "How is she doing?"

Jane waved a hand. "She has nothing to worry about. Wealth beyond imagination, and a people who adore her. If anything, she might feel like she's trapped in an ivory tower due to her celebrity. She wasn't really complaining, though."

Two Targarians wheeled in the case.

Jeff asked, "What's that?"

Mace said, "Three thousand five-carat or larger diamonds."

"You're kidding, right?"

Mace shook his head.

"What did you trade for them?"

Jenny said, "Nothing. It was a gift from her for her rescue."

Jeff smiled. "This is incredible. And good timing. We have our newest version almost finished. It's a ground-up rebuild. We identified two mistakes we had made during assembly. If all goes well, we could be ready for testing in the morning."

"Is this still the scaled down version?" Johnny asked.

Jeff nodded. "It would fit on the *Rogers*. What we don't know is how effective it will be. The math says 'very,' but the real world has a way of setting you straight. The good news is we don't need the full size diamonds to test it. We have plenty of half carat stones that will work fine."

Jasper said, "We have plans drawn up for a station to support the full size weapon should we build it. Nothing like what the Karthians had. This would be purely to support that weapon. Maybe three times the size of one of our Collins class ships."

Johnny laughed. "You do like to say Collins class, don't you?"

Jasper nodded. "It has a pleasing sound, don't you think?"

Jasper received a comm. "Your Highness, the Karthians are forming up in front of the rift."

Jasper turned. "Ladies... gentlemen... our time of peace may be at an end."

Mace said, "I'll contact Stark. We need to coordinate any defense with his ships if we want a shot at stopping them."

Jasper scowled. "Do what you have to."

A comm was opened. "Mr. Stark, as I'm sure you know, the Karthians are forming up. We should work on a defense together."

Stark asked, "How many ships do you have?"

Mace looked over at Jasper.

"One hundred twenty-two. Twenty-three counting you and the *Rogers*."

Mace replied, "We have a hundred twenty-three."

Stark huffed. "What have you been doing? Crocheting afghans?"

Jasper stuck his face in the camera image. "We have what we have. What are you bringing?"

"Seven hundred twenty-six cruisers. Sixty-seven Radicas."

"The domed ship?"

Stark nodded. "Yes. They were highly effective last time, until your ships interfered."

Mace held up a hand before Jasper could reply. "You two can butt heads later. We should move everything we have to the rift. Maybe we can keep them from coming through by keeping them bottled up."

Stark concurred. "That was our intent. Without the threat of the station, we can sit right in front of that rift."

Mace turned. "Doc, how long would it take you to install that weapon on the *Rogers*?"

Jeff rubbed his chin. With the manpower we have, eighteen hours?"

Mace took a deep breath. "Let's make it happen."

"It may not even work."

Mace shrugged. "It has to, Doc. Make it happen."

Jasper said, "You can ride out with me while they work on that if you want."

Mace nodded. "Deal. Johnny? Wanna come with?"

Johnny glanced over at Jane before returning his own nod. "Absolutely."

Jasper said, "Meet me on the *Cave* in the next twenty if you want to come."

Jasper turned and walked off as he gave orders to his aides.

Mace looked at Jenny. "Wanna join us?"

"I do."

Jane grinned. "See how easy she said that."

Mace shook his head. "Not the right time for any proposals, Jane. I suppose you're staying here with Zax and Fina?"

Jane nodded. "Go have your fun. I'll be here to see that our little ship is ready."

A shuttle ride and a walk had the four standing on the deck of the *Organ Cave*.

Jasper said, "You can sit over there if you like. If we get in a fight you're gonna wanna be strapped in."

Johnny replied, "Good view of the main display from here."

"Let's hope all we're doing is watching."

The Karthians had formed a column ten ships wide by over three hundred ships long.

Johnny commented, "Wouldn't it be great if we could just blast something through at the whole lot of them at once?"

Mace replied, "That green energy weapon might have worked well for that. Wouldn't go all the way through, but packed together like that you might have taken out a dozen ships at a time."

A Targarian scout ship moved close to the rift, staying just out of cannon range as it performed a deep scan.

Jasper looked over the resulting data. "Hmm, these ships are new. Not in our database."

Mace asked, "How many?"

"Twenty-six."

Johnny said, "Too bad there's not a way to close that rift."

Mace replied, "We don't even know why it opened or what keeps it open."

"Maybe we could ring it with those nuke ships and set them all off at once."

Jasper scowled. "Might make it bigger."

A comm came in from Stark. "They still sitting in formation?"

Jasper replied. "They are. Where are you? I count a dozen Union ships out here."

"We are close. I don't want to show how small our force is. It might provoke them to come through sooner than they otherwise would."

Jasper huffed. "Or it might make them wait longer. Your logic is flawed."

"We will be there when needed."

"They have a new type of ship," said Mace. "Any idea of what that might be?"

"We believe those to have mini versions of that station weapon. I'm not currently concerned."

"Not concerned? Did you see what that weapon did to us before?"

Stark sighed. "I am completely familiar with its lethality, or lack thereof. I suppose I could give you a small bit of my strategy to set your minds at ease. We've calculated that we can close off the rift with thirty of the Radica ships, if backed by your Collins class vessels. From that we should be able to inflict damage on their approaching ships with impunity. Your job would be to keep those cruisers at bay with whatever that weapon is you possess. I will follow up behind your ships with support against any waves of the fighter ships they may send at us."

Mace said, "I have to agree with Mr. Collins. I think your ships being here would be a deterrent to them starting an attack."

Stark's silhouette stood, shaking his head. "I believe that to be a mistake. The Karthians react to strength. At the moment, they have no idea of what forces we have. I've been moving ships in an attempt to keep their spies from gathering numbers. I believe that is why they have yet to move on us."

The following morning the *Rogers* showed up with the new weapon aboard. In addition, the Targarian engineers had extracted the mystery wormhole weapon from the *Rogers*' last encounter, adding it to her arsenal. Testing of both had yet to be done. Mace and the others transferred to their ship.

"Mr. Hobbs, where's the nearest planet, moon, or asteroid we can target? I want to know if either of these weapons works."

Liam replied, "Harkoza has a small moon."

Mace nodded. "Jump us there. Mr. Mueller, line up a battery of test firings. If these weapons function, I want to know what we can expect from them."

The *Rogers* hopped to the Harkoza moon and hovered a kilometer above the surface of the dull gray satellite. The quantum wave weapon was brought online first. A drone sensor was sent down and the weapon fired. A wave of green energy filled the space between the *Rogers* and the surface for two and a half seconds. The *Rogers* rocked from the spray of debris that rose from the point of impact. The dampening fields prevented any damage.

Mace turned to Liam. "Mr. Hobbs, take us up to ten kilometers. Mr. Mueller, let's try that again."

The test was repeated with similar results. The sensor drones sent back valuable readings before their destruction. A test of the wormhole weapon followed with little result to see.

"Did it even fire?" Johnny asked.

"Yes," said Hans. "What we need is a hard target. That soft Earth down there doesn't leave much of an indication."

A thick metal plate was flown down to the surface in a shuttle and laid out for another test. After Hans pressed the button on his console, Humphrey zoomed in with the visual sensor.

"We have a two centimeter hole in the plate. I would say the weapon is fully operational."

Mace asked, "How far out can it be projected?"

Jeff answered, "I've only had a short time to look it over. The energy feed dictates the range. With our current feed that range is about two million kilometers. Not a tremendous distance in space. Would be a formidable weapon in an atmospheric fight."

"Can the energy feed be updated?"

Jeff nodded. "I believe so. That may lead to other limiting factors, which we would have to address at that time."

"How about the size of the wormhole? Can it be scaled to create a larger hole?"

Jeff shrugged. "I don't have enough information to offer an opinion on that. When we return from this fight, I'll add that to my growing list."

Mace turned. "Mr. Hobbs, take us back to the rift. Mr. Mueller, try to come up with a few scenarios where one or the other of those weapons might prove useful."

As the *Rogers* came to a stop fifty thousand kilometers from the *Organ Cave*, Johnny asked, "So how long do we sit here?"

Mace leaned back in his chair. "As long as it takes."

Chapter 8

Five days of frayed nerves passed with no movement by the Karthian fleet. On the sixth day, starting with the back end of the column, the warships of the coming Karthian invasion turned and moved away.

Humphrey said, "It appears they are leaving, Mr. Hardy."

Jasper came over the comm. "I'm not sure what to make of that maneuver."

Mace replied, "Maybe they decided it wasn't worth it. Or maybe they're having issues on the other war front."

Stark joined the comm. "I wouldn't celebrate just yet."

Mace said, "Tell us what you know."

Stark stood and began to pace. "We have news that another one of those stations is on its way. Our strategy of blocking the rift is no longer viable."

Jasper said, "We got onto that station and destroyed it before. We can do that to a new one if needed."

Stark's silhouette stopped. "I have to wonder if we'll have that option, Mr. Collins. When you joined the fight against my ships, you allowed the Karthians to cart off the remains of several of my Radica ships. If they studied them, they may have learned of a way to defeat that technology."

Johnny said, "Doc? Is there any way to collapse that rift? Could we make a bomb or something that would close it down?"

Jeff replied, "Gnaga and I studied that idea extensively, Mr. Tretcher. Our conclusion was that we had no conclusion. We don't know how the rift was created or what force keeps it open."

Johnny said, "Well, it's just sitting there. Any tests we could conduct? Maybe load a nuke ship up with gatrellium and dark matter and set it off at the edge?"

Jeff shook his head. "As we discovered when we attempted to move around the opening, there doesn't appear to be an edge. From every angle and every approach the rift looks exactly the same. It's a mind boggling concept to think that even possible, but we experienced it, so it must be. Of course, I suppose it could also be an optical illusion of sorts."

"OK then, how about we set one off in the middle? I mean, try something... anything. If they do bring another one of those stations and Stark's domed ships no longer work, we won't be able to get close to that thing."

Jeff rubbed his chin. "I suppose a bit of experimentation wouldn't do any harm. Give me a few minutes to discuss this with Mr. Klept."

Jasper said, "Ape-man... always wanting to blow stuff up."

Johnny replied, "I think that's the first time you've called me that in a month. I've missed it."

Jasper nodded. "That's not all you're missing. And I do like the idea of trying to close that hole. If that can be done, this Karthian issue goes away."

Jeff returned to the bridge a short time later with Gnaga by his side. "We've concluded that Johnny's idea of experimentation might be a good one. With the Karthians moving away, we have the rift available for whatever we would want to try. What we'd like to do is to set off one of those nuclear ships as Johnny suggested. We would use that instance of immense power to open a wormhole a kilometer from the rift. We don't expect much interaction between the two, but our expectations are based on gut feeling and not science. We plan to also load the area with sensor probes, hoping to gain information about any possible interactions between the rift and our wormhole."

Mace replied, "So you're attempting to open another large wormhole as close to that one as you possibly can. And then study the effects?"

Jeff nodded. "Precisely. If we find interaction between the two, we hope it will lead us down further paths of study."

A jump was made back to Divinia and a ship prepared.

Mace frowned as the gatrellium was loaded aboard. "I hope we aren't wasting a precious resource. We could jump a couple hundred times with that store."

Jeff replied, "Sometimes you have to break a few eggs, Mr. Hardy."

The *Rogers* returned with the experimental ship. Sensor probes were positioned in and around the rift with the hopes of measuring some phenomenon that could be further studied, then the ship was detonated, generating a wormhole more than two kilometers wide.

As the wormhole faded, data streamed in from the sensors. Half an hour of data collecting showed no unusual activity. The hastily thrown together experiment was a bust.

Jeff stood with his fists on his hips. "I hoped to find something in that. It looks as though your fears of wasting a valued resource were right, Mr. Hardy."

Johnny asked, "Was that as close as you could possibly get it? What about setting it off inside the rift as I suggested?"

Jeff shook his head. "We can't form a wormhole with that close a proximity to another one. The initial tear in space-time will not form. I would love to see the interaction between two wormholes, but we have no way of forcing them together."

Mace held up a hand. "Maybe we do. That new weapon... it's essentially a moving wormhole, isn't it? Could we fire it at the rift and take measurements?"

Gnaga stepped up. "An excellent suggestion, Mr. Hardy. And one we can attempt immediately."

Jeff slowly nodded. "I have to agree. Mr. Mallot, if you could launch another handful of probes in and around that rift, we can fire that weapon and check for results."

Gnaga began to rub his hands together nervously. "I've wanted to perform this experiment for some time, Mr. Hardy. Thank you for your bit of wisdom."

Mace laughed. "Don't thank me yet. The result may be the same as the last shot."

Humphrey said, "The probes from the prior experiments remain in place. Would you like them tuned to look for anything specific?"

Jeff shook his head. "Full spectrum. We want everything."

Mace turned to Hans Mueller. "Mr. Mueller, place a shot right in the middle of that rift."

Seconds later, their two centimeter wormhole rapidly moved through the rift, causing a visual ripple that moved out from the center.

Jeff smiled. "I'd say we got a reaction."

The data from the probes streamed in. "Here, Mr. Klept. Look at that. The wave is bending the light from those stars on the other side. This is fascinating."

Jeff looked at Mace. "I would like to do this again. This time out to the side. I know we can't see an edge if we move around it, but there is one there nonetheless. Mr. Mueller, target as close to the inner edge of the rift as you can."

Hans replied, "Tell me when."

Jeff waved his hand as he continued to look at the data. "When, Mr. Mueller."

The button was pressed and the weapon fired. The result was different. Instead of a rippling wave moving out from the point of contact, a bright glow began to grow in intensity.

Johnny frowned at the wall display. "That doesn't look good."

Mace nodded. "Mr. Hobbs, please move us away. And do so quickly if you would."

The *Rogers* shot backwards, coming to a stop beside the *Organ Cave*. The bright glow continued to grow before spreading around the entirety of the rift.

Jasper said, "I can't say I like the looks of that."

Gnaga pointed at one of the parameters showing beside the space-time distortion. "It's getting smaller! The rift is shrinking!"

Jeff grinned. "Indeed it is!"

As quickly as the glow had started, it snuffed out.

Johnny said, "Anyone else think we need to hit it again?"

"I would say we have to," said Jeff. "This was completely unexpected."

Mace added, "If hitting it once was good, would twice be better? Maybe once on each side?"

Gnaga said, "Perhaps it would be best if we wait a bit."

Mace asked, "Are we seeing anything that looks unstable?"

Jeff pulled up several data sheets on his arm pad display. "I don't see anything that looks different than before. Mr. Hardy, it's your call."

Malcolm Stark had been listening. "I would emphasize caution. And patience. The Karthians are not a threat at the moment. Perhaps we wait as Gnaga suggests."

Jasper said, "Forget that. You want that rift open so you can attempt another deal. I say shut it down. Hit it twice."

Mace nodded. "I would agree. Mr. Mueller, target one side, then the other."

Hans typed into his console as the *Rogers* moved in again. Seconds later, the deed was done.

Hans turned as the right-hand section of the rift began to glow. "Mr. Hobbs, you can take us back out."

As the second half of the rift began to glow, the light emanating from the right side began to spread, meeting up with that from the left. As the glows joined, they burned bright. The rift again shrank. This time, when the glow collapsed, the space-time rift had shrunk by almost a third.

Mace smiled. "Gentleman, I have to say I like what I'm seeing."

"Let's hit her again!" said Johnny.

Jeff nodded. "All other parameters are holding steady. If we manage to shrink it by another third, the Karthians will have to reduce their column to no more than five ships wide."

Mace gestured. "Mr. Hobbs, Mr. Mueller, another run like the last please."

The attack on the rift was repeated, and again the diameter of the breach shrunk by a third.

Gnaga cautioned, "I'm seeing fluctuations, Mr. Moskowitz. The zeta parameter seems to have an oscillation."

Mace stroked his goatee. "Let's give it a few minutes. I don't want to cause an issue because of too much of a good thing. As Stark says, there's no immediate need. Speaking of that, do you have an estimate of when that new station will arrive?"

Stark replied, "The only information I have is that it's on its way. That could mean two hours or five months. We have no way of knowing."

Jeff said, "The zeta parameter appears to be stabilizing."

Humphrey said, "Mr. Hardy, I'm picking up movement on the other side of the rift. One moment... it's big. Very big. Has to be one of those stations. And I have ships coming in as well."

Mace pointed at the display. "Mr. Hobbs, take us in. Mr. Mueller, give us two more... no, three hits on the sides of that rift."

Gnaga raised a hand. "Mr. Hardy, I would suggest caution."

Mace replied, "If we don't close that rift now, once it's in place, that station will prevent us from doing it then."

"Knock it down," Johnny added.

Derwood raced onto the bridge, barking.

Johnny pointed. "The dog says do it now!"

The *Rogers* slipped in. Three pulses from the wormhole weapon were fired into the rift. A ring surrounding the outside edges glowed bright. The rift in space-time shrank rapidly to a point, but the glow continued.

Gnaga said, "I'm getting readings off the scale, Mr. Hardy. I would pull back if possible."

Mace nodded. "Mr. Hobbs, move us away."

Johnny whispered. "Nobody's flying through that rift. Unless maybe they have the gatrellium hull-skin like we do."

Malcolm Stark commented, "Congratulations, Mr. Hardy. Your team has accomplished what we thought impossible."

Mace replied, "The tenacity of these people is what did that, Mr. Stark. If it holds, maybe we can get down to having a peaceful existence."

"The Karthians are still out there, Mr. Hardy. And they know where we are. If another way can be found to here, they will find it. Perhaps this will buy us the time we need to replenish our military capabilities. I don't suppose you'd be willing to share whatever weapon you used on that rift with us?"

Mace laughed. "Not a chance. And I'm sending you over a list of star systems that we are laying claim to. We've been to these, explored them, and mapped them. I suggest we exchange data on our claims so as to not create contentions in the future."

Stark replied, "I take it from that you are relinquishing your claims to Earth space?"

Mace huffed. "Hardly. We claim that as a birthright. But you obviously have the people behind you, and we can't argue with that. Maybe at the moment consider us minority shareholders who do not answer to your rule."

Stark hesitated for several seconds. "I suppose it would not hurt for you to have uninhibited access so long as your visits are not aimed at subversion. And I will let the people know that it was your team that closed the rift, ending the Karthian threat."

Mace nodded. "I suppose that's as much as we could ask for at the moment. I'm certain we'll be talking again."

Stark's silhouette bowed as the comm closed.

Jasper said, "I still don't trust that snake."

Mace sat back in his command chair. "None of us does, Mr. Collins. He's given us plenty of reasons not to."

Gnaga said, "Mr. Moskowitz, I'm concerned with these parameters. That shrunken rift is emitting extreme levels of gamma radiation."

Jeff replied, "It's not enough to overwhelm our shields. It's an interesting phenomenon, though. I would place those numbers in the soft gamma ray burst category, something you might see from an extremely small magnetar."

Jasper cut in. "I say we get back to business at Divinia. I'll leave a couple scouts out here to monitor the area."

With the Karthian threat diminished and Earth under Stark's control, the *Rogers* returned to its new home at Divinia.

Johnny said, "I guess this is where we put our mailbox now?"

Mace replied, "Mr. Collins has indicated he doesn't have a problem with that. I want to see things settle on Earth for a bit before we head back. Everyone can make their own decision as to remain here or to go back there."

Zax and Fina raced onto the bridge, with Jane just behind.

Mace laughed. "They just don't quit, do they?"

Jane shook her head. "You have no idea. I don't remember having that much energy when I was a kid. And the thing is, they can switch it off in an instant. I can put them to bed and they're both out in two minutes' time."

Mace said, "I want some of what they have. How's their reading coming?"

Johnny replied, "With the digital library on the ship, they're both blasting through the books. Still at the sixth grade reading level, which means constant questions. I don't know how my angel here does it, but she patiently answers every one."

Jane half smiled. "They're starting to get complex. I don't know how much longer I'll be able to keep up."

Mace asked, "Has Fina been in the water lately?"

Jane shook her head. "We were worried about that, but she seems fine."

Jasper walked onto the bridge of the *Rogers*. "If you want, there are any number of community pools around Yentis. And lakes and such beyond the city. Hazards are minimal."

Jane smiled. "I'll arrange an outing for all the kids on the ship. Will be good for them to have a somewhat normal activity."

Jasper took control of a Targarian vacation resort complex just outside Yentis. The *Rogers* hovered over the lawn as its Human crew moved into the villas that made up the complex. The Targarians were happy to provide whatever would be needed for their Human guests to feel welcome. Jasper took pride in their response.

Jeff, Gnaga, and their team of scientists and engineers moved back to the lab in the city. They would continue to work to solve the physics puzzles now before them. Particular attention would be focused on how the endpoints of a wormhole could be moved once it was established. The possibilities for making use of that feature were almost limitless.

Mace joined Jasper at the space docks, where his new fleet of Collins class vessels was taking shape. "It's strange, I almost feel hesitant to accept that the Karthian threat is gone."

Jasper nodded. "Now we have to worry about Stark."

"I'm not so sure about that. Without the Karthians, he may have trouble bringing all the Union members into his tent. At the moment, they have the ships, he only has Humans. I could see them turning on him in an instant."

Jasper leaned his head to one side. "Maybe. All the more reason for us to continue our buildup."

Mace frowned. "We may have another issue."

Jasper turned. "What's that?"

Mace crossed his arms. "We have several hundred star systems in the region of space surrounding Earth that we've now explored. Being the first there gives us claiming rights. Without having outposts, I could see Stark's people, or the Union members, trying to lay claim to them."

Jasper scowled. "We left markers on every one of those."

"Markers can be moved. I think we might want to consider outposts."

Jasper leaned on the railing of the catwalk they stood on. "We don't have the gatrellium needed to open and maintain a couple hundred outposts. You put people out there and you have to feed them. And you have to bring them back at some point. Without a sufficient supply of gatrellium, our fleet, other than for home defense, becomes useless."

Mace smiled. "So what you're really saying is we need to get our team back out there to hunt gatrellium."

Jasper nodded. "They ain't making any more of it. If someone else gets to it first, it's gone for good."

Mace sighed. "I'll give everyone a few day's rest before I spring that on them. There's enough stress going on over the whole Stark situation. If given the choice, I'm sure at least half would just give up and return home."

Mace shook his head. "You know, I mentioned earlier about Stark needing the Karthians for leverage over the Union? Well, I think he now needs us. And I'm not talking the *Rogers*, I'm talking you and the Targarians. You give him a common enemy to talk about with the others. And I'm not suggesting you give up in any way. I'm on your side. I'm just saying he will now use you as his reason for the Union members to need him. Even without the Karthians, this whole region of space is in chaos."

"OK. Well, that just means we have to fix it."

Mace laughed. "Well, I guess we do."

Chapter 9

Two days of rest were given before a volunteer crew was asked to make a jump to Canto to check on the Knuttin Corporation. A single crew volunteered. A wormhole portal was opened and the *Rogers* slipped through.

United Front dreadnoughts were waiting. "Mr. Hardy, what business do you have on Canto?"

"We just came to check on the colony and the Knuttin Corporation."

The officer on the display shook his head. "The colony of Canto is not your concern. The United Front has it under its protection. As to the Knuttin Corporation, your inquiries will have to be directed to them."

"OK. Can you pass a message to Frado Knuttin for us? Tell him Mace Hardy is here."

"I'm afraid the United Front Military cannot be used for such purposes."

Mace tapped his finger on his armrest. "OK. Then we'll be going down to the surface to pass a message from there."

The officer replied, "You command a ship with weapons that is not registered as a United Front vessel. You will not be allowed to go any farther."

Mace returned an angry stare. "I own 24 percent of that planet."

The officer turned belligerent. "You are in violation of United Front space. You will withdraw or suffer the consequences."

Mace held up a hand. "My apologies if I got a bit heated. May we take an unarmed shuttle to the surface?"

The officer nodded. "That would be acceptable, after a search. No weapons, including personal weapons, are allowed within United Front space. Bring your shuttle back to this location. Your warship must withdraw immediately."

Johnny scowled. "I'm starting to think these people are Nazis."

Mace nodded. "It would appear so."

Mace opened a comm. "Miss Taub, could you meet me in bay one?"

"Sure thing."

Mace turned. "Mr. Crawford, that leaves you in charge. We should be back in a few hours... if Mr. Knuttin responds. If we haven't heard from him within a few days, we'll make our way back out here for a pick-up."

Jordan took command of the bridge. "As soon as the shuttle is out, let's take her back a ways."

Jenny was waiting in the bay when Mace arrived. "We going down to the surface?"

Mace nodded. "They won't allow the *Rogers* down there. If you have any hand weapons on you, go ahead and leave them over there on the table. We'll be getting an inspection from the UF before they will allow us on Canto."

"Sounds like they've really changed around their level of protection out here. Last time we just let them know we were coming."

Mace walked up the shuttle ramp with Jenny following. "They want the *Rogers* to move back out of their space. As soon as we're out, they're leaving. Not home, just out."

Jenny sat and strapped herself in. "Too much hostility in this galaxy."

The shuttle hovered and then exited the bay. Minutes later, after a full scan, it was landing inside a docking bay of the UF dreadnought *Firus*.

As the ramp lowered, four UF soldiers marched aboard. "You, out onto the deck. And no sudden moves."

"Friendly lot," Jenny whispered.

Mace unfastened his harness and stood, walking slowly to the ramp as Jenny followed. The two were soon on the deck looking back at the shuttle.

Jenny said, "I can't get tired of that blue on her hull."

"I just hope they don't spend too much time sniffing around. They would have that hull, our transponders, and any other tech we have on there they don't currently have."

"Well, not much we can do about it now. And I hate to think about swapping out one of our shuttles for something low tech just for instances like this."

Mace sighed. "I guess if we're in their space we have to follow their rules."

Two UF techs, holding scanning devices, passed by before disappearing up the shuttle ramp. Five minutes later they emerged. An officer of the deck gestured for the Humans to board their ship.

The shuttle was soon settling on the tarmac at Travia Forks. A short walk had Mace and Jenny sitting in the lounge. A commercial kiosk was used to place a comm to Frado Knuttin back in the main UF territories.

He replied several minutes later. "Mr. Hardy, I see that you are on Canto."

"Yep. We just wanted to check in and see how things are going."

Frado smiled. "They are going well. Our difficulty with the pirates and their supporters is coming to an end. As it turns out, there may be a new colony rush forthcoming, and the strength of our corporation may put us at the forefront of such a rush. Our military contracts have become quite lucrative. I'm considering splitting the corporation into two separate companies, one focused on fulfilling our military needs, the other supporting colony establishment."

Mace nodded. "Sounds like you have your hands full."

"Yes. Quite full. There isn't enough time in the day to accomplish what I need to get done. Which brings me to a question for you: the wormhole device you possess, I understand fully why you would be hesitant to provide that technology to others. What I would like to know is, would you be interested in leasing your ship to the corporation? With your crew of course."

"What'd you have in mind?"

Frado passed the image of a planet to the comm display. "As you know, our ships move at less than the speed of light. The UF has expanded to the dimension it has through the use of rifts. The rest of our travels are long voyages on starships. What this means is reaching a new star system to stake a colony can take years, even decades. With your technology, we could stake claims on an untold number of systems long before any other company could reach said systems."

Mace laughed. "So you want us to cheat for you?"

Frado pulled back. "First arrival is not cheating, Mr. Hardy. It is, however, required to register a claim."

Mace asked, "Would anyone argue those claims because they were made with a non-UF ship and crew?"

Frado smiled. "For that I have a solution. The corporation will provide individual craft and pilots for that claiming process. You use the *Rogers* to get our pilots there, they stake the claims. After, you return here where the pilots can take their claims to Canto for registration."

Mace said, "That's gonna be a problem. Your military doesn't want us in UF territory with this ship."

"That is not an issue. The systems we wish to stake claim to are outside United Front jurisdiction. I told you before of the colony process. We have to establish and build a colony to a certain level before it is recognized by our government. At that point we can begin the process of applying for inclusion in the empire. Staking a claim is the first part of that process."

Mace asked, "And what would we get as a result of this effort?"

Frado again smiled. "You own 24 percent of the corporation, Mr. Hardy. Think of it this way: if a claim is registered, it can then be leased out to a colonization company. At the same time, we provide valued services for establishing such colonies.

With your ship we could easily be the premier corporation in this space. Already, our scientists have identified eighty-nine potential system candidates. The farthest of those worlds, using our current technology, won't be explored for at least six decades. Just out of curiosity, how long does a journey through one of your wormholes take? I know our trips through a rift are near instantaneous."

Mace replied, "Actually, they're the same. It's like passing through an open door. If you have eighty-some candidates, we could probably cover those in a week's time."

Frado returned a blank stare. "You are joking, are you not?"

Mace shook his head. "If you gave me the coordinates to your home world, we could be in orbit above it in a couple minutes."

Frado sat in shock. "I had no idea your technology was so powerful. I knew you were advantaged over us, but I didn't know by how much."

Mace said, "I'll tell you what, Mr. Knuttin. We'll make the jumps for you in exchange for gatrellium. I want a hundred tons per system."

Jenny leaned in and whispered, "Kind of steep, don't you think?"

Mace replied, "Without the wormhole generator technology, they can't even make use of it."

Mace looked back at the comm camera. "Well, Mr. Knuttin? A hundred tons per colony claimed?"

The Kohamian stood and awkwardly paced. "I will have to evaluate the size of the stockpiles that are available. At the moment those are limited."

Mace replied, "Evaluate and come back with what you think is doable. As you said, we have the ship that could make this possible. It would also broaden the UF territory, leaving less likelihood of another species coming along to claim these systems. We've been doing this ourselves. And I know for a fact the members of the former Galactic Union are itching to do this as well. And I'll tell you what, if you are able to provide the gatrellium numbers I've asked for, I could possibly swing giving the corporation a minor stake in the systems we are currently claiming. Maybe 3 percent or something similar. We have over two hundred candidate systems we've identified already."

Frado sat in his chair. "I had no idea this discussion would go as it has, Mr. Hardy. All of the gatrellium in the United Front territories has export limits attached to it. Given what you've just told me, I believe I may be able to get that restriction lifted, seeing as how it will directly benefit the United Front."

Mace nodded. "Acquiring that material would be a big boost to us as well. And when I say us I mean the Targarian Empire and the *Rogers* and her crew, neither of which are hostile toward the UF."

Frado rubbed his pointed chin. "Allow me to discuss this with our military command. I have connections that go almost to the top. If such an arrangement could be signed, when would you and your crew be available to begin?"

"I would want at least two shifts of my crew. We only have one aboard at the moment. That would probably take at least a day."

Frado shook his head in disbelief. "You never cease to astound me, Mr. Hardy. Give me twenty-four of your hours and I should have a response. In the meantime, I will send over a corporate liaison. Ask them anything you like about Canto. They should easily be able to keep you occupied for the time I require."

The comm closed. Ten minutes later the corporate liaison showed. "Mr. Hardy, my name is Derette Golese. Mr. Knuttin sent me to assist you with your needs."

Mace stood, offering a slight bow as was the customary greeting of the Kohamians. "Miss Golese, this is my associate Miz Taub. I can only guess Mr. Knuttin was offering us tours of the colony?"

Derette replied, "If that's what you prefer. It was my understanding that you sought entertainment."

Mace smiled. "That'll work. What would you have available in the middle of the day?"

Derette gestured toward a wall poster advertising a sporting event. "The first annual torus tournament began two days ago.

If you would like, I can show you the favorite pastime of the Kohamian people."

As they walked, following Derette Golese, Jenny asked, "I keep hearing Kohamians. I thought these were UF people."

Mace replied, "They are. As a species they're Kohamians. As an empire they are the United Front. Think of it from the Bellias' standpoint. They are Bellia, but members of the Targarian Empire, which is now really the Collins Kingdom."

"I see. But aren't these all Kohamians?"

"That's what Mr. Knuttin indicated. They say they are open to others, but who knows."

Derette led them to a transport that dropped the threesome off at the Grand Torus Arena, located at the city's center. A short walk brought them to a room with a serving bar, a table with a variety of foods, and seating that faced a transparent wall. Just beyond it was the arena.

It was shaped like the inside of an eggshell, and the contestants flew about the walls on hoverboards. The arena, about two hundred meters long by one hundred twenty meters diameter, had goals at each end.

Mace said, "As I understand it, the teams try to work a ball down to the opponent's goal, where it's thrown into one of those red funnels. If it sticks, they get the points as designated. The goal is to reach a hundred before the opposing team."

Derette smiled. "Excellent explanation, Mr. Hardy. I take it you've witnessed a few matches before?"

Mace shook his head. "I only know what Frado described to me."

Derette replied, "There will be two demis, balls if you will, in play at any given time. Substitutions are made on the fly. The game takes tremendous balance and precise timing. Imagine a demi being thrown forward from a boarder moving in one direction to a boarder moving at a fast pace in another. I find the distant lobs the most entertaining. Would you care to wager any credits?"

Mace shrugged. "How would I do that? I suppose we have a healthy bank account here now since we can't take any off-world."

Derette's eyes grew big. "Your account is more than healthy, Mr. Hardy. It's the largest in the colony. One hundred fifty-nine million credits. Are you interested?"

"Sure. What do I do?"

Derette typed away on a keypad. A wall display illuminated, showing the members of each team in a list or rows. Going across in columns were cues that could be selected for a wager.

Mace pointed. "Number fourteen. That was my number in high school. Let's place a bet on them to score at least two points."

Derette selected the player, Kons Vakka, and then highlighted the cue, two points minimum. "And how much would you like to wager?"

Mace shrugged. "I don't know... a million credits?"

Derette pulled back. "I'm not even sure the booking house could cover such a wager."

Mace nodded. "OK, then what would a typical bet be? How much?"

Derette replied, "Kons Vakka is a goalie. The odds of her scoring two points are at one hundred eighty-four to one. Goalies rarely score. They do, however, get the occasional assist. Assists count as a quarter point. I don't recall ever seeing a goalie have eight assists in a game though, let alone a full match."

Mace said, "OK, then what would you suggest?"

Jenny asked, "Can I pick one?"

Mace nodded. "Sure. Some of those credits belong to you."

Jenny looked over the roster. "Number three. Goma Katis. I want ten credits that he scores at least two points."

Derette entered the wager. "The payout is one-point-four to one. A reasonable bet. Goma is coming off the injured list, but held a three-point-two goal average prior to that injury. She's also one of my favorites."

Mace asked, "The teams are mixed genders?"

Derette nodded. "The men have better power and speed, but the women are better strategists. They are excellent at feeding the big strikers up front."

Jenny said, "Wish we could talk to them. I'd love to get Goma's take on the upcoming game. Not that I'll know what she's talking about. I just want to get a hint about her attitude."

Derette replied, "I can take you to see them. The first game isn't for another forty minutes."

Jenny turned to face Mace. "Let's go do this. It'll add some fun to the game."

"Sure. Miss Golese, Lead the way."

Derette said, "If you'd like to make a wager, Mr. Hardy, we should do that before going down."

"OK. I want a hundred credits on Kons for a full point."

Derette replied, "They *are* your credits I suppose."

The trip to the locker room had Kohamian players walking around in various stages of dress. The Humans in escort received odd looks from most.

Derette guided her assignees to the locker of Goma Katis. "Miz Katis, I'd like to introduce you to two executives of the Knuttin Corporation. This is Jenny Taub and Mace Hardy. Jenny has selected you for a wager today."

Goma said, "What'd you take?"

"Uh, two points for ten credits, I think," said Jenny.

Goma nodded. "Safe bet."

The player standing next to her remarked. "Should have taken five. She's been on fire this past week in practice. She likes to come out with a bang, too. She's been hitting the five ring like there was nobody in front of it."

Jenny smiled. "Good to know."

The trio proceeded to the locker of Kons Vakka.

"Miz Vakka, this is Mace Hardy and Jenny Taub. They are executives with the Knuttin Corporation. Mr. Hardy has a wager placed on you today to score a full point."

Kons Vakka grunted out a laugh. "A point? Your money would have been better spent on a jug of Gookan."

Mace turned to face Derette. "What's Gookan?"

Derette replied, "It's a cheap wine, generally consumed by the lower classes. I should apologize for Miz Vakka's rudeness."

Mace laughed. "Not at all. I like a player who says what she thinks. If you manage the feat I might just have to buy you dinner or something."

The torus player stood with an angry look and a clenched fist.

Mace stepped back. "What'd I say?"

Jenny smirked. "I'd say you insulted her character. Let me guess, influencing players is heavily frowned upon?"

Derette nodded. "It's our national sport. The players, teams, and fans take it all very seriously. Undue influence is not only frowned upon, but a crime."

Mace held up a hand. "My apologies. I was only trying to make light of my obviously poor wager."

Vakka stepped forward, still angered. "You think I'm not capable?"

Jenny said, "You'd best just shut your pie hole until we get out of here. Some of these people look pretty intimidating."

Mace held his comment, bowed slightly and turned toward the door. Kons Vakka and half a dozen other players scowled as they walked away.

Back in the viewing room, they took their seats.

Derette asked, "May I have a beverage brought to you?"

Mace laughed. "Yeah, a jug of that Gookan. I'm obviously from the lower classes. I might as well drink like it."

Jenny leaned in. "I still think you've got class. At least a little."

Mace smiled. "Well, thank you, Miz Taub."

Chapter 10

A horn sounded and a dozen players from each team streamed out of doors set into the walls. On their hoverboards, the players were soon whizzing around the inside of the egg-shaped playing field, going up and over the ceiling as the flat hoverboards stayed at a fixed height to the sides of the arena, skimming along just above the surface. A mere two centimeters separated the board from the arena walls. A player leaning forward would speed up while leaning back would slow down. leaning side to side had them turning one direction or the other. The highest speeds were attained by leaning hard forward while coming down from a ceiling position.

"Wow," said Mace, "this looks like it's gonna run at an incredibly fast pace. How do they keep from colliding?"

"Skill," Derette replied. "Collisions mean injuries. Injuries mean no pay. The boards have built-in sensors that assist, making it difficult to maneuver into the path of an oncoming player, but it isn't foolproof. Goma is coming off one such injury."

"How do you keep track of who has a demi?"

Derette pointed to a hole just below one of the goals. "They will release the practice demis any moment. You'll see. It's easy for the fans to follow, quite difficult for the players. The best players are able to partially conceal a demi. The players' gloves are magnetic when balled in a fist. The demis are hollow with an iron surface. The demi will stay on the knuckles of a player who captures it up until they release their hold or are tagged by an opposing player. You see the circle on their backs? That is the tag point. Touch that and the demi is released.

"For throwing, a player will fling their arm in the direction they want to throw, unclenching their fist at just the right moment for a release. You'll have a solid understanding of how it's played by the time the game is over. Perhaps your next wager will be a more informed one."

A second horn sounded and four demis rolled out into the playing field from each goal. They were quickly captured and a melee of releases began. The demis had either a red or a blue halo surrounding them as viewed through the transparent walls of the arena. To the viewer, the walls of the other viewing rooms appeared to be solid walls. The surface of the arena looked stark white.

Ten minutes after the practice demis had been released, a third horn sounded. The demis were quickly launched at the goals, where they were either snagged by the goalies who guarded them, or they found their mark in one of the concentric rings of funnels.

Derette leaned forward in her chair. "This is exciting, Mr. Hardy. My duties do not normally take me to a torus match. This will be the first game of the tournament I've been able to attend. In about two minutes the match will begin."

Jenny asked, "How long does it last?"

Derette replied, "The shortest tournament match on record is eight minutes. It was a lopsided affair after six starters had been injured in collisions the game before. The boards have been modified since, and I don't think we've seen a game of less than nineteen minutes. Typically they run thirty to forty minutes. I believe the longest, a defensive struggle for sure, lasted over two hours."

The players all skimmed back into the opened side doors. Seconds later, a long horn sounded. The players shot out of a team doorway into the arena as ten short bursts of the horn followed. As the side doors closed, another blast signaled the two demis coming into the arena, one with a red glow, the other blue. The demis were captured and the maneuvering began.

The Forks Rangers, dressed in dark gray with yellow trim, were the home team, and the team Jenny and Mace had wagered on. The away team, the Durnis Bolts, the favorite of the farmer clans, were dressed in all black with green lightning bolts adorning their arms and legs.

"I kind of like those black uniforms," Jenny said.

Derette turned with a scowl. "Only lowlanders would wear black."

Jenny turned and whispered to Mace: "They take this stuff seriously."

Two minutes into the round, a Bolt, after building up tremendous speed, captured a pass on the fly, spun, and hurtled it toward a goal. Kons Vakka was there for the stop.

Mace raised his fist. "That's my girl!"

As the Rangers set up for a pass from Vakka, she left her position at the goal, raced up a wall and then down towards the floor. As she moved up another wall and passed over the top of the arena, she leaned hard forward, almost touching the visor of her helmet to the floor. Her hoverboard raced to an insane speed as it came down the wall. Kons Vakka turned hard at the bottom, heading toward the opponent's goal.

Derette stood. "This is not possible!"

The opposing team, unready to counter the assault of a goalie, was in complete disarray. The blue demi sailed past a goalie, striking and sticking in a funnel in the inner ring. A five point score. Viewers in the surrounding rooms could be heard through the walls as they screamed in delight. Derette was jumping up and down in her chair.

Kons Vakka had raced in, spinning on her board as she wound up for a release. The iron demi left her clench at lightning speed, soaring past the right side goalie and into the five point circle, where it clanged into a funnel. Falling from her chair, Derette Golese convulsed and collapsed. Neighboring viewers were screaming, stomping, and banging on the walls.

Derette opened her eyes almost a full minute later. "What happened?"

Jenny smirked. "I think you got a bit too excited and fainted."

Derette pulled herself up, assisted by Mace. "I must apologize. That's never happened to me before."

Mace laughed. "Don't worry about it. So long as you're OK, it just added to our entertainment."

Derette looked up at the scoreboard. "Wait... we have fifteen points?"

Jenny nodded. "In the confusion that ensued, the Rangers managed to bag another five-pointer. Was an impressive move."

Mace looked at the wager board. "What the... I thought I had a hundred eighty to one odds?"

Derette shook her head. "That was for a two point wager, though you selected one. Your wager was good for just over a forty to one payoff, it seems you've had a good night at the tournament, Mr. Hardy. Four thousand credits is quite the haul."

Jenny slapped him in the back. "Guess who's buying dinner?"

Derette pointed. "Your own wager has paid as well."

Jenny laughed. "Great. I wonder what I can get for fourteen credits?"

The game continued, with the Rangers winning after the twenty-second minute, going on to win the match four games to two. Derette led the two Humans to an upper class restaurant, where the hideous-looking Humans were offered a private booth. Derette apologized profusely for the bigoted behavior.

Mace laughed it off. "Not a big deal. This isn't our world and the people can think whatever they want."

Derette sighed. "Still, you are business clients. What happens if I bring in a client who *is* offended?"

Jenny asked, "How many of them have you had?"

"Well, none. But it would be appalling nonetheless."

Mace waved his hand as the menus were brought around. "Not an issue for us. Now, what would you expect a Human to want to eat here?"

Derette frowned. "I'm afraid I'm not familiar with Human customs or habits. I have tried one of your delicacies though. A friend offered me a sampling of honey. It was quite good."

Jenny scowled. "Bee vomit."

Mace stared in silence for several seconds. "You don't like honey? How is it possible for someone to not like honey?"

Jenny shook her head. "So a bee harvests nectar, swallows it into a honey stomach. It then carries it back to the hive, where it's vomited up for other workers who chew on it for a half hour. They spit it out and let it dry to a goo. That's your honey. You still like that?"

Mace laughed. "You've never even had it, have you?"

Jenny scowled. "And I'm not going to."

Derette smiled. "It really was quite good."

Mace looked Jenny up and down in a sarcastic manner for several seconds before turning his attention to the menu.

"Flossal? What is that?"

Derette replied, "It's a small creature that moves along on its belly. It leaves a sticky trail as it goes. Plays havoc with vegetable and flower gardens."

Mace returned a disgusted look.

Jenny said, "What's the matter? You don't like snails?"

"Thank you, but no. Sounds more like slugs. What's this one? Klovaxi?"

"Klovaxi is a fish. It's native to this planet. I've not had it, but I've been told it's excellent."

Mace nodded. "Fish. I can handle that."

Jenny asked, "Quopa?"

"That is a fruit dish covered in a sweet gravy."

Jenny winked. "I'll have that."

Derette opened a second menu. "Might I suggest a Novian wine?"

Jenny nodded. "Yes, you might."

Mace closed his menu. "Sounds good. I'll have that, too."

The Novian wine was high in alcohol, which brought about an inebriated host and two tipsy Humans. From the restaurant, the guests were taken to the most expensive hotel on Canto.

The room, a suite, had a balcony with a tremendous view looking out over a local lake with mountains in the near distance.

After a quick break in the restroom, Derette dismissed herself, apologizing for her behavior and lack of self control.

Jenny stood in the main room. "I like those curved couches."

Mace laughed. "Really? They look like something out of a pimp's playhouse from the 1970s."

Jenny put her hand on Mace's chest, pushing him back onto one of the couches. A heavy makeout session followed, ending with them passing out in each other's arms. Jenny rose a few hours later for a run to the restroom. She returned laughing hysterically.

Mace asked, "What's so funny?"

Jenny waved him toward the bedroom. "You have to see this."

Mace stood as he smiled. "OK. I'm game."

Jenny led him into the bedroom. "Tell me that's not hilarious."

Mace walked to the center of the room, pushing on a sling hanging from the ceiling. "It's a giant hammock. No bed?"

Jenny laughed. "That is the bed."

Mace tilted his head. "The Kohamians all sleep in hammocks?"

Jenny smiled. "Apparently so. Want to give it a try?"

Mace nodded. "Sure, I'll give it a rock."

Jenny climbed in first, Mace followed. The giant sling-bed was soon swinging from side to side, with Jenny laughing hysterically. After a particularly hard kick from Mace's right leg, the heavy Humans brought the hammock swing to an unexpected end. The rope leading to the ceiling from behind their heads, snapped, dumping the two mischievous Humans on their heads.

Mace rolled over to Jenny. "You OK?"

Jenny offered a pain-filled laugh. "I think I just lost a kidney."

Mace rubbed the back of his scalp. "I've got a knot coming up."

Mace stood, helping Jenny to her feet. "May I offer you a position on the curved couch, ma'am?"

Jenny nodded. "I believe you can."

The next morning came early with a knock on the suite's main door. Mace moved to answer.

Derette stepped in with a tray of beverages. "I apologize for being late."

"Late? What time is it?"

Derette paused. "I'm sorry. Are Humans not early risers?"

Mace chuckled. "Some are, some aren't. What'd you bring us?"

Derette smiled. "A cure for last night."

Mace took a sip. "Hmm. Not bad. What is it? Wait... I probably don't want to know."

Mace took a cup to a still groggy Jenny. "Drink this. It's supposed to help."

Jenny took a sip. "I have a smashing headache. No more Novian wine for me."

Mace smiled. "I think that's two of us."

Derette looked at the couch. "You didn't sleep here all night, did you?"

Mace pointed. "Yeah. I'm afraid we wrecked the bed in there."

Derette walked over to peek in the room. "Goodness, I haven't seen a rekka come down since my time at university."

Jenny stood, putting her hand on Mace's shoulder. "Yeah, well we Humans know how to party."

Mace shook his head. "We'll pay for any damages."

Derette replied, "Nonsense. The corporation owns the hotel."

"What's on the agenda for the day?" Mace asked.

"We can revisit the tournament, or perhaps have a tour of current corporation assets?"

Having seen what the corporation owned on Canto, the tournament was again selected. The wagering that followed did not go the way of the Human guests.

By mid-afternoon, Frado Knuttin was available. "Mr. Hardy, I was able to free up four hundred tons of the gatrellium resource. In exchange, our government would like the top forty worlds on our short-list to be explored and claimed."

"That's one tenth what I was asking for. Not that great a bargain for our time and effort. Tell your contacts that we would be willing to take their team to the first twenty on the list."

Frado smiled. "Excellent. I was given authority to negotiate. When can we begin?"

Mace scratched his goatee. "Well now I feel like I underbid. Anyway, have your teams meet where your dreadnoughts stopped the *Rogers* on our way in. We need to return to drop off our shuttles to make room for yours."

Frado nodded. "They will be waiting. Mr. Hardy, if this goes well, it could be the first step in expanding relations with your people."

Mace replied, "Well, my people are all on the *Rogers*. Other than that we have Jasper Collins. Earth is now ruled by another."

Frado frowned. "I'm sorry to hear that, Mr. Hardy. We'll keep that between us for the time being so as not to cause any uncertainty."

The *Rogers* returned to Divinia, dropping her two shuttles. Once back at Canto, two UF shuttles were waiting. As they landed in the docking bays, their crews stepped out onto the deck. Mace was called to docking bay one.

Frado Knuttin was standing with a smile. "Mr. Hardy."

"Wasn't expecting you to come," Mace said.

"It was a last moment decision. I decided I could not afford to miss out on such an adventure. These twenty worlds will be claimed as United Front territory. It will by far be the single biggest expansion of our holdings in our history. Think of it, twenty new worlds within a week."

Mace smiled. "Will be more than that, Mr. Knuttin. This is twenty new star systems, not just worlds. I'll be dropping a shuttle in a system, then moving to the next. Once the second shuttle is away, I'll return and wait for the first. You should be able to cover most systems in a day or two. The week figure won't happen unless you only want to claim each identified planet, which I don't believe you'll want to limit yourself to. If you prefer, we can just do those twenty and be done in a few days."

Mace thought for a moment, holding up a finger. "Or I have another option. If you ready another eighteen shuttles, I can pick them up, drop them off, and reclaim them in a couple days when they are all done. You could have all twenty systems covered in two to three days."

Frado grinned. "I do like that option."

Mace nodded. "And I'd be willing to do it for say... another five tons of gatrellium per system?"

Frado agreed. "I'll give the order. The shuttles will be here in the next few hours. Shall we begin?"

Mace slowly shook his head. "Just one thing missing, Mr. Knuttin: gatrellium... five hundred tons of it."

"It is on its way. Unfortunately, it's a three week journey from our storage facility."

Mace sighed. "OK, how about this. See if you can authorize having a wormhole opened to wherever your transport is. We could take delivery of the resource immediately and be on our way here."

Frado said, "You could do that?"

Mace crossed his arms. "Might take fifteen or twenty minutes to set up, but yes. Contact your people and give me the coordinates. And none of this is because I don't trust you. I do. I don't trust your government. Governments have a way of negating deals once their goals have been reached."

Frado frowned. "I know of what you speak. Let me see what I can arrange."

Frado walked back aboard his shuttle, returning almost an hour later. "Our leadership has agreed, but with conditions. One quarter of the gatrellium will be made available for transport now, with another quarter moving after each set of six shuttles have been delivered."

Mace nodded. "Acceptable. You have coordinates?"

The coordinates were given and passed back to Divinia. Jasper, using the full wormhole generator of a Muhatha, took possession of the first ore hauler, confirming its cargo.

After a short comm from Divinia, Mace said, "Looks like we're set, Mr. Knuttin. By the time you strap yourself in, we'll be at the first location on the list."

The Kohamian returned a broad smile as he made his way up the shuttle ramp.

Mace opened a comm to the bridge. "Mr. Hobbs, jump us to the first target."

Seconds later, the *Rogers* slipped through a wormhole to the first of twenty worlds. Scans relayed nine planets surrounding a red sun.

Mace opened a comm. "Mr. Knuttin, you are free to go. Planet four looks like it might even be habitable. If you want, we can stick around for a few minutes to make sure you're safe."

Frado replied, "That will not be necessary, Mr. Hardy. Our scans show only natural signals occurring. We will be fine. And thank you again for making this happen."

"The locations on your list aren't anywhere near Earth space, so it wasn't a problem for me. That and the fact your people haven't shown aggression. I can see the protection of Canto being strategic and not aggressive. Its proximity to the rift gives it value to the UF."

Frado said, "Yes, we are strategists. However, we are not all saints, so I would warn you to continue to be as cautious as you have been."

With the first shuttle away, the *Rogers* made a jump to the second system. A return to Canto had two more UF shuttles exploring planets. Three hours later, the last of the explorers were released.

Chapter 11

Liam asked, "Where to?"

"Take us back to Mr. Knuttin's shuttle. I want to make sure everything there is OK."

The jump to the star system they'd designated as Gellos was completed in seconds. Scans indicated four ships in the area of where Frado Knuttin's shuttle was expected to be.

Mace yelled, "Mr. Hobbs! Take us in! Mr. Mueller, prepare for defensive fire!"

Three minutes passed as the *Rogers* raced in from the edge of the solar system. The UF shuttle, her engines disabled, tumbled with a slow roll, three unknown vessels surrounding her. A hail was sent but not accepted. Two of the ships turned and began firing at the incoming cruiser. Hans Mueller returned a set of plasma rounds, first disabling the weapons of the two ships, followed by their drives.

The remaining vessel turned all its weapons on the UF shuttle, shredding her hull and breaching the containment of her fusion reactor. With a bright flash, she disintegrated completely. The third ship turned to run.

Mace yelled, "Target her engines! Don't let them escape!"

A pair of quick bursts from the microwave cannons knocked the ship's propulsion offline. The *Rogers* circled the alien vessel, taking out her weapons one by one.

Mace glanced over to see Johnny was already looking at him.

"Got my back?"

Johnny nodded as he stood.

Mace opened a comm. "Miz Taub, meet us in bay one."

Jenny replied, "Where you planning to go? We don't have any shuttles."

Mace rocked his head back. "Mr. Hobbs, take us in and connect the grapple. We'll be floating over."

The assault gear was gathered and the three Humans got to the task of cutting through the enemy hull. Twenty minutes passed before they were greeted with a hail of laser fire. A combination of plasma rifles, AR-15s, and Johnny's thunder glove were used to first gain a foothold and to then force their way into a main hallway. The fighting was fierce, ending when the Humans reached the bridge.

The alien attackers were holding Frado Knuttin and his crewmen at weapons point.

Frado said, "Careful, Mr. Hardy. They obviously don't show mercy."

"We have a language translation for them?"

Frado shook his head.

Mace sighed. "I guess we do this the hard way."

An hour after the tense standoff had begun, the translation algorithms had a lock.

Mace said, "You will release our people immediately."

The captain of the vessel scowled. "You have invaded Korvan space, attacked our vessels, and killed many of our crew. Our fleet will soon be here to deal with you."

"Is this your planet? Your system?"

The captain replied, "Our research lab on the surface says it is. What claim do you have to these planets?"

Mace held up a hand. "We're just explorers. Our scans didn't reveal any signals, so we thought it was all uninhabited. Why did you fire upon our ship and destroy our shuttle?"

The captain scowled. "It was you that made the aggressive move. We only sought to protect ourselves."

Mace looked at the legless Kohamian sitting in a chair. "What happened to your legs?"

Frado returned a half frown. "They were aboard the shuttle, charging."

The captain banged a fist. "You will pay for this intrusion!"

Mace replied, "OK, first off, you have no broadcasts showing this as Korvan territory. That's something that is universally done elsewhere. Second, it was your ships that fired first. We were only defending ourselves. And, as you can see from your sensors, we didn't kill all your people. They are still there. Now, I'll apologize for killing your people here, but that was only done because you wouldn't respond to a comm. Had you done so, we could have resolved this peacefully."

Humphrey came over the comm. "Mr. Hardy, I did a scan of that planet. I find no sign of a research lab."

Mace asked, "Mr. Knuttin, where'd these ships attack you from?"

Frado replied, "They emerged from a deep hole in the planet. We had no indication of their presence until we were almost directly above them. We attempted to run. They caught us here."

Mace got back on his comm. "Mr. Mallot, there's supposedly a hole in that planet big enough to house these three ships. Find it, scan it, and tell us what you find."

Humphrey replied only seconds later. "I have the location. However, we'll need to go down there for a scan."

Mace turned to face the captain. "You have anything to add before our ship goes to investigate? Such as, why are there three warships guarding a research lab?"

The captain replied with an angry tone. "This system has been a target of Quathan rebels. Twice they have attempted to establish a base here. This Is Korvan territory. They have no right."

"So that's a military base down there? Not that I care, I just don't want any more violence. We aren't an aggressive species. We seek peace. I'm hoping this is all an unfortunate misunderstanding and that we can part ways amicably."

Mace crossed his arms. "Mr. Knuttin, I think we have to agree that this system is occupied and claimed."

Frado nodded. "We agree."

Mace said, "Good. Then we'll be leaving. Captain, we apologize for the intrusion. I know it doesn't bring back your dead or repair your ships, but it does mean we are leaving and are not likely to return for other than diplomatic relations."

Humphrey said, "Mr. Hardy. I have five new ships just showed on the sensors. They are different than the three we have here."

The captain said, "Quathan rebels! And you've left us defenseless!"

Mace sighed. "Mr. Hobbs, intercept the incoming ships. Captain, please tell me you have a language translator for them."

The captain scowled. "They speak Korvan."

The *Rogers* rushed to stop the new threat. A hail was answered with a different story. The Quathan ruled the Korvan Empire and had done so for decades. The three ships being guarded by the *Rogers* were the rebels.

Mace turned to the captain. "Is this true?"

"The Quathan invaded the palace and overthrew our king. We fight for Queen Meliene. She is the only true and rightful ruler of the Korvan Empire. The Quathan council are ruthless thugs."

Mace winced. "So we stumbled upon your base and crippled your ships. And now your enemy is here to put an end to you. That sound about right?"

The captain looked up. "And to the queen. She's down below. With her death, the true kingdom will never return."

"We stepped right into this one," said Jenny.

Johnny followed. "We can't just turn them over. Who knows who's right here?"

Mace nodded. "Captain, do you have another system you could move to?"

The captain nodded. "Much less secure than this was, but yes."

Mace looked at Johnny. "Jasper's gonna hate us, but we need to leave this situation as close to the way we found it as we can. The Quathan don't know the queen is here. All they see are these rebel ships."

Johnny asked, "What do you propose?"

Mace stroked his goatee. "Captain, can you provide the coordinates to that other site? If so, and if your queen has another ship, we can safely transport her there."

The captain frowned. "How do we know we can trust you?"

"You don't. As I can see it, you don't have much of a choice in the matter. Accept our help or let the Quathan capture her."

The captain gave the coordinates. A comm was opened to Jasper and after a short run by the queen's shuttle, a wormhole was opened and the queen passed through.

Mace turned his attention to the five ships, opening a comm. "This is Mace Hardy. This territory is claimed by the Knuttin Corporation in the name of the United Front. You are in violation of our borders. Withdraw your ships or face retribution."

The hail was answered, "You have rebel ships. You must turn them over to us immediately."

Mace shook his head. "They invaded our space. They are being dealt with accordingly. You will leave now or risk the same fate. This system is property of the United Front. Are you looking to start a war, Captain?"

Several seconds of silence passed. "We will withdraw. However, if it is found that the United Front is harboring Korvan rebels, it will be you that has started a war."

Mace nodded. "Noted. Now, leave immediately."

The captain bowed before giving a command to his ships. They sped away in the direction they had come from.

Mace turned to the captain. "Can your ships be repaired?"

The captain replied, "It will take a full rotation of that planet."

Jenny checked on her arm pad. "Nineteen hours."

Mace began to pace. "Here's what we'll do. You'll repair your ship's drives, and when ready, we'll transport you to the same location as your queen. And as for this system, Mr. Knuttin, it is now officially claimed. We'll take you back to Canto, where another shuttle can be brought out to do the scans and plant the markers. The queen lives, you get your system, and we all go home."

Frado said, "You would make a fine diplomat, Mr. Hardy."

Mace laughed. "Diplomat, doormat, so long as the job gets done, you can call me whatever you want."

A jump was made to Canto, where another shuttle was brought forward. Frado Knuttin remained behind. His thoughts of a thrilling exploration and laying claim to the first new system in the UF Empire had proven to be just that, thoughts. Henceforth he would be more than satisfied with hearing about the results.

The following day, the Korvan rebel ships were ready for transport. The captain and his crew marveled at the Human technology as their ships passed through to their new home base. The next day, jumps were made to collect the shuttles. All were returned without further incident. The UF Empire had grown by another twenty star systems.

Upon return to Canto, the crew of the *Rogers* was inundated with pleas to continue, and with offers from other corporations for their services. The Knuttin Corporation was not the only entity with stores of gatrellium.

Mace sat in his chair on the bridge. "Do we run everything through Frado or do we strike our own deals? We've already had enough offers to fully cover the gatrellium needs for a few thousand jumps."

Johnny replied, "As you've repeatedly said, they aren't making any more of it. Whatever we can stockpile would be to our advantage."

"I think we stay with Mr. Knuttin," said Jenny. "He's always treated us fairly. And we own almost a quarter of his company. Let him broker the deals and delve out potential colonies as leases. I would think that would leave us in the driver's seat for the foreseeable future."

Mace nodded. "Agreed. I'll have a talk with him about the importance of getting as much of the gatrellium as we can. The more we have, the less anyone else could have. If Stark or one of the Union members got wind of our endeavor here, they would strike out to make deals of their own. And we don't want them getting more of this stuff. The less they have, the more confined they stay."

Johnny replied, "I think we have our decision."

A comm came in from Jasper. "We have major problems."

Mace asked, "What happened?"

"The scouts I left at the Karthian rift are reporting activity. They say the portal just opened slightly. Not enough to fit a ship through yet, but it definitely got wider."

"Crap. That puts our trade deal here on hold. Let me have a conversation with Mr. Knuttin, then we'll be back."

"You might want to hurry. The rift could be pushed wide open if they've figured out how."

Mace nodded. "Be there as soon as possible."

A comm was opened to Frado Knuttin and a meeting hastily scheduled. Frado arrived on a shuttle in docking bay one of the *Rogers*.

Mace walked up the ramp to meet him. "We have trouble. Remember me telling you about the Karthians and the rift? Well, they figured out how to open it up again. They're working on it right now. We need to go so we can try to counter whatever they're doing. I can't say how long we'll be, so our efforts for further exploration here have to be put on hold."

"Unfortunate. However, this may give a bit of breathing room so leases can be set up in the optimum manner. I'll circulate the word that these twenty systems will be it for the time being. Most will take at least a decade for anyone to get a ship out to. This may give us a chance to get the process right before continuing."

Mace took a deep breath. "Thanks for the understanding. Now, we have to leave. I'll check back as soon as I can."

The shuttle departed for Canto as the *Rogers* jumped to Divinia.

Jasper, waiting with his fleet, opened a comm. "Let's go see if we can put a stop to this."

Mace asked, "How many ships do we have ready?"

"One hundred forty-two."

"Have you contacted Stark?"

Jasper scowled. "I didn't, and he has no interest in my hails anyway, unless I'm calling to turn the Targarians over to him."

"Give me a minute. He's gonna want to be out here."

A comm was opened and the current status of the rift delivered to Malcolm Stark. A representative of the Union fleet would be there shortly.

The *Rogers* followed the *Organ Cave* to the rift.

"Can't say this is a good development," Mace said.

Jasper replied, "Nope. Got word about five minutes ago that it widened again. Their smaller ships can now fit through."

"We could go in and try to shrink it."

Jasper nodded. "That's why I invited you out here. You have the one weapon that will do that."

"Mr. Hobbs, take us in. Mr. Mueller, hit the two sides of that rift with the wormhole weapon."

As the *Rogers* approached, a green wave of energy blasted through the opening, blistering the skin of the *Rogers* and knocking half her transducers offline.

"Jump us out!" Mace yelled.

Liam replied, "Wormhole generator is down!"

"Well, back us out then!"

Liam calmly turned. "Already moving in that direction. We'll be clear in fifty seconds."

A series of wormholes opened, and a dozen of Stark's Radica ships came through.

A comm opened. "I sent these along in case you needed them."

"A little late. They just fried half our systems with that green wave."

Stark shook his head. "Completely preventable with only a modest level of planning."

Mace scowled. "What's done is done."

Humphrey yelled, "Another wave coming through!"

Mace looked into the comm. "Any way you could divert a couple of those ships our way?"

Stark's silhouette typed away on a keypad on his arm. Three of the Radica ships powered up their domes and headed for the *Rogers*.

Humphrey yelled, "Fifteen seconds to impact!"

The Radica ships sped past the *Rogers'* position. A minimal amount of the green wave made it through, though another three transducers fell when it hit.

Jasper said, "I'm alerting the repair dock at Divinia."

"We aren't heading that way. Mr. Hobbs, turn us around. We're following those Radica in. They can keep that wave off us while we shrink that rift."

Johnny smiled. "And that's why you're the captain."

The ships moved into position. A double shot from the wormhole weapon saw the rift again shrunk to only a ball of light.

Humphrey said, "Parameters are stable, Mr. Hardy. That did it."

Mace let out a long breath. "Mr. Hobbs, take us back to the *Organ Cave*. Mr. Collins, we would appreciate a wormhole open to Divinia."

Humphrey said, "Before we go, have Mr. Collins scan our hull for breaches in the gatrellium."

Mace turned to Johnny. "And that's why every good captain has an ace crew."

Two potential weak points were identified and corrected. The *Rogers* once again slipped into the repair dock for a week's worth of rehab.

Chapter 12

With the rift crisis averted, the ships of the former Targarian Empire returned to Divinia. Malcolm Stark left three of the Radica ships parked at the rift for use if the Karthians again attempted enlargement. The crew of the *Rogers* received a needed rest.

Mace walked into the resort lounge, where Johnny was sitting at a bar with a smile.

Johnny held up a beer. "Check it out. Tres was able to reverse-engineer one of my Mangrove Darks. I can now have as many of them as I want."

Mace laughed. "Here comes three-hundred-pound Johnny."

"Truth is, I've felt a lot better of late. Those nutrient bars aren't the tastiest, but dropping forty pounds was worth it."

Johnny stared at his bottle. "Maybe I can have Tres work on the calorie count of these things."

Tres entered the lounge. "So, a Mangrove Light?"

Johnny returned a half-hearted smile. "Sounds a little too frilly for me. Guess I'll just have to limit my consumption." He turned back to Mace. "How go the repairs?"

"The gatrellium skin was in bad shape. They've replaced almost half of it. At least in that form it's 100 percent recyclable. Doc says they have another two days."

"And what's our new adventure after that?"

"We always need more gatrellium. That means we go back on our own or pay another visit to Canto."

Tres asked, "When do we expect to have the Targarian fleet up to strength where nobody will bother us?"

Mace shrugged. "Could be six months, could be a year. We certainly aren't there yet. What bothers me most is Stark and his crew are building ships much faster than we are. A year from now they're still likely to be more powerful. And with the spies they have running around, I don't know how really secure our technologies are. I wish we could make more of this UF relationship. They would be an ally that would easily keep Stark away."

"I'm still not sold on the UF," Johnny said. "Who wouldn't trade five hundred tons of gatrellium for twenty star systems?"

"Yeah, I'm not overly fond of them either. I like Frado, but the feeling I've gotten from the rest of them seems very one-sided."

The next two days passed without incident. The *Rogers* emerged from the repair docks, good as new once again. Mace gathered a crew and made the jump to Canto. Frado Knuttin was eager to move on to the next twenty star systems on their list.

This time, the UF government wanted thorough scans. The shuttles would be in the systems for almost a week. No interactions with other sentient species were initially reported.

The *Rogers* waited in one of the star systems for the first shuttle to return. Once aboard, they jumped to pick up a second. Upon return to Canto, an urgent message from Jasper was waiting.

Johnny opened a comm. "What's the problem, old man?"

Jasper returned a serious look. "Where have you been? The Karthians are coming through the rift!"

"What? Why didn't you try to notify us?"

Jasper scowled. "I did. Your UF friends refused to give your location. Kept saying it was none of my business. That you were under contract and would be done in a week."

Mace asked, "What's the status? Where am I needed?"

"You're needed here! Now! As I said, they're coming through the rift. Close to two thousand ships so far, with more right behind. And of worse note, they keep widening that rift. A couple more pushes and that monstrous station will fit through. There's two of them now, and they've figured out how to marginalize Stark's Radica ships. You should get back here now. This is the big invasion we feared."

The comm was closed. "Mace opened another to Frado Knuttin. "I have bad news."

Frado smiled. "Something go wrong with our shuttles?"

Mace nodded. "Yes. Eighteen of them. They're stuck out in those systems."

"You can't go get them?"

Mace shook his head. "We're heading home. The Karthians have invaded with more than two thousand ships. We have to leave now."

Frado returned an uneasy look. "We have crews on those ships. We can't just leave them."

"I wish I could help. This is much bigger than your current problem. I can send each a comm telling them to find a way to survive, but I don't have time to go get them. I'm sorry."

The comm was closed as the *Rogers* jumped back to Divinia. The full crew was brought aboard, with family members left behind at the resort complex.

Mace opened a comm to all sections of the ship. "As most of you know, the Karthians have come through the rift. A large force is heading toward Harkoza as we speak. We intend to make our best stand there. If we fall below 50 percent of our ships, we pull back here to Divinia. If our defenses here fail, we fall back to Earth. For any who want to return to Earth, the time has passed. We have to make our stand. You are all like family to me, and I will do my best to protect that family. For all of you who are believers, may God bless us all and get us through this day."

The comm closed. A wormhole was opened to the Harkoza system and the *Rogers* slipped through to where Jasper was waiting with a hundred sixty-five ships, Malcolm Stark with eight hundred.

Jasper opened a comm. "Scouts place the Karthians at six hours out."

"Do we have a ship count?" Mace asked.

"Nineteen hundred," said Jasper, "plus one of those stations."

Mace pulled back. "They can move those that fast?"

Jasper sighed. "The fleet is coming at 60 percent light-speed."

"We have to do everything we can to protect our wormhole generators. If they fall into their hands, they could jump to whatever system they want."

"I haven't mentioned it before, but I had a system built into the new Collins ships. If they detect anyone aboard the ship who is not Targarian or Human, a self-destruct timer for the generator is started. I'll pass you the override code, but give it to no one. And don't give out word of its existence. Once set, you have eight minutes to disable it. The alert flash will only show on the command chair. My people all know to contact me if that warning flashes. They don't know what it is, but they know it's important."

"We'll safeguard it. Are the Karthian ships all the same cruisers we saw before?"

Jasper shook his head. "About a third of them are smaller. We're calling them frigates. We don't yet know what they're capable of."

"Nineteen hundred ships. And we have what? Nine hundred-ish?"

Jasper nodded. "I haven't told you, but our little surprise solar flare ships we used against the Quelli … I have four hundred of them. We'll be making use of the first ones in about three minutes. I'm patching through a feed from one of our scouts. You see their first mistake?"

Mace nodded. "Flying in a tight column?"

Jasper grinned, "Makes for easy pickings. We're hoping that with their current speed we can fry fifty or sixty ships with a dozen of those solar ships."

"You have any more of those under construction?"

Jasper nodded. "Four docks. They currently take a week to turn around. I wouldn't place much of our strategy on their use. Solar flares are unreliable and ships have to be either flying in a straight line or sitting still for it to be a useful weapon."

"What about the station? You targeting that as well?"

"Another dozen solar ships. We plan on having two rows of ships waiting on the flares. One will hit the station and the front of the column. A second, anywhere from two to six seconds later, depending on the speed of the flare, will impact the column further back from an angle. We hope to get some of the ships taking evasive action."

An assistant walked up to Jasper. "One minute, Sire."

Jasper nodded. "Here we go."

Mace asked, "Can I patch this through to Stark?"

Jasper scowled. "I suppose he will know of it soon enough."

Mace passed the feed to the other ships. "Stark, watch the column front. We're about to see our first action."

"The solar flare weapon," said Stark. "Yes, I know."

Johnny turned with the mic muted. "Now, how could he possibly know that?"

"He either has a mole here on this ship, or on the *Organ Cave*."

Johnny clenched a fist. Humphrey typed away on his console.

Jasper said, "Here it comes."

Twenty-four micro-wormholes opened at the same time. Half a second later they expanded. Million-degree solar plasma suddenly smeared across the sensor display of the scout ship. Forty-seven Karthian ships were incinerated, another sixteen heavily damaged. The flares aimed at the station were off, but several decks going down one side were scorched and opened to the voids of space, the inhabitants instantly annihilated.

Six seconds later, the second set of wormholes opened. They were perfectly positioned to catch the large volume of ships that were turning away from the column. Another eighteen were vaporized, with thirty two others taking heavy damage. The great Karthian fleet spread out, coming to a crawl as the situation was evaluated.

Jasper gave a command. "Phase three!"

Another sixty wormholes opened as the solar flare advanced. Seventy-five Karthian ships were destroyed and another forty severely damaged.

Jasper slapped his hand on his hand rest. "Yes! I love it when a plan comes together!"

After several seconds of confusion, the Karthian ships began to move forward, this time spread apart and changing directions at random intervals.

Jasper said, "As expected. We'll be lucky to get a one to ten ratio now. I think those flare ships have seen their finest moment."

"Park them for a while. Another opportunity will present itself. We just knocked out an eighth of that force without firing a shot."

Jasper pushed another image to the comm display. "They have another six hundred parked at the rift already. If that builds much we're gonna see two fronts of attack at the same time. There are three other Sarkesian worlds that are equal distance from that rift."

The Karthian threat continued to come, moving to within two hours of a strike.

Jasper stood and paced in front of his comm camera. "Order the evacuation."

Mace asked, "What you have going on?"

Jasper replied, "I'm evacuating the colonies at Gerthis and Swankek. That will free up nearly a hundred of those microwave cannons."

Mace tilted his head. "Are you planning to move them somewhere else?"

Jasper nodded as a wide wormhole opened. "Here."

The microwave stations moved through in columns of four from Gerthis. A second wormhole opened to Swankek. The orbital stations were moved into position around Harkoza.

Jasper said, "We're gonna need the support. At this stage I'd rather sacrifice those stations than ships."

Mace nodded. "A wise move. And better for your crews."

Jasper scowled. "Not the crews on those stations. That's two hundred of my citizens I just sent to their death."

"And possibly twenty-five hundred lives you saved. Such is the burden of commanding during war."

Jasper sighed. "I bet those soldiers are wishing they were commanders about now."

Mace said, "We'll be pulling the trigger right alongside them, Mr. Collins. Your Targarians have always struck me as people of honor. They'll sacrifice themselves if it means others will have the chance to live."

As the approaching fleet reached only an hour away, Stark added his own attack to the mix. Fifty of the Radica ships, newly modified to regain their prior advantage, came through wormholes directly in the path of the immense station. Following right behind were two hundred of Stark's cruisers.

The cruisers raced in under the cover of the Radica ships as the green waves of energy were rejected. The cruisers quickly attached themselves to the hull of the station. Breach holes were cut and Human Marines stormed aboard with one-way tickets. As the Karthian ships surrounding the station closed, Stark's cruisers detached, jumping back through newly opened wormholes.

Malcolm Stark said, "We'll see how they like having ten thousand Marines on that station."

Mace said, "I doubt it makes it to Harkoza."

Stark's silhouette bowed. "There's no substitute for boots on the ground."

Fifty Karthian troop transports were diverted to the fight on the station. Fifteen minutes later, it dropped from the speed of the fleet and was soon out of range of the scout ship sensors. The extra cruisers and Radica ships joined the ranks of the fleet at Harkoza.

Mace said, "Nicely done. We might actually have a chance in this fight."

As the attacking fleet drew within half an hour of Harkoza, Stark came over the comm. "I just wanted to offer status of the station assault. It seems the Karthians have changed tactics there as well. Our progress is steady, but slow. We've captured five out of the sixty-six decks. Moving up or down a deck is difficult."

Jenny came onto the bridge. "Start cutting your way through. Make your own transits."

"That has been attempted several times. They are quick to swarm the breach, preventing us from breaking through."

Mace asked, "What weapons are your forces using?"

"They are equipped with plasma rifles and AK-47s. The Karthian body armor is proving extremely tough against our bullets. And they have some kind of dissipater unit that negates most of the plasma charge. Our hand grenades have been the only effective weapon, and our teams have limited supplies."

"What they need is this thunder glove," said Johnny.

"You have a hand weapon that would be useful?"

Johnny replied, "Well yeah, but I only have one."

"Mr. Hardy, how do we get that weapon aboard the station? If we don't push forward at a fast pace, that station will be here at Harkoza joining the fight."

"I thought it had stopped?"

"Only for a moment. It's headed this way again."

Johnny said, "This glove doesn't go anywhere that I don't."

"Then you must go to the station. I will gladly send a ship to get you aboard."

Johnny turned. "I don't wanna go fight with them. I don't know your people or the tactics they use."

Jenny said, "I'll go... with you that is. I'll get your back."

Mace sighed. "Maybe we send a team."

Liam Hobbs said, "If you think for a minute you are going, Mr. Hardy, you are sorely mistaken. We need you in this coming fight."

Jordan Crawford added, "He's right. This time neither of us can go. You because you're needed when this fight starts, and me because at some point you will need relief. This is going to be a fight that could go on for days."

Mace tapped his fingers on his armrest. "OK… Johnny, you and Jenny. But this is voluntary. If you aren't comfortable, you don't go. The decision is yours."

Johnny chuckled. "Comfortable. I'm sure I won't be comfortable either going or staying. I'll go under one condition: if we make a breakthrough, every effort will be made to bring me back to this ship. I don't want to be stuck out there."

Stark replied, "Every effort will be made to recover you and Miz Taub, Mr. Tretcher. A ship will be there to collect you momentarily."

Johnny stood. "Comm me as often as you can. I want to know what's happening here."

Mace nodded. "Will do. You better go see Jane before going to the docking bay. Stark will have a shuttle here in a few minutes."

Johnny left the bridge with Jenny following behind.

"I hope we're doing the right thing here," Mace said.

Jordan Crawford replied, "We are. If they don't get the push they need from that glove, Stark can bring them back."

Mace turned to the comm. "You hear that? If their help is ineffective, you bring them right back. They are vital parts of this crew."

Stark nodded. "I'll make sure of it."

"You do that. Now, what are our plans for a defense here?"

Stark pushed a short list over the comm. "Our Radica go in first, followed by the cruisers, with our smaller assault ships coming to bear when the battlefield has turned chaotic. Our cruisers each have a modified shuttle. The assault craft carries a team of twenty-five Marines. The shuttles have been fitted with a fast breaching collar which should allow boarding of a vessel in less than thirty seconds. That assumes an average hull thickness. If there is trouble, we still have the plasma cutters."

"That's gonna be a mess out there."

"Complete chaos if all goes well."

Chapter 13

A shuttle landed in docking bay one. Johnny said goodbye to Jane, Zax, Fina, and Derwood. Jenny gave a long goodbye kiss to Mace. The shuttle lifted out of the bay and disappeared into the void.

As Mace walked onto the bridge, Humphrey said, "Fifteen minutes. We'll have them on the sensors any moment."

"Jasper, what are your plans?"

"We're following a similar strategy to Stark. The Collins go in first, followed by the cruisers with shuttles and Marines. We've studied Stark's assaults on that previous station. Got the recorded data from the stations data store we downloaded. Unless they've changed tactics, we know how they fight and have been training to counter it."

Mace looked around the bridge. "I guess that leaves us. Anyone have suggestions as to how we play this?"

The bridge was silent.

Mace held up his hands. "Come on, people. No opinions?"

Liam said, "Run and shoot. That's about all we have."

Mace replied, "OK. We have our cannons, and that green weapon. Is there a way we can make good use of the wormhole weapon?"

Hans said, "If we can locate their reactors, and if it will make it that deep into their hulls, we could take ships out in that manner. Otherwise I would suggest using it to hit their gravity drives. We could just fly around targeting drives."

Mace nodded. "I like both of those suggestions."

Jordan said, "We don't have shuttles, so a boarding party is out. And I don't think we would want to do that anyway as we wouldn't be able to stay with a shuttle to protect it. Us against a single ship, yes. Against that armada, no."

"OK. Mr. Mueller, it looks like we're all here to support your efforts."

Hans replied, "I'd prefer it if you assigned one or two weapons to me and gave the others to someone else. I can multitask, but not to the level we will need here."

"Anyone else want to take one on?" Mace asked. "I can take the green weapon if all I have to do is fire it at indiscriminate targets. Mr. Mallot, you think you could handle the wormhole weapon if Mr. Mueller sticks to his cannons?"

Humphrey nodded. "Would be my pleasure."

Mace replied, "You Canadians are too nice. But OK, I think we have our efforts lined up. Mr. Crawford, if you can, support Mr. Mallot. Be his eyes for the bigger prize."

Mace opened a comm. "Mr. Moskowitz to the bridge."

Jeff arrived seconds later. "You rang?"

Mace pointed to a chair beside him. "Have a seat. I have control of the green energy weapon. I want you to identify targets for me."

"Do we have a navigation plan?" asked Liam.

"Keep us on the outskirts of the fight. If we start taking a beating, get us out of there. We'll have to play this on the fly. If we find something that works, we keep at it. If not, we look for something different. Mr. Crawford, once you see that Mr. Mallot has a handle on things, I want you to get some sleep. Take a pill if you have to. When I'm ready to hand over command, you'll need to be rested. If this fight lasts as long as I think it might, we're gonna need you awake and ready to go."

Humphrey said, "Five minutes."

Mace opened a comm to all decks. "The fighting will be getting underway in a few minutes. Make sure you're strapped in as much as possible. Things could get rough. We're just going to be flying and shooting. Keep your stations as operational as you can. If you have issues, ask for help. You've all been through this before to some degree. This will likely be worse. And as I've said a hundred times prior, there's no finer crew. When it starts, just do your best. This could be a long fight, and it's a fight we have to win, if not here at Harkoza, then at whatever location we fall back to. Fight the good fight. That is all."

Humphrey pushed an image of the incoming horde to the main display. "Here they come."

Jasper said, "Wait until they're within range of the microwave stations. We need all the firepower we can get."

The image on the wall display showed the two sides clashing. Green symbols flowed into red and yellow as blue ones continuously fired their weapons. The display was quickly an incomprehensible mess of colored icons that both flashed and changed colors.

Mace nodded toward Liam. "Mr. Hobbs, pick a spot and go."

The *Rogers* lurched forward into battle. Within seconds, the first rumbles could be felt as plasma rounds for the opposing ships impacted the hull. Hans Mueller began to return fire, making use of both the microwave and plasma cannons.

"We have a hull breach on designate 447," Hans yelled. "Mr. Hobbs! Bring us back around and I'll finish them off!"

Liam replied, "Turning. Number 447 coming up on port."

Hans fired. "She's burning!"

The quick victory was met by three hard blasts to the *Rogers'* hull, rocking everyone inside.

"Damage report!"

Humphrey fired the wormhole weapon. "Minor! Transducers still at 100 percent!"

The starboard drive of a Karthian cruiser took a hit, taking the drive offline.

Jordan pointed to the next approaching ship on the display. "This one, coming in hot to port. Wait! It's turning away. Hit 523, coming up from below!"

Mace fired the green energy weapon.

Jeff said, "Miss. Try this one... 162."

Again the green energy weapon let loose its potent round. The target evaded the slow pulse with minimal effort.

Mace said, "We have to get closer. They have too much time to react."

The plasma cannons caused little more than an inconvenience. The dampening fields surrounding most ships—or the composition of their hulls—made the plasma weapons almost useless. Once a ship had taken damage, plasma regained its significance. As Hans loosed round after round from the microwave cannons, one ship after another took hits with most only causing minor damage—damage that was easily repaired.

The opponents slugged it out for an hour before the great station joined the fight. Johnny and Jenny were aboard. The thunder-glove weapon had only been modestly effective, allowing the Marines to take an additional five decks. The shuttles that had delivered the men had all been cleared away. The fight on the station would see the end of one side or the other.

Johnny said, "We can't get clear shots up or down any of the stairwells. They're defended too well."

Mace asked, "What are the black smudges on your battlesuit?"

"It's from the walls of those stairwells, I've had countless rounds impact right beside me. We can't quite get to them or them to us. The thunder glove worked great for the first three decks. That's when they began moving their people back about two meters. I just can't get in a good shot now."

Jane said, "Can't you hold that out on a stick or something?"

Johnny frowned. "I built it so only I could shoot it. The glove senses my hand."

Jasper said, "Well, can't you cut off your hand and put both on a stick?"

Johnny shook his head. "Har, har. Aren't you the comedy king. If you had any better ideas, I'd be grateful, though."

Jasper replied, "Have you tried going outside and up or down?"

Jenny replied, "They've tried just about everything. The external guns have been modified and now skim the surface. They pick us off before we get anywhere."

Jasper said, "I'm guessing they brought more nukes with them?"

Johnny nodded. "Those are of course the last resort. Stark wants this station taken so it can be studied and possibly used in defense of Earth."

Jasper said, "I know I'll hate myself for releasing this. I'm sending the data we retrieved from the last station. Maybe his people can figure out a weakness."

Jeff stood. "Wait... let Gnaga and me have a crack at that. We know that station fairly well, but we haven't looked at it from an assault perspective. Can you give us a half hour?"

Johnny replied, "We aren't going anywhere."

Jasper said, "I'll gladly hold it."

The *Rogers* continued fighting, taking up a figure eight pattern to better assist Hans, Humphrey, and Mace with their weapons fire. Three Karthian cruisers had been taken out of the fight. Jeff met with Gnaga as they conferenced in the remainder of the science and engineering team on Divinia.

Half an hour to the minute, Jeff emerged from their discussions. "We may have a way to move from deck-36 up to deck-12 and down to deck-60. There's a plasma feed tunnel that runs between the reactor rooms on every eighth deck. You have one on deck-36. When you enter the room—"

Johnny said, "Hold up. I'm heading there now."

Mace asked, "Can I take it there's a reason you wouldn't want to be caught in this tunnel?"

Jeff replied, "If the bulkhead doors are open, anyone would have a clean shot at you from any of the connected decks."

Mace said, "And if the doors are closed?"

Jeff cleared his throat. "If they're closed, you have to open them. If Johnny can connect to their system, we believe we can do that from here."

Johnny said, "I'm at the reactor room."

Jeff nodded. "Turn to your right and walk to the back wall."

"If I turn right I'm facing a wall."

"What do you see if you turn left?"

Johnny looked the other way. "The hallway wall is on my left. About a meter out from that are what I would guess are the reactors. I see four of those. They look about three meters a side and four meters tall. About a meter of floor between each one."

Jeff said, "Pass through your helmet's camera feed."

Seconds later an image appeared on the wall display. "That far wall, down the hallway wall. Go to it."

Johnny complied. "OK, there."

"Is there a door on the wall looking to your right? Should be about halfway down."

Johnny nodded. "I see it."

Jeff flipped the diagram on his display, matching it to what Johnny was seeing. "Walk down that wall and past the door. The next wall you come to, turn to your right. You should see a console station on the back side of each of those reactors."

Johnny walked. "OK. Got it."

"I need you to log into a console for me."

Johnny chuckled. "And how am I supposed to do that?"

Jeff pulled up an image of the console keyboard. "You see the key with the symbol that looks like a house ?"

Johnny nodded. "Got it."

"Press that key, then enter the following number sequence..."

"Hit me with it."

"228933429. When complete, hit the key with the double down arrow."

Several seconds later, Johnny replied, "I'm in."

Jeff said, "That's a wireless interface ... according to the data we have. Patch the connection through the comm."

"Done."

Jeff typed away on a keyboard. "The door back on the wall... it should now be unlocked. When you open it, you'll find a switch on the back side. Figure out how to engage that switch. That will show the door as closed if anyone should notice on a console elsewhere. I have a video feed of that tunnel. After that switch is again closed, I'd give it a couple minutes before going in."

Johnny opened the door, looking down into the tunnel. "I'm not gonna fit through there."

Jenny stepped up. "I can."

She pulled a packet from an external pocket on her battlesuit, removing a bandage and several tabs of tape. Using the tape, the door switch was set to the closed position.

"Excellent," Jeff said. "The alert on the console is off."

Jenny looked into the tunnel. "I don't see a ladder. What am I supposed to hold on to?"

"There's no gravity in the tunnel. You should be able to easily pull yourself in one direction or the other."

Jenny nodded. "I can do that. If I make it up to deck-12, what's the plan?"

Jeff shrugged. "Look for a way to get others up there."

Jenny winced. "Come on, Doc. Give me something. Can I access a console and open doors? Turn off power?"

Johnny said, "How about the gravity thing we used to clear those spider-bugs off the *Rogers*?"

Jeff stood silent for several seconds. "Genius. When there, find a console. Enter the number as was just done. 228933429. When complete, hit the key with the double down arrow. From there I'll guide you to the gravity controls."

Johnny said, "Well, why don't we just do that here?"

"They have these floors locked out from the main systems. We can control the gravity here, but not elsewhere on the station."

Jenny leaned into the tunnel going up. "I'll signal back when I'm there. In the meantime, Johnny, stick your head in and make sure nobody comes into this tunnel from below."

Jenny began her climb.

The *Rogers* continued to weave, turn, and fire, all the while taking only minimal damage while making a dent in the Karthian lines. The Stark ships had come in with their boarding parties at the ready. More than a hundred Karthian cruisers were under manual assaults. In a troubling turn of events, fifty of the compromised cruisers exploded all at once, killing the Human Marines that had gone aboard.

Stark came over the comm. "Hardy, the Karthians are using drone ships. We just lost half our assault teams. Have your people scan for bios before boarding any ships. If they're empty, disable them if you can and move on to another."

Mace turned to an image of Jasper Collins. "You catch that?"

Jasper nodded. "I did. We're making adjustments."

Jenny Taub reached deck-12. "The door is locked."

Jeff said, "You'll have to force it. The lock is weak. And remember to disable the switch that shows it as open."

Jenny pushed on the door. "OK. It's bowing. If I can get my boot around I can... too tight a space."

"Put your shoulder into it," said Johnny.

"I can't get leverage. Jeff, what's behind this tunnel wall on the opposite side from the door?"

Jeff pulled up a diagram. "On that floor... you have piping."

"The wall of this tunnel is thin. How much space is behind it before we hit the piping?"

Jeff replied, "Quarter of a meter? A foot maybe?"

Jenny backed down the tunnel several meters. "OK. This ain't gonna be pretty, but I need space."

A low power plasma round entered the tunnel wall opposite the door. Water sprayed into the tunnel as the force of the concussion that followed pushed Jenny down.

Johnny looked up the tunnel into the chaos. "You OK? What was that?"

Jenny replied, "I needed space to get leverage on that door. Let's see if I got it."

The thin tunnel wall had ruptured, and along with it a fist-sized water pipe. The pressurized water sprayed into the tunnel, forming globules before floating off in both directions.

Jenny growled. "I need windshield wipers. Can hardly see a thing."

Johnny asked, "Can you get back to the door?"

Jenny replied as she grunted. "There now... hold on."

The lock of the access door gave way. Jenny sprang through the door and flopped onto the floor as water sprayed into the room.

"I'm in."

Seconds later she was at the console. "Number is in. OK, Doc, I have access."

Jeff said, "You'll see a symbol on the top right of the display that resembles tools. Select that. On the next page, the fourth row down ... you'll see an up arrow, a down arrow, and a deck number. Set it to deck-36, then tap the up arrow several times."

Jenny followed the instructions. "It's showing the gravitational pull on that deck is changing, but only by hundredths of a point each tap. Will take me a minute to run it all the way up."

Jeff scratched his chin. "Wait a sec... to the right, you'll see a symbol with a bunch of stacked bars. Select it and tap until the value displayed stops changing. That should be the increment value."

Jenny complied. "OK. We're there."

Jeff took a deep breath. "Go back to the up arrow and tap once."

Johnny said, "You're messing with the gravity on this floor, right? Don't you think we should test something at maybe halfway first? And we need to let our guys know what's coming first."

Jeff nodded. "Sorry, you're correct. Jenny, bump the increment level down by half."

Jeff patched into the comm with Stark. "Let your men on the station know that we're about to conduct a few gravity experiments there and for them to hold tight. If this works we may have a way for them to push forward."

Stark replied, "Consider it done."

Jeff said, "Jenny, when the increment is set, tap the up arrow once, followed by the down arrow."

Jenny followed the request.

Johnny said, "OK, definitely felt that. Began to float off the floor."

Jeff smiled. "Excellent. Bump the increment to full, set the deck to deck-30 and wait for my command. Stark's people should be able to storm the deck with their gravity boots on while the Karthians are floating around trying to figure out what happened. As they feed me the all clear, I'll tell you when to reset deck-30 and move to deck-29. We'll do this going up until they've broken through."

Word was passed to the Marines and the experiment begun. As expected, the chaos created by the complete lack of gravity gave the Human Marines the advantage they needed. In seconds, every stairwell was crowded with Marines, firing non-stop. Deck-30 was quickly overrun and the gravity restored. Deck-29 followed with deck-28 immediately after. By deck-25 the Karthian defense had folded. Thousands scrambled as the big Humans pushed ever upward. Decks 5 through deck-1 turned into a Karthian bloodbath. The soldiers had no time to surrender and instead fought to the bitter end.

The same strategy saw decks 40 through 66 cleared within another hour. The station was completely under Stark's control.

Johnny said, "Any way we can arrange for a pick-up?"

Mace replied, "Mr. Hobbs, take us to that station."

Jeff said, "I'm sending the coordinates to a docking bay on deck-36. We should be there in a moment."

Jenny nodded. "Be right down."

Chapter 14

Stark came over the comm. "Mr. Hardy, I thank your team for their ingenuity. I'll have to ask later how you pulled that off, but it worked, so we'll move on and be happy with the result for now."

Jasper interrupted. "The other station is on the move. Looks like it's coming this way with another nine hundred ships."

Stark said, "I must go. We must prepare to board that station as well."

Liam said, "We're in position for pick-up. Miz Taub and Mr. Tretcher are on their way over."

Mace asked, "What are our numbers looking like?"

Jasper replied, "Our boarding ships are failing. We've lost thirty shuttles with their crews and the soldiers aboard them. Only eight have been able to grapple their ships. We've also lost twenty-six cruisers and two Collins. Their losses are worse, but not by the numbers we need them to be."

"At least we have that station out of the fight. How have the microwave stations fared?"

"Good. Four lost. And while they aren't taking down any ships, they are poking a lot of holes. Those are making our plasma weapons at least marginally effective."

Johnny and Jenny walked onto the bridge. "Wasn't too bad. Didn't even get shot at."

Mace turned. "Mr. Moskowitz, will they be able to make use of that station and its weapons?"

Jeff nodded. "I don't see why not. Should I pass that information to Stark?"

Mace replied, "Only if you can give them some insights. They have the same data on that station now. If Stark fails to get his people aboard the other station, we'll need the one we have to fight against it."

As the space-battle continued, Malcolm Stark sent his ships and shuttles to pick up the Marines who had taken the station. A second assault was planned for the new threat. As the ships approached, a contingent of Karthian ships broke free from the fighting, catching Stark's shuttles as they docked for the pick-up. The Karthians paid a heavy price, while knocking out most of the shuttles under Stark's command. There would be no assault of the approaching station.

Mace passed the data Jeff had accumulated on the station's operation to the Stark team. The smaller defensive weapons could soon be seen firing as crews became familiar with their operation. Minutes later, the great green energy weapon sent a wave of quantum death out into the void of space.

Jasper came over the comm. "That was your doing, wasn't it?"

Mace nodded. "I didn't see any other way. That other station will be here shortly. We have to have a way to fight it. We need those men to be effective."

Jasper scowled. "Should have just nuked it like the last one."

"We're doing what we can. Have you managed to straighten out your assaults?"

Jasper stood and paced back and forth. "No. They have countered everything we've tried. I'm pulling those forces back. Tired of seeing them getting slaughtered."

Mace said, "Not that it's a big help, but we're rejoining the fight now."

"They've begun targeting the microwave stations as I feared they would. We've lost a dozen in the last fifteen minutes. And we're now at dead even on the ship casualties, down seventy-six total."

Mace frowned. "That's a big change."

Jasper nodded. "We're making adjustments, but at the moment it's looking bleak. Especially given the fact that another nine hundred ships will be here shortly."

"Before, you had said the 50 percent loss level was your cutoff. Does that still hold true?"

Jasper shook his head. "I don't think we can afford to let the losses go that deep. As soon as those microwave stations are done, we'll likely be pulling back. Those are all that's keeping us in this fight."

"You evacuated a colony to bring those stations here. Can you do that again?"

Jasper frowned. "No. The evacuation is still underway, and those are our smallest colonies. If the Karthians stay together as one large fighting force, when they do attack one of my worlds, we may pull stations from the others forward at that time. I won't be leaving them unguarded while we fight over a world that has already been abandoned."

The *Rogers* swirled, jinked, and spun, weapons firing at any Karthian vessel that came near. Her shields were holding, having not lost a transducer. That changed as four highly charged plasma rounds impacted the forward hull at the same time. The ship jolted, throwing anyone who wasn't fastened-in to the deck or against a forward wall. Three transducers were lost.

Humphrey said, "Mr. Hardy! We have a weak point on decks four and five forward!"

"Mr. Hobbs, try to keep our nose pointed away from any incoming."

Liam shook his head. "That's an impossible order, Mr. Hardy."

"Can those transducers be repaired or replaced?"

"Not while in this torrent of plasma," said Jeff. "Anyone going out there would be killed by the first strike we encountered."

Mace frowned. "Mr. Hobbs, take us out of the fight. Jasper, we're making a jump to Divinia. We need a repair dock for fifteen minutes."

Jasper replied, "Already full of ships. What do you need?"

"We have three transducers out. All close together."

Jasper shook his head. "Gonna have to handle those on your own. We have critical repairs going on."

Mace turned. "Mr. Hobbs, jump us to a neutral point in space where we can effect repairs."

The *Rogers* rumbled. "You have to rid us of our tail first, Mr. Hardy. They're too close."

Mace armed and fired the green energy weapon. The short distance prevented an evasive maneuver. The Karthian ship slowed and turned away, explosions coming from its sides.

Liam said, "Jumping away."

Seconds later, the *Rogers* was in dead space, a quarter light-year from the fight. "Mr. Montak, we have three transducers out. Can you get your team out on the forward hull to replace them?"

Bontu replied, "Gladly. I'll report status as we progress."

Jeff said, "We're looking at twenty minutes. That other station will be arriving about the time we get back."

The Mawga crewmen got to work on the repairs. As usual, the work was completed a few minutes ahead of estimates. A jump was made back to the fight.

The *Rogers* circled and fired in the seemingly never ending mass of Karthian ships.

Humphrey gave status. "The second station is three minutes out. I show nine hundred twenty-two Karthian ships in its wake." A rumble was heard and felt as a plasma blast impacted the gravity drives.

Jenny commed forward, "The starboard drive is showing fluctuations in its efficiency levels. I'm trying to track down the issue but I'm not sure what I'm looking for."

Mace turned to Jeff. "You think you and Mr. Klept could give her a hand? If we lose a drive, we're sure to start taking a beating from those cruisers."

Jeff nodded. "We'll take care of it."

A violent strike on the hull sent Jeff hard to the deck.

He slowly stood, rubbing his left elbow. "Felt that one through the suit. I'm OK."

Jeff hurried away. In the minutes that passed, the second Karthian station arrived. A bright green quantum wave of energy emerged, striking the first station dead center, breaching its dampening field. Debris flew from the hull and outer rooms. The Human-conquered station returned a blast of its own. The Karthian station turned and moved away from the impact and the glancing blow caused only moderate damage. A counter-shot by the Karthians dug into the prior breaches, collapsing the outer bulkheads.

Johnny said, "Is there nothing we can do to stop that weapon?"

Mace gestured toward the display. "Stark has his Radica ships coming up."

Johnny shook his head. "Should have had them there before."

Mace frowned. "I'm sure he wanted to. They're needed in this fight with the ships too."

A third strike from the Karthian station blew into the center decks of the captured vessel before the Radica ships could move into place. Fires raged and explosions exposed new areas as reactor containment and hydrogen stores failed.

Johnny said, "They're really taking a beating."

The *Rogers'* hull rumbled. "We're taking a beating."

Jeff came over the comm. "We have a problem. One of the feeds to the starboard drive has cracked. It's holding for the moment. If it ruptures, we could lose that whole drive."

Mace pressed the trigger on the small green energy weapon. "Can it be fixed?"

Jeff shook his head. "Not without a repair dock. There's a larger assembly it fits in that has to be removed."

"If we had another complete assembly, how long would it take to swap out?"

Jeff thought. "With a dock, a half hour. Without? I couldn't say."

"Is there anything we can do to partially secure it?"

Jeff looked at the damage. "We could try an over-weld, but that may cause more damage than do good."

Mace nodded. "I'll leave that to you to decide what's best."

Again the *Rogers* was rocked with a powerful blast. Jeff flew almost out of camera range, across the room, coming down hard on the back of his helmet.

A hand went up in the air. "I'm OK."

As he stood and looked at the crack in the feed, he said, "Crack just got longer."

Mace winced as the weapon he commanded threw out another wave. "Do what you can."

Four hundred Karthian cruisers engaged the Radica ships protecting the station as the remaining force joined the fight.

Jasper came over the comm. "We probably have a half hour before I pull my people out of here."

Stark replied, "You do that and the Sarkesian people will be left with no defense."

Jasper shrugged. "I gotta do what's right for my people. I can't go home defenseless."

Twenty minutes later, a multitude of nuclear explosions brightened the void of space, taking most of the four hundred approaching Karthian cruisers and nearly half of the Radica ships with them.

Stark said, "That was all the nukes we had. It was also the last of our tricks for this battle. I'm open to strategy suggestions."

Jasper replied, "Unless something changes, we'll be pulling out in about fifteen minutes. Bad news for the Sarkesians, I know, but I have to start thinking about my own people."

Mace said, "We'll be moving out with Mr. Collins."

Stark was silent for several seconds. "Understood."

Mace shook his head as he attempted another shot from the green weapon. "That's ten thousand Marines on that station. When we leave, they'll be overrun. I count at least a hundred troop transports waiting at the back of the Karthian reserves.

That's at least five hundred troops on each one. They board that station and they *will* take it back."

Johnny replied, "Not much we can do."

Another set of Karthian cruisers closed on the Radica ships protecting the captured station. With no protection from Stark's fleet, the Radicas were quickly overrun. As the last Radica turned to flee, the captured station released a green wave, striking the attacking Karthian station dead center. Debris scattered as the outer hull was breached.

A return shot dug deeper into the captured station, penetrating two additional bulkheads and spreading from two decks of damage to four.

As the *Rogers* continued to get rocked with shots, Jeff said, "Mr. Hardy, failure of that drive is imminent. Could happen at any moment."

Mace returned a frustrated look. "Have you attempted the weld?"

Jeff shook his head. "We thought it too risky."

"Well, now that failure is imminent, that risk is irrelevant, don't you think?"

Jeff nodded. "It is, but we're talking replacement of this assembly versus replacement of the entire drive."

Mace sighed. "Just do it. We need any extra time it might afford us."

"Consider it done. Mr. Heeb, start the torch."

The comm closed.

Two hard strikes reverberated through the *Rogers'* hull as the new Karthian ships joined the fight.

Johnny looked over at Hans Mueller. "Mr. Mueller, let me take that for a while."

Hans continued his relentless firing of the plasma and microwave weapons. Johnny unfastened his belt, moving to the weapons station and placing his hand on Hans' shoulder.

"Swap out. You're spent."

Hans said, "I can do this."

Johnny leaned in. "Fresh hands and eyes, sir. You need a rest. You've been at it non-stop for five hours."

Mace said, "Mr. Mueller, take a break. That's an order."

Hans looked up. "Can you unfasten my belt?"

Johnny reached down, popping a clip. Hans rolled out of the chair onto the deck. Fatso Geerok hurried over to assist as Johnny took the station, snapping and pulling the belt tight.

Geerok said, "Come on, Mr. Mueller. I'll get you to the bunks."

Hans replied, "Just give me a moment, please."

Geerok shook his head as he reached down, pulling the big German up by the belt. "You stay here, one of those blasts is gonna knock you around."

The pudgy Mawga admiral strained, but carried the worn out Human from the bridge.

Johnny glanced over his shoulder as he began pushing the trigger button. "Wow, didn't know Geerok had that kind of strength."

"That's two of us," said Mace.

The new Karthian station continued to trade blows with the now immobile captured station. A deep strike released containment of a hydrogen store, igniting the contents and sending a rolling cloud of debris from the affected decks, setting nearly an eighth of the once great station ablaze. Fires raged and then snuffed out as the oxygen in each new hull breach was released.

Jasper said, "Five minute warning, Mr. Hardy. Be prepared. They're gonna be chasing us. Can't jump if they're too close."

Mace nodded. "We'll be ready."

A comm was opened. "Mr. Moskowitz, tell me good news?"

"Almost done. The fluctuations are subsiding. Good call on the weld."

"Sometimes we get lucky."

Three heavy jolts rocked the *Rogers*. The image on the wall display of the gravity drive room turned to a bright flash as the attempted weld failed. A small explosion sent shrapnel flying from the feed. When the image cleared, a wincing Jeff Moskowitz was lying against a back wall.

"Jeff! You OK?"

Jeff slowly nodded as he looked around the room.

Jenny was standing over Gnaga. "He's injured. Unconscious. We need some help."

She turned her attention to Maala Heeb. "I'm afraid Mr. Heeb didn't make it. Took a big chuck of that shrapnel to his face shield."

Hooba rushed into the room. After a moment of staring at his dead friend, Jelog Hooba knelt to assist Jenny Taub with the unconscious Gnaga Klept.

Two additional strikes rocked the ship, sending Jenny and the Mawga scientist to the floor.

Jasper said, "We're pulling out."

"We're with you." said Mace.

As the *Rogers* turned from the battle, two Karthian cruisers followed in close pursuit.

Mace scowled. "Johnny, Mr. Mallot, we need those two ships off us or we're dead here!"

Johnny said, "I'm hitting them with what I can. They keep coming."

Another heavy jolt had Jenny picking herself from the floor and opening a comm. "We have Gnaga strapped in. He needs attention."

Mace replied, "We have two ships we can't shake. Don't have the speed."

Humphrey yelled, "One is dropping away. Two more are approaching!"

The *Organ Cave* swooped in with twin shots to the Karthian ship's drives.

"We have distance!" Liam yelled. "Wormhole opening!"
The *Rogers* slipped through to Divinia.

Chapter 15

The *Rogers* pulled alongside a lengthy line of ships at the repair dock. A shuttle was dispatched to collect Gnaga Klept. Jeff Moskowitz and Jelog Hooba left with their friend, heading to the Targarian medical facilities.

Jasper came over the comm. "We lost nearly half our ships out there. A lot of good people died today."

Mace replied, "We lost Mr. Heeb. What are the chances of getting into one of those docks for a full gravity drive replacement?"

Jasper took a deep breath. "Slim to none in the immediate future. We have to prioritize getting as many ships fully operational as we can. You can still fight. That puts you near the back of the list."

"Before your jump, did you see if Stark was leaving too?"

Jasper shook his head. "We were only seconds behind you. Last I saw he was still fully engaged."

Five minutes later, a comm came in from Stark, a dark silhouette in his usual chair with an index finger propping up each temple.

"The Sarkesian worlds are lost."

"We did what we could," said Mace. "The station?"

Stark let out a long sigh. "The weapon was offline. The Karthian troops were flooding aboard. I gave the order I hoped I'd never give."

"Nukes?"

Stark's silhouette nodded. "Nukes. They were to fight to the last man, allowing as many Karthians onto that station as they could before setting off four of those weapons. We lost comm to them two minutes ago."

Mace took a deep breath. "The hazards of war and yet another reason you do all you can to avoid it."

Stark looked up. "Exactly what I was trying to do before Mr. Collins forced our hand."

Mace shook his head. "You can't pin this on him. For all you know the Karthians were planning to double-cross you anyhow."

"I suppose now we'll never know."

Mace asked, "What's your next move?"

Stark was silent for several seconds. "We wait and watch as they devour the Sarkesian worlds. They take with them one of our gatrellium mines. A small one, but much needed. Speaking of such, I know you possess technology that allows a jump through a much smaller wormhole. I don't suppose you'd care to share that with us?"

Mace frowned. "Here's the rub, we give that to you, and we're giving it to all the Union members. We give it to all the Union members, we give it to anyone who conquers them. We might as well put that on a banner and fly it around to every world we know, broadcasting it to the masses."

Stark was again silent in thought. "I suppose I agree with you in that respect."

Mace asked, "Do we have an ongoing defense?"

Stark replied, "We believe the Karthians will consolidate at Harkoza as they sweep through the Sarkesian worlds. The Quelli are the next logical Union member to attack, with a world only six months journey from Harkoza. After that, we have the Targarian worlds of your illustrious King Collins."

"The Quelli have any defenses?"

Stark shook his head. "Only their ships. Two hundred of the remaining ships in our fleet."

Mace said, "If we really have six months, how many more can you produce?"

"We had production of sixteen per week of our newest design. We are losing a quarter of that production with the Sarkesians. The math says roughly three hundred."

Mace tapped his fingers on his armrest. "We're turning out about ten a week. That's another two hundred fifty or so by that time. Given our losses, we'll be in the neighborhood of four to five hundred ships by then. If you can convince the Quelli to fall back and fight with us here, we might have a decent shot at holding them off. Jasper could call in the several thousand microwave stations he has at his other worlds. As far as that goes, we could pull our orbiting ones from Earth."

Stark replied, "I don't see that happening, Mr. Hardy. Earth would not give up her only defense, and I would not ask her to do so. I hope you realize the Karthians will also be reinforcing what they brought through. With that rift wide open, we may see another of those stations, perhaps even two."

"Would you be willing to defend with us here at the Targarian worlds?"

Stark thought for a moment. "You would have the Human backing, but I cannot promise the ships of the other Union members. They are a stubborn lot, and only seem interested in participating when they think it suits their immediate needs. I pressed to stay longer at Harkoza, hoping to inflict as much damage as I could. The other members, excluding the Sarkesians of course, were insistent we leave immediately after your departure."

Mace crossed his arms. "So we essentially have six months to prepare."

Stark nodded. "It would appear so."

Mace leaned forward. "You ever gonna let me see your face?"

Stark was silent for several seconds. "Perhaps that day will come. Unfortunately that day is not today. There are still those who wish me gone from a position of power. I don't wish to give them the slightest opportunity to do so, as it would invariably be at the expense of myself or my loved ones. I'm certain you understand."

Mace half smiled. "Sadly, I do. Are you back at Earth?"

"For the foreseeable future."

"We'll be here if you have any news. We'll pass on anything we learn to you there. Until then, I'm sure we both have busy schedules."

Stark bowed as the comm closed.

Mace turned. "Johnny, I'm heading to the med facility to check on Gnaga."

"I'll be heading down to the surface with Jane. Once she has me and the kids settled, she'll be back to visit with him."

The shuttle ride to the med facility at the repair dock was short. Mace was soon turning the corner into the room that supposedly held Gnaga Klept.

A Targarian doctor, pulling the sheet up over the patient's head said, "I'm sorry. They expired."

Mace rubbed his temples as he turned to walk back into the hall. In a room immediately across from him, the back of Bontu Montak's head could be seen.

Mace walked into the room to see a groggy Gnaga Klept looking up. "Mr. Hardy..."

Mace shook his head. "Glad to see you're still breathing. I had the wrong room number and apparently the fellow across the hall was... well, he passed. How are you?"

Jeff was sitting in a chair, shifting his shoulder. "Concussion. He shouldn't talk. He needs to rest."

Mace turned to Jelog. "Mr. Hooba, I'm sorry for your loss."

Jelog replied, "It was his time. I know it is Human custom to mourn the loss of a colleague. Mawga do not. In our culture, we say they have merely departed this existence to go to another. We do not believe it to be better or worse, just different. Perhaps one day our paths will again cross."

Mace nodded. "Still, sorry. Jeff, how's the shoulder?"

"Getting stiff. Got knocked around a bit more than I'm used to. That battlesuit works great for small impacts, not so much for full body slams. Where do we go from here? Do we wait on an attack?"

Mace said, "Well, I just had a talk with Stark. He says the Karthians will be busy eradicating the Sarkesians for a few weeks. When they're done, he thinks the Quelli are next. That's six months. Targarian space is another six or seven after that. Technically, we might have as much as a full year to prepare. We just have to keep in mind they will be adding to their ranks during that time as well."

Mace pulled up a chair. "Has anyone looked at that shoulder?"

Jeff shook his head. "No. And I'm not going to ask. There's far too many critically injured about for me to pull someone off for a bruised shoulder. You just mentioned the Quelli. Are we not going to help defend their worlds?"

Mace offered a partial frown. "They have no other defenses. Just their ships. If we're to make a stand it will have to be here where we have the addition of the microwave stations. I wish it wasn't so, but it is. Unfortunately, the Quelli will be on their own, as no other Union members want to step up for that fight. Stark promised support from Earth if they come here after, but I doubt any of the other species will supply their ships in support of the Targarians. At least not after their run-ins with Jasper."

Mace stood. "I forgot. We left the Kohamians out in their shuttles. I need to jump back to Canto to bring them home. I'm sure they're quite unhappy with us at the moment."

Jeff said, "Couldn't be helped."

Mace walked toward the door. Still, it needs to be done. I'll be back when I'm finished. Should be able to collect them all in a day."

Mace hurried back to the shuttle and was soon aboard the *Rogers*. "Mr. Hobbs, set a jump point to Canto and take us there."

Liam replied, "We only have half a dozen people aboard. And we're down a gravity drive."

Mace nodded. "I'm aware of those facts, but we need to bring those UF people back. Can't leave them stranded like that or they're gonna be miffed at us."

Liam turned to his console. "Should we inform someone?"

Mace opened a comm. "Mr. Collins, we'll be gone for the day. Need to finish up our work at Canto. If we're needed, leave a message with them as we'll be jumping back and forth bringing those shuttles home."

"Take your time. Things will be a mess here for the next couple weeks as we get our fleet back in order. We lost a lot of good commanders out there."

Mace nodded. "I just hope we can make their sacrifices worthwhile. We'll be back shortly."

Bontu Montak walked onto the bridge deck as the *Rogers* slipped through a wormhole to Canto.

"Can I help?"

Mace asked, "Who else is aboard besides you?"

"Five of my crewmen. Is there something you need?"

Mace gestured toward the exit. "Have them monitor the reactors, drives, and other stations. It's just us aboard."

Bontu frowned. "What if we have trouble? Is this wise?"

Mace leaned back in his chair. "We need to do this to save face with the UF."

Bontu nodded. "I will have them cover the stations, Mr. Hardy."

The captain of a UF dreadnought hailed the *Rogers*. "Captain, first, my apologies. Second, we're here to collect the shuttles that were stranded. If you could give me the coordinates for the first two, we'll be on our way."

Two additional dreadnoughts moved in close. "I'm sorry, Mr. Hardy. We've been asked to detain you for breach of contract. The Adjutant General will be here in two days for your preliminary hearing."

Mace returned an irritated look. "There won't be any detention, Captain. You either allow us to retrieve your people or we leave and they remain where they are."

The captain returned an angry look. "You would defy the United Front? In our own space? You realize this gives me authorization to shoot, do you not?"

A hail came in from Frado Knuttin. "Mr. Hardy. I am sorry, but you will have to comply with the council's demands."

Mace let out a deep sigh. "No, it's I who am sorry, Mr. Knuttin. Sorry I got involved with trying to assist your people. We were called away to war. That war is ongoing. I have a short amount of time available to collect your people. You need to allow me to do that before I have to leave again."

Frado replied, "You must allow me to talk with my connections, Mr. Hardy. Perhaps I can smooth things over."

Mace replied, "How long will this take?"

Frado shook his head. "I couldn't say, but you must allow me to try. And I'm looking at the image of your ship. It looks as though it was a fierce battle. Can I assume you were victorious?"

Mace scowled. "Hardly. They kicked our asses. They are wiping out an entire species as we speak. In six months they'll be wiping out a second one. After that, our heads will be on the chopping block again."

Frado bowed his head. "I can see the concern in your eyes, Mr. Hardy. Know that I shall do my best."

Mace sighed. "I know you will."

Mace returned to the captain. "Sorry to make you wait. That was Frado Knuttin. He's attempting to speak with your command."

The captain replied, "In the meantime, Mr. Hardy, I'll be sending a detachment over there. We wouldn't want any incidents to happen so near to our colony."

Mace shook his head. "Yeah. No. We'll be waiting for word from Mr. Knuttin."

The captain leaned toward his comm camera. "I'm afraid you misunderstood, Mr. Hardy. My people will be there momentarily."

Liam Hobbs attempted a power-up of the starboard gravity drive. Plasma spewed from the directional funnel into space. Liam jumped from his console frantically, running in front of the comm camera. "We have a breach of the hydrogen store! The ship is about to blow!"

Mace stood. "What? How?"

The comm channel closed. Liam returned to his station.

"What's going on?"

"I'm trying to buy us some space ... and... yes! There they go!"

Liam slammed a button on his console. A micro-wormhole opened in front of the *Rogers* and her functional gravity drive pushed her through. In an instant, the *Rogers* was back in Targarian space.

Liam turned, "Sorry, Mr. Hardy, we needed a way out of there and that's all I could think of."

Mace grinned. "That was brilliant! And an excellent job of acting. I seriously thought we *were* about to blow."

"They were being a bit beastly. We were only attempting to make right on our pledge."

Mace thought for a moment. "We know where those shuttles are supposed to be. How about we go get them anyway. We can drop them off a couple hours out from Canto and not have to mess with those... *beastly* people."

"Have I ever said I liked you, Mr. Hardy, because you always try to do the right thing? Most would just abandon the mess and move on, but you persist, in an attempt at least, to do what's proper."

"If I didn't at least try, as a kid my mom would give me the belt across the back of my legs. I learned early on it was worth avoiding the pain."

"First jump coming up," Liam said.

Nine hours passed before the last of the shuttles were dumped into Canto space. The *Rogers* returned home and a secondary skeleton crew was brought aboard.

Mace turned to Bontu Montak as he walked up the ramp of a shuttle. "You sure you won't join us, Mr. Montak? It's nice down there. We have a run of the compound."

Bontu nodded. "The crew and I prefer to stay here. This has become our home."

"Last chance..."

Bontu slowly shook his head. "They have no desire to set foot on any planet that is not Rhombia, Mr. Hardy. They are no longer comfortable on Earth either. As I said, this is our home now. And do not worry, we have plenty of entertainment with watching your Human movies."

Mace chuckled. "Just don't watch too much of that stuff. It'll rot your brain."

Mace was soon on the surface. Zax and Fina raced out to greet him as Johnny followed.

Zax said, "Mr. Hardy, welcome back to Divinia!"

Mace laughed. "Well, thank you for welcoming me. I take it you like being back on-planet?"

Zax nodded. "Fina has been teaching me how to fish."

Mace looked up at Johnny. "Maybe they aren't adopted after all. You sure you weren't a donor for those embryos? They did have you on that drug for a few days."

Johnny nodded. "I'm sure. Besides, I try to catch fish on a hook. These two are catching them with their teeth. I've tried to tell them that's not the proper way, but they won't listen."

The two kids darted off across a blue-green Targarian lawn and Derwood shot out of the building after them.

Mace laughed. "At least they're keeping Derwood healthy."

Johnny chuckled. "That dog used to get up several times in the middle of the night to check on us. He sleeps solid through now. They're constantly giving him and Molly a good workout. I take it the Canto mission was successful?"

Mace frowned. "Yes and no. We got the explorers back to Canto, but we had to sneak them back. The UF wanted to arrest and hold me for some adjutant general hearing. Liam managed to spook them far enough away that we could make a jump. He put on a pretty convincing show in front of the comm camera. For a moment I thought the *Rogers* was about to blow."

"Hmm. He's always been kinda by the book. Good to know you can count on him in a pinch."

Mace nodded. "I feel like that with most of our crew. They keep giving and giving, no matter what I ask."

Johnny patted Mace on the shoulder. "You treat them like family, and they're acting like family. You're just getting back what you've given."

Two wet kids, each carrying a fish in their mouth, raced past Mace and Johnny and into the building.

Johnny sighed. "Gotta see to this or Jane will accuse me of teaching them that way on purpose."

Johnny approached the door, rubbing the sides of his head as a scowling Jane came out to stand in the doorway.

Chapter 16

The coming threat of the Karthians loomed over every activity. Weeks passed before the last of the Sarkesian colonies fell. Healthy males were packed onto ships and sent away to be worked to death in Karthian mines. Women, children, the elderly and the infirm were mercilessly butchered. The once great Sarkesian species, an original founder of the Galactic Union, was rapidly on its way to extinction.

As Mace sat in a long chair with Jenny, overlooking the lake at the compound, a comm came in from the Quelli Alpha, the leader of their species.

"I must humbly ask for your assistance. King Collins has refused our pleas. We cannot defend our worlds on our own. The Karthians will be coming this way next. I beg you to convince the King we need his support."

Mace sighed. "I feel for you, I really do. But if we are to stop the Karthians, it will have to be here at the Targarian worlds. The defenses here at least give us a fighting chance. I would offer this—see if you can convince one of the other Union members to allow you to move your people to their worlds. That would at least force the Karthians to fight us here at Divinia first. If we then lose here, we will all know that our time is very limited."

The Quelli leader stroked his mane in thought. "To abandon one's home is a difficult task to contemplate. And to accept another into your home, when you aren't prepared, is another difficult task."

Mace said, "I'm afraid those are your only options. Stay and fight, or convince another species to take you in, at least temporarily."

The Quelli Alpha bowed as the comm closed.

Jenny said, "He needs to be talking to Stark. The Zinka have the space, but they don't have the infrastructure to support billions more people."

Mace nodded. "If we all pooled our resources we could make this happen, but it would be at the expense of us building ships, which are required for our survival. Unfortunately, I think the Quelli have no choice but to make the toughest of choices. They'll have to choose who gets moved to someone else's colonies. And that depends on someone accepting them."

Jenny sighed. "War... I like it less every day."

A frantic comm came in from the Quelli leader. "They are here! The Karthians! How is this possible? You must convince the King to come!"

The comm channel closed.

Mace opened a comm to Jasper. "The Quelli say the Karthians are there. Do you have any people there?"

Jasper replied, "Let me... wait, I have an incoming message. *Karthians at Talicon.*"

Mace said, "How? Do they have wormhole generators?"

Jasper scowled. "They've destroyed or disabled enough of our ships. They may have acquired it from there."

Mace shook his head. "This changes everything."

A comm came in from Stark. "I can see by the look on your face you've already received the news."

Mace replied, "They must have the wormhole generator. Did the Quelli see how they arrived? Were wormholes detected?"

Stark shook his head. "We don't know. I've just sent a scout ship to gather information. I should have an idea of what we're looking at in a few minutes."

An aide to Stark walked into camera view, whispering into his ear. Stark nodded as he opened a holo-display over his arm.

"It's the full force, including that station. The Quelli fleet has pulled back. Military posts on the ground are being wiped out."

Mace moved Jasper's comm into the channel. "We should begin our preparations. If the Sarkesian worlds only took a few weeks to overrun, the Quelli will likely be the same. Mr. Stark, try to convince the Quelli to move their ships here. Jasper, we need to be prepared to move those microwave stations as we talked about before."

"They're ready to move," said Jasper.

Stark said, "This creates a new problem for us. We will only have a few minutes advance warning before the fighting begins. All strategies and tactics must be fully defined before they arrive."

Jasper replied, "What would you suggest? For us, we plan to stay as close to our microwave stations as possible. Not sure what else we could do."

Mace said, "We're just a single ship. We'll just do what we did last time. We managed to knock out seven of their ships. Two thirds of those kills came from our extra weapons."

Stark replied, "How many of those can be produced in the few weeks we might have?"

Mace shook his head. "Zero. We don't yet know how the wormhole weapon works. And the green wave generator took months of tweaking to get it to work at the level it does. And it's really only been useful when following one of those wormhole shots, which is difficult to coordinate at best."

Jasper huffed. "So we're reduced to just clubbing each other over the head until only one side is left standing. I'm not placing a lot of confidence in our chances."

Mace stood and paced. "I have one other potential option. The United Front."

Jenny scowled. "They want to arrest you."

Stark asked, "What do we have to offer?"

Mace stopped. "Territory. We have the Sarkesian worlds, and soon the Quelli worlds. And we've posted mining claims on about two hundred other worlds. We could offer the UF part or all of those territories in exchange for assistance."

Jasper scowled. "I understand where you're coming from, but I can't say I fancy that option. We may be trading one aggressive species for another."

Mace nodded. "That may be true, but to my knowledge, the UF at least allows second class citizens. And that's only an issue if they decide to take over all the other territories here."

Jasper replied, "I'll have to chew on that idea for a bit."

Stark said, "For the moment at least, we keep that as an option. All the uninhabited territories in the galaxy don't do us any good if we're dead."

Jasper asked, "What about the Dellus and Gorange and other Union members? Will they join us here in a grand defense?"

Stark replied, "I will be addressing them shortly. It may be difficult to convince them of the benefit of an allied defense. If they hold back and we are victorious, they are sitting with a still powerful fleet. If we fight the Karthians to a stalemate, again they have an advantage. If we fight and lose, they will in turn lose."

Mace said, "Maybe we could entice them with promises of territory. Expansion is their ultimate goal. We have worlds identified that we could offer."

Stark nodded. "Another excellent suggestion. I'll use that if my other efforts fail."

Mace crossed his arms. "Should I make a trip to Canto to discuss that option with the UF? Time may be of the essence."

Jasper said, "How many ships do they have guarding that planet?"

"Last visit it was eight. Why?"

"If you jump there by yourself they are likely not to let you leave this time. If we send thirty of our Collins ships, they might just listen to your offer. And if they refuse it, you'll still be able to come home."

Mace nodded. "I like that idea. The Kohamians respect strength. When can we go?"

"Give me an hour."

Mace shook his head. "Actually, the *Rogers* won't be ready until tomorrow. And I'd rather make the trip in my own ship."

Jasper said, "You do realize that if they have the wormhole generators they could be *here* tomorrow, right?"

"I do, and if that turns out to be the case, none of this will matter anyway."

The following Yentis morning, the *Rogers* jumped through a wormhole to Canto. She was met immediately by three dreadnoughts.

The captain Mace had talked to previously was no longer in charge. "Mr. Hardy, prepare to be boarded."

Mace held up a hand. "Not so fast, Captain. I need to speak with your superiors about a very lucrative deal."

The captain shook his head. "I have no time or patience for your games, Mr. Hardy. Stand down all weapons and shields. You are under arrest for crimes against the United Front. You will comply or face the consequences."

Mace smiled. "Sorry, Captain, it is you who will comply with my request. I need to speak with your superiors about an urgent matter."

The captain stood from his chair with an angry expression on his face. "My next warning will be in the form of weapons fire. Stand down or—"

A micro-wormhole opened with thirty Collins class warships streaming through.

Mace said, "Again, I would like to speak with your superiors."

The captain scowled. "This is an outright act of war!"

Mace leaned forward. "Contact your superiors or I'll make it an outright act."

A Kohamian admiral was patched into the comm. "You have invaded United Front space. I advise you to leave immediately."

Mace said, "Admiral, I apologize for this intrusion, but I must speak with someone in command. It's urgent. And I'm not talking about the command here at Canto. I need to discuss a potential defensive alliance with the United Front and I don't have time to dicker with lower level field commanders. This is an urgent matter and requires higher up attention from people with authority to make such alliances. You know my history.

You know for whom I speak. Please connect me with your superiors."

The admiral sat silent for several seconds. "Give me a few minutes, Mr. Hardy. Your request is not of a usual nature."

Three minutes passed before another individual showed on the comm display. "What is the meaning of this intrusion?"

Mace replied, "Our territories have been invaded by another empire. By ourselves we may not able to defend against them. I've come here with an offer that might interest you. In return for assistance, we have a number of previously populated worlds that we would cede to your control. At the moment, that is fourteen prior colonies in eleven star systems.

"The previous occupants have been wiped out by the invaders, leaving the worlds open for claim. Should you be willing to offer sufficient assistance, we would acknowledge your claim to those worlds. I can send you data on the worlds in question. You decide whether or not you have interest and what you might be able to offer in return. At the moment, we need ships and weapons. We are outnumbered and we're being outproduced.

"I know the United Front has gone through a period of strengthening your empire and that you're now in an expansionist mode. Here are fourteen worlds that are ready for colony establishment, mining, whatever you want to use them for. They are also relatively close to a rift that leads to this other empire."

The individual on the display rubbed his protruding chin. "While our interest level with regards to expansion is high at the moment, we are quickly discovering we lack the means to travel the great distances needed to manage and defend such colonies. There has been much discussion about the twenty worlds we just laid claim to with your assistance. Some will take decades for us to reach. Of much greater value to us at the moment would be your wormhole technology."

Mace sighed. "I'm certain you understand that we cannot part with that technology for obvious reasons. For one, it makes us vulnerable to immediate attack. It's the one technology we cannot afford to give away."

The Kohamian diplomat smiled. "It would appear to me to be the only option you have, Mr. Hardy. I might be able to persuade the council to trade temporary defense of your worlds for such. I can tell you also that no amount of far territories will elicit a defensive pact from our leaders."

Mace took a deep breath, letting it out slowly. "Let's say we were to offer the wormhole tech, would the United Front be willing to supply as much might as we need to defeat the Karthians? If we can eliminate the force in our territory, I believe they would then leave us to ourselves, turning their aggression elsewhere."

The diplomat nodded. "I will pass this information on immediately. Expect a reply within the hour."

Mace said, "We'll be here. Oh, and ask your local admiral not to send any more ships to greet us. If he does, we leave."

The diplomat bowed. "Consider it done."

The comm closed.

Mace turned in his chair. "Opinions?"

Jordan Crawford replied, "The wormhole tech is the one advantage we've had over these other species. We give that away and we're at their mercy, as you suggested. We need years of build-up to be able to defend what we have. Our production is weak, as is the rest of our technology."

Johnny nodded. "What he just said. If we give that up, the UF has the means to rapidly expand, including into our space. And from what we've seen, they would be far harder to stop than the Karthians. I would have to vote no on this."

Jasper said, "You already know my thoughts on doing that. It's a bad idea."

Mace looked at Jeff. "Mr. Moskowitz?"

"I'm of mixed feelings. Other than *protecting* this colony, they haven't shown us any expansionist aggression. On the other hand, they haven't exactly been cooperative with us. I would have to say I lean in the direction of the rest of you. Perhaps find out how quickly they would be willing to respond to something as a last resort?"

The Kohamian diplomat returned to the comm after just over an hour. "Mr. Hardy, the council would be willing to entertain a trade of your wormhole technology, in its entirety, for a one-time defense of your worlds from these Karthians."

Mace nodded. "Any technology trade would have to happen after this defense. And the result of such defense would have to be the complete annihilation of the threat. If that could be agreed to, I will take this back to my people for discussion. Oh, and one other question: how soon could the needed resources be made ready? Assuming we will provide a means of transporting any assets to the battlefront."

The diplomat replied, "I have been given authority to agree to terms if I find them acceptable. Given the size and nature of the threat you sent my way, we would require four days to assemble the necessary force."

Mace bowed. "I'll be back with an answer in a Canto day. We can move forward or part ways from there."

The comm closed. The *Rogers*, along with Jasper's escorts, returned to Divinia.

Jasper said, "You aren't seriously considering that deal, are you?"

"It could be what saves the Targarian worlds, as well as Earth. I am considering it. I'd like to talk with Stark first. He has a good grasp of thinking out the angles we might not see."

A comm was opened. "Mr. Stark, we have a dilemma and a possible solution. I need your opinions and insights. The United Front has agreed to provide the means for us to defeat the Karthians. In return, we have to turn over the wormhole technology."

Stark rubbed his chin. "I've been mulling over this very idea. It would allow us to rebuild, but at the same time make us vulnerable to a new and possibly more powerful species. What happens when the boundaries of our empires come together? Such as on Canto? Can they be trusted to be respectful of our claims or should we fear them as we fear the Karthians? It's a dilemma... with no easy answer."

Johnny chuckled. "I expected something insightful. He's only repeating what we already know."

Mace said, "That offer is on the table. Take a few hours and tell me what you think. We don't have to tell them today. Oh, and if we decide to do this, they said they could have a force ready in four days' time. I would expect it to be at least a week given all the unknowns. The tech would not be turned over until the mission was completed."

Stark's silhouette sat facing the camera for several seconds. "I'll have an answer for you in two hours."

Chapter 17

Two hours came and went. After four, Mace opened a comm to the reigning Human king.

Stark answered, "We continue to work on the pros and cons of the agreement with the United Front. You stated they don't need an answer for another eighteen hours. The issue is quite complex. A hasty answer would be remiss."

Mace nodded. "Just wanted to check in since you went well past your suggested deadline."

Jasper opened a comm. "We have trouble. The Karthians are finishing up their efforts with the Quelli worlds. The remaining Quelli fleet has taken refuge with the Zinka. The Karthian fleet could be coming this way at any moment."

Mace replied, "I guess that ends our discussion about the UF. We don't have time for them to assemble a defense anyway."

Stark said, "I'll begin preparations to move our force to Divinia. I believe the Gorange and Dunden Heap will be joining us. The Dellus, Zinka, and Quelli are opting to stay away."

Mace sighed. "I figured as much. We'll just have to deal with it."

Jasper said, "We've detected wormholes opening at Talicon. We don't have any indication as to where they are connecting to. Talicon is the Quelli home world. Wait... scan results coming in. It looks like Nineka. That's the Dellus capital. They jumped around us!"

An aide whispered to Stark. "I have confirmation. Eleven hundred ships are in the Nineka system. The Quelli have indeed jumped. The Zinka are not committing. The Gorange and Dunden Heap have given their word to join us here should we be attacked before them."

Jasper said, "Stinkin' Zinka. They've been backstabbing everyone from the beginning. The Dellus are fools for trusting them."

Stark looked over information above his arm pad. "The Karthian station has arrived at Nineka."

Mace said, "That's one massive wormhole they're opening."

Stark nodded. "Indeed, the cost of gatrellium must be astronomical."

"What kind of force do the Dellus have available?"

Stark replied, "Just over four hundred ships if the Zinka show. Without them, I'd say... two-fifty? This fight will be over in a matter of hours."

Johnny said, "If they're already moving to Dellus space, what happened to the Quelli? They couldn't have moved that many out of those colonies already."

"Flat-out genocide is what's happening," said Jasper. "The ships they left behind are pulverizing the Quelli cities. Full-on eradication."

Bontu Montak came onto the bridge. "The Dellus? Is it true?"

Fatso Geerok stood from his chair. "It's true. Nineka is under assault. Rhombia will follow."

Mace said, "And all we can do is watch. I'm sorry, Mr. Montak. There's nothing we can do."

Bontu replied, "I understand the situation. You must wait for the time you feel you can make the best stand. No need to apologize."

Johnny said, "Too bad we can't make a jump to the Karthian home world and rain down terror on their people."

Stark replied, "Their planets, similar to Divinia and Earth, have many levels of defense. I think it unlikely that with our current force we would get within striking distance."

The Dellus Admiral Dlukov opened a comm to Jasper. "Your Highness, we beg your assistance. Help us now and we will submit to your kingdom and rule. Our ships are already seeing heavy losses. The traitorous Zinka have abandoned us."

Jasper remained firm: "I can't help you, Admiral. Our defensive stand will be here. You could salvage your fleet and send it this way. It won't help your worlds, but it would give your fleet a fighting chance."

The admiral scowled. "I would just as soon die here in my own territory than defend someone so callous as to even ask such a thing."

Jasper nodded before closing the comm. "Then go ahead and die."

Johnny raised an eyebrow. "Cold."

Jasper huffed. "Real. They picked their friends. Now they pay the price."

Mace said, "So that brings us back to the issue of the UF. Maybe it's not too late to enlist their help."

Stark stood from his chair, his arms clasped behind his back as he began to pace. "I no longer think we have a choice, Mr. Hardy. The agreement with the United Front is now our best option. My advice would be to travel there immediately to initiate the deal. It does us no good if the Karthians attack beforehand. We may not last long enough to bring any aid through."

Mace asked, "Jasper?"

The Targarian king scowled. "I don't see that we have a choice, either."

Mace turned. "Mr. Hobbs, take us to Canto. Gentlemen, I'll give you an update when I return."

A wormhole opened in front of the *Rogers*. The bright blue cruiser moved into UF space. The three dreadnoughts were in the same position as when the *Rogers* had last been there.

Mace opened a comm. "Captain, you can inform your superiors that we are ready to sign a deal."

The captain held up his hands. "I'm sorry, Mr. Hardy. The deal you sought is no longer available."

"What? Why? We had another fourteen hours."

The captain shook his head. "We no longer need the wormhole technology from you. We just signed a protection deal with the Mawga for that information. They have opened wormholes to allow our fleet through. Should the aggressors attack there, we will defend. It seems you no longer have anything of value to offer."

The comm closed. A new comm came in from Jasper.

"I can't believe it," said Mace. "The Mawga just destroyed us. Where'd they get the wormhole tech?"

Johnny replied, "Well, we were about to do the same to them."

Mace shook his head. "Not true. We would have offered protection to this whole region, not just Earth and Targarian space."

Jasper said, "The Mawga had taken possession of a Quelli Muhatha, giving them access to a wormhole generator. But we have another issue. The Australians. The forces the Kaachi stole from us are entering that fight at Nineka."

Mace let out a deep sigh. "We have to go and try to get them. They should be here with us."

Jasper frowned. "Mr. Stark, are you prepared for a jump to Nineka? Our lost Australians just showed up. The Kaachi brought them out in defense of the Dellus."

Stark replied, "We lose our defensive advantage with those microwave stations."

Mace shook his head. "Doesn't matter. We only have to get them out."

Jasper said, "I have two scouts there right now. The Kaachi have some new boarding ship that has allowed them to attack and clamp onto those Karthian ships."

Mace said, "Mr. Hobbs, take us to Nineka. Mr. Collins, Mr. Stark, I'll be expecting your ships there momentarily."

"We'll be there," said Jasper. "And I'm bringing a hundred of the microwave stations from my Kehouth colony. I'll have the population transferred from there as well."

Stark walked off the screen as he said, "We will be there momentarily, Mr. Hardy."

The Human-commanded ships massed ten minutes from the fighting that was occurring around Nineka. The Dellus fleet was completely engaged. The Kaachi, bringing another eighty warships along with the Australians and the boarding ships, were in the process of getting into the fight. Wormhole openings were detected on the far side of the planet. Zinka and Quelli ships came through. A third set of wormholes was opened near Stark and the Human ships. The Gorange and the Dunden Heap ships moved into formation.

Mace looked over the wall display. "This is everything we have."

Stark said, "I've informed the others our mission here is to retrieve the Australians and to leave. I got an immediate response from the Zinka and Quelli. You'll see their reply any second."

Again wormhole openings were detected as the Zinka fleet and their Quelli friends left the battle space.

Jasper scowled. "I hope those cowards are next."

Mace said, "What's our plan here? The Aussies are already engaged."

Stark said, "We have no choice but to attack from the opposite side of that station. We can't engage that beast without risking our remaining Radica ships."

Jasper nodded. "Well, let's get at it. People are dying out there."

Mace said, "Johnny, send out a general comm. See if we can get the Aussies to connect. And do it on the normal Kaachi frequencies as that's probably what they would have those ships restricted to."

"Mr. Collins," said Stark, "if you can make your fleet a distraction, we will attempt a run into where the Australians are and provide them with an escort out. The Gorange and Dunden Heap will assist with that mission."

Jasper replied, "Say when and we'll move."

Johnny said, "I have a comm to one of the boarding ships. Pushing it to the big wall."

An image of an Australian officer wearing a modified Kaachi battle suit showed on the display. "Mr. Hardy, glad to see you're joining the fight."

Mace replied, "We've been in from the beginning. The Dellus have been holdouts. We need you to send word to your other ships to pull their personnel back. We're coming in to bring you home."

The officer replied, "We're here to fight, Mr. Hardy. After you abandoned us, the Kaachi have provided for us."

"We didn't abandon anyone," said Mace. "They took you and cut off communications. We've made every effort to find you but were not able to. The Kaachi said the Dellus took you. The Dellus said they didn't know what we were talking about. Looks like the Kaachi are the ones who deceived you."

The officer returned a skeptical look. "That's not the information we had, Mr. Hardy. Stark's people told us of your treachery and asked that we stay with the Kaachi as a sort of insider force. We know of your alliance with the Mawga, and now with the United Front, meanwhile leaving us exposed. They equipped us and trained us for just such a fight. We fight here so we don't have to fight at Earth."

Mace shook his head. "You've been led astray, Colonel. You should have been brought home a long time ago. Stark's people lied."

Mace switched the comm to Stark. "So you lied to us about the Australians. All the time you knew they were with the Kaachi."

Stark slowly nodded. "It is true. I believed having a force inside their force would give us leverage when it came time for action. It was a mistake on our part. We didn't know they were still alive. It seems the Kaachi hid them away, telling us they were killed in a tragic accident, and then continued to feed them false information as if it was coming from us. The evidence they presented of their demise was convincing. Of course, us having knowledge of them being there in the first place would not have gone over well with the Australians back on Earth, so we remained silent on the issue."

Mace returned an angry stare. "You set them up and then abandoned them. This must be a difficult undertaking for you right now. And I'm thinking our strategy here just changed. You, the Gorange and the Dunden Heap will be the distraction, while we—Jasper and I—go in to escort the Australians."

Stark nodded. "I have no issue with trading positions. Tell us when you are ready to begin."

Mace switched comms back to the Australian, patching Stark in. "Colonel, it seems the Kaachi have been feeding you bad intel. Stark says they lost direct contact with you, and the Kaachi told them you had all been killed. Anyway, doesn't matter at the moment. We're coming in to escort you out. We'll be taking you back for a full debrief. Any decision you want to make from that point on will be your own. Is Coran Daughtry available?"

The colonel replied, "General Daughtry was executed by the Kaachi for high treason shortly after we went through the wormhole. He attempted to take control of a ship to bring us home. We were told his attempt would have been detrimental to Earth's defense and that King Stark authorized it. He was a good bloke."

Stark's silhouette stood. "I authorized no such thing. Whatever you have been told by the Kaachi is untrue."

"Who are you?" asked the colonel.

"That's Malcolm Stark," said Mace. "He won't show his face out of fear for his family, or so he says. I'd take what he says with a grain of salt as well. There's usually motive behind what he wants you to believe, although in this instance he's probably telling the truth. Anyway, get your people back to their ships. We're coming in to bring you home."

Stark's fleet, along with those of the Gorange and Dunden Heap, moved into the fight. Jasper's ships, along with the *Rogers*, raced towards the Australians. As the forces clashed, the Australians moved their forces back to their ships and the Targarians opened a path for their retreat. As they came into free space, a wormhole portal was opened to Divinia. Stark and the others disengaged, leaving the Dellus and Kaachi to fend for themselves. Hours later, word from a scout came telling of the complete destruction of Nineka.

After a meeting with the Australians, they were sent back to Earth to be with their families. The ninety-six hundred who had survived several years of captivity would only have a few days before they would be called upon to defend their people. Their homecoming would be short-lived.

Gnaga Klept stood on the bridge. "I must apologize for my people. Our leaders followed the Dellus. If you were not of their species, they viewed you as nothing more than an asset or liability, to be used or discarded. I believe your Australians were hidden away, trained for a future use where the Kaachi would put them into battle for some conquest. That conquest never came. Our leaders saw the Dellus as the embodiment of power and prestige. Our people will now suffer because of it."

Mace replied, "When all is said and done, we may all end up suffering for our choices. Better to believe in something that gives you hope than to have nothing but despair. And you don't have to apologize for the decisions others have made. Just as I won't be apologizing to anyone for what Stark has done... or will do."

Gnaga nodded. "As always, I thank you for your kindness. I know the galaxy would be a better place if the people on this ship were in command of her. For that reason, I have committed myself to this cause."

Mace patted Gnaga on the shoulder. "Your being a part of this team is why we've made it as far as we have. Now we just have to bring all our efforts home for one final fight."

Stark came over the comm. "The scouts report the Dellus are no more. The Karthians are now moving through the Kaachi colonies. They're finding little to no resistance now that the fleets have been destroyed. We expect the next move to be toward the Mawga worlds. We've given warning and have several scout ships positioned nearby. If the Karthians do attack there, we'll quickly ascertain the strength of the United Front."

"Has there been any sign of UF ships at Rhombia?"

Stark shook his head. "Not as of yet. We believe the Mawga Muhatha, with its full wormhole generator, is sitting in UF space waiting to make a transfer. Other than that speculation, we have count of a hundred and twelve cruisers in the Mawga fleet. They would only last minutes against that Karthian horde."

Fatso Geerok interrupted. "Have we found out how the Karthians are moving their ships? Do they have a single ship with a generator or a fleet of them?"

Stark replied, "A single ship generates the wormhole to move that station. The remainder move through hundreds of smaller wormholes. Again, they must be using a tremendous amount of gatrellium to move that fleet around. Far beyond the stockpiles we possess."

Jasper sighed. "You mean the stockpiles we used to possess. We'll soon be down to the mines in Targarian space, all of which are nearly depleted."

Mace asked, "How are our supplies here?"

"We keep building those ships and we'll be out in a year. And as you know, if we run out we will be stuck here with nothing but half light-speed to move us around. Communications between our colonies will be limited to light speed. Our comms, although instant, are only viable for a short distance."

Johnny chuckled. "And the news just keeps getting better."

Mace sat in his command chair. "Any value in a jump to Hoorka space? Maybe they would have gatrellium to trade."

"They use it for their own ships," said Gnaga. "I don't see that as a possibility."

Mace sat rubbing his temples as an aide came to Stark's side.

Stark said, "Gentlemen, the Karthians are in the process of annihilating the Kaachi people. Their capital of Hathius has been all but destroyed. We have reports of freighters loaded down with people being incinerated as they try to reach space. The Karthians *must* be stopped."

Gnaga sat in a chair. "Will I be the last of the Kaachi?"

Jasper said, "With every one of these kill-offs, we're also losing valuable ship production."

Stark replied, "Perhaps you should have shared your technologies while you had the chance. Your ships fare much better than ours, and yet you won't divulge your secrets."

Jasper scowled. "Yeah, well, secrets get stolen or traded. The Karthians, our cruel enemy, are only able to do what they do because they stole the technology from the battlefield where your people were too sloppy with its protection. And we see what the Mawga did with it—traded it like an old bicycle for protection from the Karthians. With our ships, if they become too damaged to fight and too damaged to run, we set off the self destruct. The crews of those ships may die in the process, but they protect the rest of us by preserving what little advantages we may have. So don't come preaching to me about sharing when you don't do it yourself."

Stark replied, "What technology do we have that you do not?"

Jasper crossed his arms. "Your dome ships, the Radica. I don't recall you volunteering anything on those. And what did we just learn? You knew the Kaachi had the Australians. Did you tell us so we might try to do something about that? No. Was too embarrassing knowing you got played. You know, it's a good thing you're the King, 'cause you ain't much of a human being."

Mace stood. "This conversation isn't leading anywhere good. Let's keep focus on the prize and not on our past mistakes."

The comm was silent for several seconds before Stark replied, "You are of course correct. Mr. Collins, I apologize for my past transgressions. I can do nothing about those at this moment. Perhaps in the future, when this is over, I can make remedy. For now, however, we will just have to make do."

Chapter 18

Word soon came of the Karthian jump to the Mawga capital. As the ships took formation for their assault against the tiny Mawga fleet, a wormhole from the United Front opened and dreadnoughts streamed through, just over a hundred in all before the portal closed. The ships moved into a line, only a kilometer apart.

Jasper said, "They stick that close and the green energy from that station is gonna rip into them. When those Karthian ships start moving they'll only have five minutes before they're within range. I hope they have more than that coming."

The modern UF dreadnoughts were styled much differently than the older military surplus vessels the Knuttin Corporation used for its fleet. They also differed from the boxy ships of the UF protection fleet at Canto. The dreadnoughts at Rhombia were long and tubular, like the barrel of a gun. The flat surface on the face of the ships gave no clue as to the power of the microwave cannon that sat behind it. Their bright red hulls shone brilliantly against the black void of space.

Johnny said, "I sure hope those are as powerful as Mr. Knuttin claimed."

"I think we're about to find out," said Mace.

Two hundred Karthian ships began to move forward. The UF dreadnoughts all fired at once. From each warship, a continuous blue beam stretched out toward the attacking ships, wobbling as their aim took shape as a slowly expanding spiral. The dreadnoughts began to move forward as they fired.

"I don't get it," said Jasper.

Gnaga replied, "The spirals of energy will continue to spread out, acting as a net to guide the Karthian ships to a desired location."

Jasper huffed. "And what happens at that location? They're firing from too far away to be effective."

As predicted, the Karthians ships, while avoiding the incoming beams, moved into four confined areas. As they sped forward, four new wormholes opened in close proximity. Intense microwave beams emerged, striking the vessels one by one as they attempted to alter course. When struck, the destruction of each vessel was complete. The dozen cruisers that managed to dodge the short bursts coming from close by were forced into the incoming beams fired from the original ships. After less than a minute, all two hundred of the attackers had been destroyed.

Johnny said, "We need to get us some of those."

Stark said, "They could have been ours if not for our stubbornness. We can only hope they will weaken that force further."

"No such luck," said Humphrey. "That station is jumping."

Mace asked, "Do we know where to?"

Humphrey shook his head. "From the distance of those scouts it's hard to say. We do know it wasn't to Targarian space."

Johnny replied, "Yeah, that's pretty evident. Stark? You have spies with Gorange and Dunden Heap? Or Zinka?"

Stark typed into his arm pad. "One moment... it seems the Zinka are the losers of this round. Just over nine hundred Karthian ships, and that massive station, are closing on the Zinka capital. Their fleet is moving out to engage. We should have visual coming any second."

A video feed of the battle space showed on the display wall. Beams of light and tiny flashes filled the screen. The occasional green wave of energy was followed by a bright flash.

Jasper said, "I'd say they're getting their asses kicked."

As the two sides moved together, the display filled with hundreds of explosions.

Humphrey said, "Mr. Hardy, I'm detecting high levels of gamma radiation. It would appear the Zinka were able to set off those detonations in and around that Karthian fleet."

"Results?"

"The feeds are coming from Mr. Stark's scout ship. It needs to be closer for any determinations to be made. At the current distance we don't have enough resolution to say."

Stark said, "The scouts are moving in."

Humphrey replied, "The sensors counted at least eighteen hundred nuclear blasts. Depending on the shielding of the Karthian ships, they may have caused significant damage, if only to the crews."

Stark's scouts updated the data on the display.

Humphrey said, "Trajectories coming in. Sir, a third of the ships in that field are now drifting in straight lines. That indicates to me that either their drives are offline or their crews are incapacitated."

"And the Zinka ships?" asked Mace.

"I'm only showing eight ships identified as Zinka vessels that are making random moves."

Johnny winced. "Kamikazes. They sacrificed their entire fleet. Probably did the most damage possible. Their people are now gonna pay regardless."

"How many Karthian ships are still showing movement?"

"Six hundred and twelve. Three more just joined those ranks."

Jasper said, "I thought they had shielding against those nukes?"

"Could be that's only on new ships," said Mace. "How many nukes do you have ready?"

Jasper replied, "Fifty-two, but I hoped to use those against that station. Would have to follow Stark's Radica ships in for that. Not sure if it will have much impact as the armor and shielding on that station is substantial compared to a cruiser. Detonating in close proximity might not yield any worthwhile results."

Stark said, "I can get your ships in close if we want to try."

Humphrey pushed a live feed to the display. "The Zinka fleet has been destroyed. Ships are moving on the planet. Their other twelve colonies have no defenses. The Zinka capital will be finished within hours."

Mace frowned. "I now have to wonder if they're avoiding us because of these defenses."

Stark replied, "A sound strategy. If they take out those who are easily defeated, they take their ship production as well, and any future trading between them. It would be the strategy I would use. I expect the Gorange and the Dunden Heap to be next."

Johnny asked, "Why aren't they taking captives to work in their mines from each of these worlds? Why just the Sarkesians?"

Gnaga answered: "The Sarkesians are a sturdy lot. They are well suited to mining and other physical tasks. I suspect their mines are full. They have no need for more miners. Or any other laborers for that matter."

Johnny shook his head. "Doesn't make sense. If you've beaten their fleets, why not put the people to producing or mining or whatever else you could have them do that enriches your kingdom? Those Zinka colonies all have value—make the Zinka extract the maximum from that value. They aren't viewing the labor as an asset."

Geerok said, "Could be their interests only lie with Humans. We saw that as a common theme in the Galactic Union. Why would the Karthians be any different? They've seen your abilities."

Johnny sighed. "Let's hope that's not the case. Although I guess being a slave would be one step up from being dead. A short step, but at least you might have the opportunity to fight for your freedom."

Jeff came onto the bridge. "Mr. Hardy, we think we've been able to recreate the wormhole weapon we have here on the *Rogers*."

Gnaga said, "You had a breakthrough?"

Jeff nodded. "Just now. We'd like to be taken down to our lab at Yentis. We'll be working on our prototype from there. If all goes well, we should have it up and running in as short as a few days. And we think it might be scale-able."

Mace gestured toward the doorway. "Go make it happen, Jeff. We may not have more than a few days."

Mace turned as Jeff left. "That weapon could be our salvation. It worked consistently during each of our recent fights."

"Punching pinholes isn't highly effective," said Jasper. "If it can be scaled up, won't it use more gatrellium?"

Mace nodded. "It would. But imagine punching a hole that was say... a few meters wide? And all the way through. I'd give up a kilogram of gatrellium for each time we could do that. Would be a game changer. And if they can reproduce it, we can make more. We could push the Karthians back through that rift and keep them there."

Stark said, "And I suppose there would be no sharing of this weapon?"

Mace laughed. "Not a chance. It's bad enough that two new species have the wormhole generators in the first place. Either, if they so desire, can now move an entire fleet to any of our colonies without warning. If there was ever a time when Humans faced extinction, that time would be right now. This weapon could put us back in the game."

Jasper said, "I'm ordering resources to be diverted to assist in any way we can."

The scouts continued to monitor the Karthian fleet at the Zinka capital. Part of the fleet was dispersed to the other Zinka colonies to do their dirty deeds. Groups of ships were sent back to the rift. Speculation was there were numerous crews injured by the Zinka nuclear assault. The powerful Karthian fleet had been reduced to only five hundred ships.

Jasper said, "We're now talking about numbers we could fight. If they jump to the Gorange or Dunden Heap worlds, we would have a force to match them."

Mace asked, "Would you commit microwave stations to such a venture?"

Jasper nodded. "I would. And as many as half of the roughly fifteen hundred stations we have."

Mace raised an eyebrow. "You do realize that station is still out there, right?"

Jasper scowled. "That station is big and slow to move. Its range is also less than that of our microwave cannons. We could sit back and pick away at it if we wanted."

"Well then, why don't we go now? Hit them at the Zinka capital while they're regrouping."

"I'm thinking of doing just that. Stark? You in?"

Malcolm Stark's silhouette tapped his fingertips together. "My only concern is that we risk diminishing our own force as well. Let's say we manage to cut their remaining fleet in half and they turn and run back to the rift. What would be our cost? Half our own ships? If so, that is too high a price to pay. They will be sending more ships through that rift. They have them readily available. On the other hand, if we choose to hold back and they reinforce, are we then in an equally bad position?"

Mace scowled as he shook his head. "You're sounding cautious. What happened to that all-out fearlessness and confidence we usually see?"

Stark sighed. "Our world was being run by another species. It's easy to jump into a fire when you have little to nothing at risk. We have a free Earth. Every decision we make has an effect on our people. I'm merely thinking out loud here, hoping to pull benefit from your reactions. As you can see, I'm not getting the result I had hoped for."

Jeff came over the comm. "Mr. Hardy, I know you've been waiting on a result. I just wanted to let you know our first test was a failure. However, it did identify a few shortcomings with our initial design. We hope to have those corrected later today."

"You look terrible, Doc. When's the last time you slept?"

"I've managed a few short catnaps. This work is too important for sleep, Mr. Hardy. If it functions as I believe it will, we'll have a formidable weapon, something for which there may be no counter."

"Just don't burn yourself out, Doc. Mistakes don't help us either."

Jeff Moskowitz nodded. "Noted."

Mace rubbed his chin as the others looked on. "I take it you're all waiting for me to make a decision?"

Johnny laughed. "The Kings need your guidance."

Mace rolled his mouth back and forth in thought for several seconds. "Let's do this. Mr. Collins, how long will it take you to get those microwave cannons ready to move?"

"Twenty minutes."

Mace nodded. "Let's get this rolling, then."

Mace stood as Humphrey Mallot said, "New ships are streaming through the rift. One moment... scouts are reporting another fleet of nine hundred ships."

Mace sat back in his chair. "Are they all cruisers?"

"Most. It would appear there are some support ships mixed in there."

Jasper said, "That's it, then. It looks like we wait for them here."

Mace shook his head in frustration. "How have your colony moves been going? Any way to close a couple more? The more of those microwave cannons we can consolidate in one place, the better off we'll be."

Jasper scowled. "Still working on moving the ground-based stations from the last one. We've moved three colonies now. Those were our smallest, excluding the Phaleron colony which has one of our gatrellium mines. We're still recovering twenty to thirty kilograms a day from that one."

"Any way to move the weapons and leave the mine open until the last minute?"

Jasper tilted his head to one side. "I suppose those guns aren't doing much good there anymore. I'll get my people started on it immediately."

Humphrey said, "The Karthians are jumping. That's both the fleet at the Zinka capital and the one at the rift. The destination is... Dunden Heap space."

A hail came into Stark from the Dunden emperor. "The Karthians are here. Will we be receiving any assistance?"

Stark slowly shook his head. "As we've said before, our best chance against them is an all-out battle here at Divinia. I realize the enormity of what I suggest, but your fleet at least has a fighting chance if you join us here. We cannot protect your worlds."

The emperor looked down at the deck of his command ship for several seconds before turning to his fleet commander.

"Order all ships to Divinia."

The officer returned a shocked expression. "Sir?"

The emperor turned with a scowl. "We've lost, Commander Fless. As a species, we might as well take as many Karthians with us as we can."

Stark's silhouette bowed. "Your selfless decision will be remembered, Your Eminence. Your ships will be welcome under my command. We will do all we can to defeat these savages."

The comm closed. Seconds later, a Muhatha and one hundred thirty-six cruisers of the Dunden Heap fleet joined with those of Malcolm Stark. The destruction of the Dunden colonies continued for two days. A further jump to the Gorange capital of Nellivue had the Gorange scrambling to defend. Their great cities were deep underwater, making for a difficult assault from above. The one hundred sixty-seven cruisers of the Gorange fleet jumped through to Divinia.

The Gorange commander opened a comm. "Our cities are under siege. As previously decided, our fleet is best utilized here. The Karthian ships cannot reach our people. Their lasers and plasma weapons will not penetrate our oceans. They will have to bring down soldiers, and those soldiers will be fighting in our seas where we have an extreme advantage."

Malcolm Stark replied, "You are a species of honor, Commander Krog. I wish we had the means to offer assistance."

The commander nodded in appreciation. "We have abandoned the Fellonce and Lewitis colonies. Their seas were too shallow to defend. Our other nine are deep ocean worlds."

Mace joined the conversation. "Your assistance here at Divinia is greatly appreciated, Commander. If we can't make this stand, the Karthians will have destroyed us all."

Jeff came over the comm excitedly. "Mr. Hardy! It works! We successfully formed a meter-wide wormhole, and then moved it from one location to another."

Mace asked, "So you can reproduce this weapon?"

Jeff nodded. "And an additional bit of good news is the gatrellium cost. Our test apparatus opened a meter-wide wormhole and moved it forward for half a kilometer. The gatrellium consumed remained under a kilogram. I believe with a few tweaks we can reduce that amount by half."

Mace said, "Excellent work, Doc. When can we put it in production? And is the design ship-worthy?"

Jeff nodded. "It is. We should have production drawings ready by tomorrow. I've already sent ahead the designs we know will not change. By the end of this week we should have our first dozen coming off the production line."

Mace's smile began to fade. "The Karthians are at Nellivue. We probably don't have a week. What else can you do for us?"

Jeff replied, "Let us finish the tweaks here. Mr. Collins, if you'd like we can add this weapon to your arsenal on the *Organ Cave*."

Jasper nodded. "I would like."

"And, Mace, we should be able to make modifications to the one on the *Rogers* at the same time. That at least gives us two. I don't believe it possible to speed up the production of the others. We will already be cutting corners that we shouldn't. There's still a slight possibility that these weapons could malfunction. If that were to happen, the open wormhole would likely move through the ship. For that reason the weapon should be isolated in its own room, and placed as close to the forward hull as possible. It is also a directional weapon. The ship will have to be aimed in the direction you want the wormhole formed."

Mace asked, "How far can the wormhole be moved? And is it still created at a one kilometer distance?"

Jeff rubbed his chin. "I suppose it could be kept open for as long as you want to supply gatrellium to it. And the one kilometer is an arbitrary number to begin with. That is a distance that we're guaranteed to not have interference from a nearby mass—namely, us. If you wanted to begin the space-time fracture at say... fifty-thousand kilometers, I don't see why that would be a problem."

"I'm assuming you could program in a few firing sequences for us. If I wanted to pass in a target and have the wormhole open near it and then move through the target for instance, would that be possible?"

Jeff nodded. "I'll have my people put something like that together, Mr. Hardy. A point-and-shoot interface would definitely make it easier to control."

Jeff moved on to continue his work. The Gorange warships joined the fleets at Divinia. All told, the Human-led armada totaled seven hundred forty ships, with two new Collins class vessels coming online every other day. The Karthian onslaught would soon be upon them.

Chapter 19

Reports came in from the Gorange capital. Submerged cannon platforms that rose to the surface to fire kept the Karthian ships in high orbit. Bombardment from above had little to no effect on the Gorange defenses or cities. The ultra-deep oceans of Nellivue had the Karthians at a loss as to how to form an assault. Attempts to bring shuttles of soldiers down to the surface had failed miserably.

A full day passed with no progress by the attackers. The newly created wormhole weapon had been installed on the *Organ Cave* and was ready for a test.

Jasper sat in his command chair, with the others connected over comm feeds. "I need a good test target."

Johnny said, "Why not target that Karthian station? You have its exact location. Do you need to have the *Cave* there to open the wormhole?"

Jeff replied, "He will need to be within sensor range. The wormhole generator needs the direct feeds from the sensors to form the initial fracture."

Jasper said, "Jumping to Nellivue. Give me a sec... OK, I have the target on the sensors. Now it wants a destination. Am I limited on where that can be?"

Jeff replied, "You should only need the coordinates, same as a normal wormhole."

Jasper tapped his fingers on the arm pad of his chair before moving them to a small console. "OK, I have a destination target set. Let's see how she fares."

Seconds later, a wormhole opened a kilometer away from the Karthian station. Million-degree plasma sailed through the meter-wide opening. The wormhole moved slowly toward the station, scorching the exterior armor as the heat overwhelmed the inertial shielding that was its major protection. The station pulled away as the outer layers of protective armor began to melt and burn.

Mace asked, "Was that the Nellivue sun?"

Jasper grinned. "It was. And all indications say that was a success. What I would like to know is, can that wormhole be moved at a faster pace?"

Jeff replied, "The speed is limited at this time. We're hoping to explore that once we have more time."

Jasper frowned. "This could be the weapon we need, but not if it moves that slow."

"Can't we shove a nuke through there?" said Johnny. "Not one of the ships, but maybe a nuclear missile? Something they wouldn't have time to react to?"

Jeff replied, "That station is impervious to nuclear explosions. They don't carry the impact in space as they do in atmosphere. The nuke's primary function out in the void is the gamma radiation they expel, and the station is well shielded. As to a nuclear missile... I suppose that would work. It would need to be in flight and a wormhole opened in front of it for it to fly through. They would still have a moment's opportunity to destroy it. My guess is it would only work once or twice before they began to vaporize them as they came through."

Mace asked, "Specifically, what are you working on right now with regard to this?"

"The stability issue I spoke of before. Our focus is to address the factors surrounding that possibility. I expect that may take some time."

Mace nodded. "I'd like you to switch gears. Focus on moving that wormhole at a faster pace. We just saw where that is a critical need."

Jeff winced. "I would think removing the potential for killing yourself was a critical need as well, but if you insist, we'll take your guidance."

"I insist."

Jasper said, "You make this work and I'll build a ten story monument to you right here on Divinia. Doc Moskowitz, the scientist who saved us all. I can see that written on the base in meter-high letters."

Jeff half smiled. "While flattering, totally unnecessary. My contributions are no more meaningful than yours."

Jasper nodded. "Fine then, I'll build us both monuments."

Mace cut in: "Doc, I'm sure you're eager to get back to your work. How are the updates to the *Rogers* coming?"

Jeff replied, "The *Rogers* should be ready in a few hours. The team will let you know when it's complete."

The comm closed.

Jasper said, "Well, at least in the meantime I have something to play with. Let's see how many of those cruisers we can catch off-guard."

Jasper typed away on his console. The image of a Karthian cruiser appeared. A meter-wide wormhole was opened to the Nellivue sun and a jet of ultra-hot plasma streamed through. The cruiser quickly turned to move away as a heavy black scorch mark ran down the side of the ship.

Jasper said, "I could sit here and do this all day."

Johnny gestured toward the display. "If we get more ships with these weapons, maybe we could open five wormholes in a circle or something where we could catch them no matter which way they turned."

Liam replied, "Right now they only need to back up as the pilot of the station did. Word will be passed around to the other pilots."

Jasper continued to target Karthian cruisers for most of an hour. By the time the hour was up, the entire Karthian fleet was continuously on the move and changing course. No further damage was being done.

Johnny said, "Now you're just being a pest."

Jasper replied, "If that's all I get, I'll take it. I'm a distraction, which keeps some of their focus off the Gorange."

A giant wormhole opened just above the Nellivue atmosphere. A rush of solar plasma streamed through, burning brightly as it fell toward the ocean's surface. A massive cloud of steam arose as the seawater boiled off, expanding rapidly, covering a hundred square kilometers in only a few seconds. The wormhole remained open for only a second before the extreme heat caused its collapse.

Humphrey said, "I think we have a problem, Mr. Hardy. That steam cloud is superheated. Calculations say it could raise the ocean temperature in that region by as much as a half degree. They do that a few more times and Nellivue's oceans will see irreversible damage. That may allow the Karthians to destroy their primary food sources. A couple degrees difference could completely interrupt their food chain. If it's like Earth, you kill the plankton and you kill the fish that feed on plankton as well, and then the fish that feed on them."

Jasper said, "We have a lock on the ship that created that wormhole. I'll be back in a minute."

Mace said, "Hold up, if you know which ship that is, we don't need to destroy it, we need to take its gatrellium. It must have a massive store if they can afford to burn the gatrellium it took to open that large a portal."

Jasper replied, "Boarding party?"

Mace nodded. "That's what I was thinking."

"They were foolish enough to send that ship out on its own. We'll handle this one. I have the crews here that are ready."

The comm closed before Mace could reply. Seconds later, a new comm opened with a sensor feed from the *Organ Cave*. Humphrey Mallot pushed it to the display wall.

"Wow, sir, they have the ship in a grapple already."

"How long before the closest ship is within range?"

"Seven minutes."

"Can they get aboard during that time?"

Humphrey nodded. "Looks as though they're already aboard. And Mr. Collins is leading the charge."

Mace stood. "You're kidding! Why would he risk himself?"

Johnny laughed. "If you don't know the answer to that by now..."

"I know the answer—he's a crotchety old fool. Mr. Mallot, do we have the feed from his helmet?"

"Patching it through."

The image on the display jerked violently as Jasper bulldozed his way down a hall firing his plasma rifle full tilt. Explosions rocked the Karthian ship as the intruders penetrated all the way to the room that held the gatrellium store. A Targarian soldier took aim at the generator.

Jasper grabbed his rifle. "Hold on."

Jasper Collins walked across the room to a console, where he entered coordinates. A sizable wormhole opened a kilometer in front of the two entangled ships.

Humphrey said, "We have a wormhole opening."

Mace asked, "Where?"

"Here."

Jasper gave the order to move, and the *Organ Cave* plowed forward with the Karthian ship still attached. Seconds later the two ships were sitting in Targarian space near Divinia.

Jasper blasted the generator with his rifle before rejoining his troops in the hallway, pushing hard forward until the bridge was reached and the Karthian commander surrendered.

The remaining Karthian crew was escorted from the ship.

Jasper came over the comm. "The ship is secure. We got just over a ton of gatrellium. They were preparing to open that flare wormhole another half dozen times."

"Well done," said Mace, "but you really shouldn't risk yourself over a raid like this. We need you here when that fleet comes this way."

Jasper smirked. "Like you wouldn't have done the same. The raid was a success. We're now trying to determine if we can spot the other ships that open these wide portals. Could be a quick windfall of gatrellium for us, and it would keep that station where it's at until they get a new ship out there."

Johnny said, "I do like that idea."

Mace nodded. "Keep us informed."

Fifteen minutes later, a second large wormhole opened above Nellivue and another mass of solar plasma rushed through. As before, the plasma illuminated the atmosphere before making contact with a region of the great oceans of the Gorange capital planet. A massive cloud of steam shot halfway to orbit, spreading out like a shockwave, soon covering another area of more than a thousand square kilometers.

Humphrey said, "Mr. Hardy, global surface temperature is up a full five degrees. Atmospheric up twenty-two. Another strike like that and the Gorange will begin to feel the effect down deep."

Mace opened a comm to the Gorange commander. "Commander Krog, is there anything we can do?"

The translators kicked in as the Gorange commander spoke through the saltwater that surrounded him in his bridge. "I fear I must return our fleet to Nellivue to protect against further attacks. Other than fighting alongside us, I know of nothing I could ask, and I know that is not something you can provide while still protecting your own people. These are difficult times, Mr. Hardy. It appears our strategy has failed and we are now forced to sacrifice ourselves to try to save our people."

Mace bowed his head. "I thank you for the assistance you and your people have given, Commander. If you figure out a way for us to help, please ask."

Wormholes were opened and the Gorange fleet moved through. The Karthian cruiser that had delivered the previous solar flare, and its four escorts, were caught off guard and quickly dispatched. Half the Karthian fleet came in response, chasing the Gorange commander and his ships from the area. A third portal ship was moved in, and again a portion of a massive solar flare was redirected down into the atmosphere of Nellivue. The result was another massive steam cloud and a rapid rise in surface temperatures. Reports from the Gorange indicated a deep ocean temperature rise of nearly half a degree over the course of a few hours. The Karthians were determined to have their victory.

Two additional plasma clouds were redirected before Humphrey turned with a stunning revelation. "Mr. Hardy, I think the solar flare weapon may be losing its effectiveness."

"How so?"

"The initial blasts have thrown a tremendous amount of water vapor into the atmosphere. The latest plasma was directed into one of those steam clouds. It seems most of that heat is now being absorbed in the high atmosphere or reflecting back into space. I've run several calculations, and frankly, it appears the amount of plasma reaching the ocean surface has decreased by an order of magnitude. My projections say that amount of decrease will happen again shortly, rendering that strategy almost useless as a weapon.

"It would appear the planet, using the nature of physics, is protecting itself. Damage to their environment has been done, but that will reverse in time."

Mace opened a comm to the Gorange commander. "Mr. Krog, I'm sending you an analysis done by one of our crew. I believe your planet may no longer be in danger from that attack. Don't sacrifice yourselves. Your people are gonna live."

"We've run analyses of our own, Mr. Hardy. Given the current conditions, our cities will be running out of food in ninety Gorange days. Our aqua farms are all near the surface. The current crops are already showing signs of devastation from the high temperatures. Items in harvest may be the last of what we have to eat. Even the crews on our subsurface ships are suffering from the heat. We have methods of warming our ships. Cooling was done using ocean water. That surface water is now thirty degrees warmer."

"I understand, Commander. I just wanted to let you know what we're seeing, and that is that the current Karthian tactic is no longer effective. All I ask is that you don't sacrifice your people in vain. The Karthians can do no more harm to your people."

The commander was silent for several seconds. "I will take your suggestions under advisement, Mr. Hardy. Thank you for your concern and your efforts."

The bulk of the Gorange fleet charged in, destroying the Karthian portal ship before turning to flee. The assault came at a cost of twenty-two Gorange cruisers and their crews. Once away from the Karthian fleet, a jump was made back to Divinia. The Karthians soon abandoned the plasma bombardment of Nellivue, pulling back to re-evaluate their options.

In the days that followed, Jasper Collins decided to abandon another colony. The twelve million citizens of Rhogatar were loaded on transports to be brought back to Divinia. The ground-based microwave stations would be disassembled and moved to Divinia as well, along with their space-based counterparts. The list of Targarian colonies to defend had dropped to nine.

Mace stood on a catwalk with Johnny and Jasper as they looked down on the ongoing construction of Collins class ships.

"Who could've imagined we'd be standing out here like this today? Looking down on the construction of a starship with an alien planet filling the view... a slew of alien species running around, all seemingly wanting to kill each other or to dominate us. It's like we've been swept away into some epic Hollywood movie. Jasper Collins, of all people, is now the King of an entire species, ruling over a dozen colonies."

Jasper replied, "Nine colonies now. Probably less if we have time."

Mace nodded. "And, Mace Hardy, bartender turned marauding warship captain, giving it his all to save the Human race."

Jasper said, "And Johnny Tretcher, the ape-man, as big as ever."

Johnny laughed. "Hey now, I'm still down twenty pounds. But yeah, it's been an incredible ride. You know, the astronauts used to talk about what it was like to be in space looking down on Earth. Those who visited the International Space Station came back speaking of feelings of awe and transcendence. I get those feelings every time I look down on one of these planets. Always an incredible sight."

Jasper leaned on the rail. "I'll have to say, it has been an adventure. I used to think about how lucky I was to have inherited that cave. I spent my childhood and most of my adult life feeling that way. Now it somehow doesn't even feel real. All we had or did before seems of little consequence. That huge cave is like some incredibly minute piece of a monster Earth that is part of a massive galaxy."

Jenny Taub walked out on the catwalk to join them. "What are the men of Earth talking about today?"

Mace put his arm around her shoulder. "How different things are from what they were. Look down at that planet below... how's that make you feel?"

Jenny leaned on the rail. "Makes me feel small. Like I'm some tiny bug infesting this big beautiful galaxy."

Johnny replied, "Infesting is about right. Only there's a lot of other bugs who want to kill or control us."

Jenny nodded. "There is that."

The foursome watched from above as two large sections of a Collins were welded together. It was a moment of peace and reflection they had not experienced in weeks. It was a moment they doubted would last long.

Chapter 20

Jeff met with Mace in the dining hall of the research lab building. "Mr. Hardy, I feel we're this close to making progress."

"Nothing yet though, huh?"

Jeff frowned. "I'm afraid not. The wormhole must be stable before it's put in motion. Moving it forward a meter wide has proven difficult. It's like it develops its own inertia field that wants to hold it in place."

Mace leaned forward on the table. "Could you leave it as a micro-wormhole during the initial move and then expand it as it got close to the target?"

Jeff sat staring for several seconds before he stood. "Genius, Mr. Hardy. We can push a tiny wormhole around quickly, possibly even changing direction from its initial heading. The expansion is almost instantaneous. And a micro-wormhole moves at near the speed of light. This could possibly be our solution. I must get back to the others to talk this over."

Mace half waved as Jeff left the room. "Glad I could help, Doc."

Johnny walked in seconds later. "Doc eat something bad? Looked like he was scurrying for the bathroom."

Mace shook his head as he smirked. "No, he just has something new to try and was eager to get back to work. Listen, I wanted to ask you about what we do if we fail here. I mean, I know we fight as long as we have the *Rogers*, but what if we lose? What if the Karthians overrun this place? If we fall back to Earth, what's our plan? Stark will be in charge of everything but the *Rogers*."

Johnny walked over to a machine, which dispensed two nutrient bars. "Are you talking ground game?"

Mace nodded. "Possibly. If our fleets fail, and the Karthians wipe out our microwave stations, do they just wipe us out or do they enslave us?"

Johnny grabbed a beverage from a cooler. "Maybe we hide out in the cave?"

Mace thought for a moment. "It is shielded heavily. And we have gatrellium stored in there along with a fusion reactor. We could stuff the tunnels with nutrient bars and stay hidden in there for a year... except for the entrance being exposed."

Johnny sat. "So maybe we camouflage the entrance. A few big rocks and maybe a hidden door?"

Mace crossed his arms. "That's a possibility."

Johnny took a bite of a nutrient bar, before stopping mid chew. "Wait... how about we take one of these holo-projectors we have on our suits and just broadcast a false image? Could make it look like dirt and leaves or something. Just like the surroundings."

Mace nodded. "I think that's a brilliant idea. With a reactor sitting inside the cave and a holo-projector sitting right at the entrance, we could project a large enough image above and around it that you wouldn't even know the gift shop or drive were sitting out there. The whole property could be made to look forested and unused."

Johnny sat forward. "How big an image could we project?"

Mace shrugged. "We'll have to go ask. But I do like the idea of having a place to fall back to."

"We have the site at Alpha Centauri that no one knows about either. If we can't make the cave, we could take refuge there. It's big enough we could even park a shuttle in there in case the *Rogers* gets discovered."

"You, sir, are on fire today."

Johnny grinned. "I like being on fire. Usually I just fizzle."

Mace tapped his fingers on the table as he ran images through his mind.

Johnny took a swig of his beverage, wiping the corner of his mouth on the forearm of his battle suit. "When do we get started?"

Mace stood. "I think right now. Bring your food. I wanna have a quick talk with Jeff."

The talk was started and over in five minutes. The holo-projector used for the main wall display on the bridge of the *Rogers* would provide an image a kilometer in diameter if given sufficient power. Power, with the fusion reactors, was something they had. A quick trip was made to acquire the holo-projectors, along with a number of other items they felt would be needed.

A gravity wall and an environmental system would make the carved-out cave at Alpha Centauri livable. A half-dozen semi-truck-sized food containers would keep the crew and family of the *Rogers* fed for over a year. Volunteers were pulled together and they made a jump to the planet closest to Earth's solar system.

Mace took charge of the construction once inside the cave. "I want two generators up here and two more in the back. Add in circuit breakers so we can switch between them. I want two holo-projectors up here, one on each side of that cave mouth. We'll have each of them projecting the same image. If one goes down, we're still in business. The gravity wall can go here, and the environmental system over here."

Johnny said, "We have three of the ESs. We won't need more than one of them on Earth."

Mace nodded. "OK. A backup here would be a good thing as well. I'll make a note to bring another gravity wall generator, too. Might as well be as redundant as we can if we're gonna be trapped here. Once this stuff is in place, we can work on the interior. I'm thinking we put bathrooms here... sleeping quarters here... dining over there, and a big lounge area out here in the middle."

Johnny said, "You know what would be good? We should swipe a dozen of those virtual simulators from the Ronceverte center to put in here. If we could possibly be stuck here for a year, we're gonna want some entertainment. They would be good for keeping the kids occupied, as well as getting them educated."

"I'll add those to the list."

"A healthy armory would be worthwhile as well."

Mace entered the extra items into a recorder on his arm pad. Anything else?"

Johnny scratched the side of his face. "Hmm, what about a small lab for Jeff and his crew? You know we're gonna need to fix something if we're stuck here for that long."

Mace nodded. "Excellent. Again, you're on fire."

Johnny slapped Mace on the back. "Johnny Fire... that's what they call me."

The two men walked the cave at Alpha Centauri, building up a list of needed items. Once back at Divinia, Jasper assigned two thousand Targarian construction workers to assist with the build. A week after their initial survey, the last of the living quarter walls was mounted into place.

Johnny said, "I can't believe that went that fast."

Mace replied, "Incredible what can be done if you have the dedicated resources and materials. Now all we have to do is stock it."

Johnny half smiled. "And then we do it all over again on Earth."

Mace stroked his goatee. "Yep. And we already know what we need."

Johnny sat back on a stone slab that had been cut from a wall. "I can't believe the Karthians haven't attacked."

Mace winced. "They have to be waiting on reinforcements or something. Nellivue is still covered with a thick cloud of water vapor."

"Maybe they're waiting for that to settle."

"According to Jeff, that will take years. If they survive this they'll probably have to relocate while the planet recovers. He said the oceans there are expected to warm by as much as four degrees. The whole ecosystem will get trashed."

"You think they'll do that to Earth?"

Mace shook his head. "Don't know. If they win, and they decide they want to enslave us, there's nothing stopping them from destroying the whole place."

"I guess we just have to win then."

The week that followed saw a buildout of the insides of Organ Cave. The cold damp stone was replaced with elevated floors, walls, ceilings, and rooms with doors. All told, the cave would now comfortably house a hundred eighty Humans. Food stockpiles were moved into place and a holo-projector hooked up.

The projected image covered the cave, the gift shop, the science lab constructed for Jeff and his team, and the field where shuttles would normally land. A newly constructed shuttle was powered down and parked in the field. A second was moved into a cave at Alpha Centauri. Neither small ship would hold all who would possibly stay if the time came, but they did give options where there otherwise might be none.

A return trip was made to Divinia. Mace and Johnny joined Jasper in his palace, where they found him watching an old black and white movie.

"You know they do have those in color now," said Johnny.

Jasper waved his hand. "Shush, it's coming to the good part."

The two men sat, taking in the remainder along with their old friend. "Always liked a happy ending."

Johnny laughed. "Never took you for a sentimental guy."

"That's because you're an ape. So I take it your hideaways are complete?"

Mace nodded. "Both Alpha Centauri and the cave could now house all of us for more than a year if needed. Each has a shuttle parked there with a wormhole drive. I can't believe Jeff was able to pack all that gear in there and still leave room for passengers."

Jasper flipped off his holo-display. "That was my Targs. They're crazy good at engineering and design. Too bad our efforts aren't spent toward building a great society instead of war. I think we could make this place the envy of the galaxy. Instead, just about everything we have is put into the war effort. Starting next week we'll have a third production line going for the Collins ships."

Johnny asked, "What are our numbers now?"

"We have a hundred ninety-two Collins, two hundred forty cruisers. Combined with Stark's ships and the others, we're almost back to nine hundred."

Johnny nodded. "That's better than I thought."

Jasper shook his head. "Don't think it will matter. The Karthians just brought in another fleet of five hundred ships. They have fourteen hundred parked at Nellivue now. If the pattern holds, they'll have another five hundred show up in three days. That's when I expect them to make their move."

Mace made a trip to the science lab. "Doc, any progress?"

Jeff replied, "Significant... on paper. We're assembling a new prototype. Come, I'll show you."

Mace followed Jeff Moskowitz into the assembly lab. "We're hoping this will open a micro-wormhole and then move the beginning location forward while the destination remains where it was. As the wormhole reaches its target, we inject the gatrellium and dark matter, thereby widening the opening. If it works, we'll be able to target the Karthian ships directly, using our plasma cannons."

Mace asked, "How's that gonna work?"

Jeff gestured toward a far wall. "Imagine that wall is the ship in question. It would have a powerful dampening field surrounding it. The wormhole allows us to travel through that field into the ship itself. We can even go through the outer hull. If we expand the wormhole and follow it up with a shot from a plasma cannon... well, imagine what that cannon will do if it doesn't have the dampening field or armor to go through. A single shot might be enough to take out a ship."

Mace nodded. "When can we have it?"

Jeff frowned. "We don't have a working unit yet. We need to prove the concept with this miniaturized prototype before spending the effort to build something full size."

Mace tilted his head. "Miniaturized?"

Jeff walked to a table. "This is it. We have a micro-reactor here. This is a gatrellium store. And this a hydrogen store. When we put this to the test in a ship, a wormhole will be opened a kilometer from us. The destination will be a kilometer beyond so we can easily check for success."

Mace asked, "And your weapon?"

Jeff crossed his arms. "For this experiment, we'll be firing a low power plasma burst and testing the resultant impact. If it checks out, we should see the same result from a full strength cannon shot."

Mace looked over the device sitting on the table. "So this has a wormhole generator packed into it? Impressive. I could probably carry that thing on my back."

Jeff shook his head. "It's quite dense. Two hundred sixty kilograms. Our efforts were on miniaturization to fit on a ship—and for safety for this lab."

"You think any weight could be trimmed off?"

Jeff thought for a moment. "I suppose, but we're talking in the neighborhood of perhaps 5 percent. Still too heavy for a single person to carry if that's what you're after."

"Can it be miniaturized further?"

Jeff winced. "Doubtful. The generator components can't be manufactured any more compact and still perform. I suppose it may one day be possible, but today is not that day."

Mace nodded. "OK. When's this one ready for its test, I'd like to watch."

"Come back in an hour. I'll have it on a shuttle by then. Or if you prefer, I can pass video to you through a comm feed."

Mace held up a hand. "No, I'll be back. I'm heading over to Jasper's palace. Anything I need to ask him for?"

Jeff shook his head. "Thank you, I think we're set. I'll give you a comm when it's ready."

Several minutes later, Mace walked into the palace. Workers were busy putting the final touches on an opulent throne room. A solid gold high-backed throne chair, adorned with jewels and luxurious cloths, sat in the center of the room. On either side, a fountain of blue water flowed from the high ceiling, trickling down over a hundred small ledges before ending in a pool that circled in front of the throne.

The throne was raised, as was the pool, having a glass wall two meters high that allowed viewing of a variety of fish inside. A grand walk proceeded into the room and past the throne. The opposite side of the walk was shielded by a glass wall, behind which much of the more beautiful flora and interesting fauna of Divinia could be viewed. A spare jet-black King's battlesuit sat in the chair. An internal mechanized skeleton gave the otherwise empty battlesuit the occasional movement, leaving the Targarians who would see it not knowing whether it was the actual King or not.

Jasper walked up behind Mace. "I thought it a waste of time, but my people insisted. I give plenty of speeches over the comm. They thought this would give the people a better way to connect with their king."

Mace replied, "Take a look at history and you'll see how important symbology can be to the masses. Even something as simple as a flag can give people something to rally behind and be proud of. You make this *their* throne room and about *their* king and it could be a positive for you. And speaking of symbols, I think that's one thing missing from Earth. We need something that ties us all together. Don't show this to Stark though. Earth is not in need of a throne for Stark to sit upon."

Jasper sighed. "They plan on opening this to the public in a couple weeks. I just hope we have a couple weeks."

"Well, we're doing all we can toward our defense. Aside from that, the people need their daily lives to continue. I know if I were back on Earth, that would be the thing keeping me from going insane. We all need something normal that we know, understand, and can cling to. You know, fighting for your life is a good motivator, but fighting for a cause? That's a great motivator. Aside from their lives, you represent the cause the Targarians are fighting for."

Jasper nodded. "Makes sense."

Mace gestured toward the throne. "You do look imposing sitting up there. I suppose being a real-life giant to these people helps."

Mace followed Jasper into the palace, where snacks were had and further discussion made before Jeff opened a comm.

"We're ready, Mr. Hardy."

Mace nodded. "Thanks. I'll be over in a few minutes."

The comm closed as Mace turned to the King. "You coming? First test of an updated wormhole device."

"Absolutely."

Jasper looked around at one of his four aides who were always at the ready. "Mr. Gooti, you can take over here. I'd rather not be bothered with any further decisions on the throne. Make your best judgment and we'll go with that."

Muumur Gooti bowed before leaving to take on his new duties. Jasper followed Mace to a shuttle that took the men to the science lab. Jeff herded them into a second shuttle that was flown to the location where the wormhole was expected to open wide. When the second shuttle stopped, the three men stood in front of a wall display.

Jeff spoke into his comm. Seconds later, a meter-wide wormhole opened, showing on the display.

Jeff handed Mace a controller. "Do us the honors?"

Mace accepted. The small cannon on the shuttle was powered up, and Mace took aim. A plasma bolt struck a target that appeared through the wormhole. The space-time portal collapsed seconds later as Jeff sent the shutdown signal from his arm pad.

"Give me a second to pull up the results... and we have a success. I believe we'll have a working weapon the Karthians can't defend against when we build the full size unit."

Jasper nodded. "Then let's get you back and get that built. When will it be available?"

Mace replied, "He believes it's gonna take most of a week."

Jasper winced. "Tell me what you need to make it happen sooner."

Jeff shrugged. "Time is what we need. I don't suppose you have any of that lying around, do you? The manufacturing can be accomplished in about three days. The remainder is all tuning, which is a manual trial-and-error process."

Jasper replied, "Just keep at it, Doc. We're gonna need everything we can throw at them when the time comes."

Mace returned to the palace with Jasper.

Chapter 21

A comm came in from Jasper's scout ships. "Sire, another block of ships is coming through the rift. Seven hundred twenty this time."

Jasper nodded. "Thank you, Commander. Let me know when they arrive at Nellivue."

The commander bowed as the comm closed.

Jasper scowled. "Looks like our three day buffer just ran out. Last bunch of ships fell into formation at Nellivue in about an hour. I expect these will do the same. After that, nothing is stopping them from coming here."

A second comm opened to Jasper. "Your Highness, we have wormholes opening near the Dethika colony. It is Karthians, Sire. Coming from the rift."

Jasper frowned. "Thank you, Admiral Baakun. Take up the positions as we discussed previously. We'll be sending ships your way momentarily."

Jasper turned to Mace. "I presume you'll want to be getting back to the *Rogers*."

"We'll be taking our civilians back to the cave on Earth. On the jump back we'll go straight to Dethika."

Jasper placed his hand on Mace's shoulder. "Mace, I'd just like to say that it's been an honor to know and fight alongside you."

Mace huffed, "Yeah, well, this fight isn't over yet. So save those thanks for when we kick their asses."

Jasper grinned. "Consider it done."

Mace hopped a shuttle back to the compound at Yentis. The *Rogers* hovered above a broad field, her rampway lowered to the ground. The compound buildings were emptying with the Human civilians associated with the *Rogers* crew streaming up the ramp.

Mace opened a comm to the bridge as he walked toward her. "Mr. Crawford, how are we looking?"

Jordan replied, "Five minutes, Mr. Hardy. I suggest you start jogging if you'd like to speed this up. At the moment you'll be the last aboard."

"Have Mr. Hobbs prep for a jump to Earth. We'll be dropping all non-essentials at the cave. Their job will be to make it fully operational. The rest of us will be coming back to fight."

"We're all set, Mr. Hardy. Just waiting for you."

Mace picked up the pace, using the built-in exosuit structure to sprint the distance from the shuttle pad to where the *Rogers* was waiting. As he ran up the ramp, the access lifted and closed, and the *Rogers* shot upward through the atmosphere. Seconds later, a micro-wormhole opened and the *Rogers* slipped through.

Stark came over the comm. "I take it this is our cue to move forward?"

Mace nodded. "It is. Jasper didn't notify you?"

Stark's silhouette shook his head. "I'm afraid Mr. Collins has no desire to converse with me, even when it's his worlds that are being attacked."

"He's stubborn that way. Anyway, the Karthians are jumping to his Dethika colony. After our drop here, we'll be going back."

Stark said, "Your people are welcome to stay in any of the community centers. They each have plenty of empty rooms, including Ronceverte."

Mace shook his head. "We're covered, thanks. And if you didn't know, the Karthians sent in seven hundred twenty new ships just a few minutes ago. That puts them at over two thousand in their fleet. We don't hold them at Divinia, they're coming here."

"Yes, unfortunately I believe my prior efforts have seen to that eventuality."

The *Rogers* settled in the field near the cave.

Mace said, "It's a shame we didn't have another week. We have a new weapon in the works that might even things up."

"Yes, the wormhole weapon. I understand the initial tests went well."

Mace frowned. "You still have spies on Divinia? I guess I can't fault you for it. Yes, the wormhole weapon. Can't say it will do us much good if we can't build it."

"You could always move production here."

Mace sighed. "I wish I could. Mr. Collins wouldn't approve. Regardless, we don't have it and it doesn't look like we'll have it in time to save Divinia. Listen, I have work to do here. I expect to see your ships out at Dethika when we get there."

Stark stood. "We will be there momentarily."

The comm closed.

Johnny said, "I think he's right. We should move Jeff and his lab here. It's possible they could have that finished before the Karthians made it here."

Mace nodded. "I agree. But I don't want to give Stark a reason to want to see Jasper and the Targarians wiped out. If the production of that weapon was moved here, he would have incentive to only fight long enough for it to be built and put into play. After that, he would bail on the Targarians."

"Yeah, but we would have the weapon then."

Mace turned to face Johnny. "And Stark would have it too. He runs this planet. Anything located here is his to take."

Johnny half frowned. "While that's true, if he really wants it, what's to stop him from holding our people hostage until we turn it over?"

Mace shook his head. "We wouldn't turn it over. Doing so would doom everyone else to his domination."

"I'm starting to think we should have taken everyone to the Alpha site instead."

"I don't think he'll bother us unless he's sure he can get his hands on that weapon. If we manage to defeat the Karthians, we'll be the power to be dealt with. The *Rogers* would crush anything he could put in the sky."

Jordan Crawford cut in. "Sorry, Mr. Hardy, but we're ready to go. Everyone is off who's getting off."

Mace nodded. "Mr. Hobbs, set in the jump for Dethika and make it happen."

Jane and Jenny walked onto the bridge.

Jane said, "Let's kick some Karthian ass. Jenny and I want to man a boarding shuttle."

Johnny replied, "You do know you won't be going anywhere without me tagging along, right?"

Jane smiled. "I wouldn't dream of it."

Mace asked, "You have someone covering your stations?"

Jenny nodded. "We do. Even though they aren't really needed. Those stations run themselves."

Mace shook his head. "Not entirely true. We've lost drives and reactors, and each time we needed the expertise of this crew to recover and keep going."

"Our trainees are competent," said Jane. "They know their stations. Besides, if our being out on a shuttle helps take out a single Karthian ship, it's worth the risk."

Johnny looked at Mace. "I'd say their minds are already made up on this one."

"I just wish I had a valid reason to say no. Anyone else have a reason they'd like to throw out?"

Liam Hobbs said, "Their odds in that new shuttle aren't any worse than ours here. It has the same shielding and same speed. They may not have weapons to fire, but if they can get aboard, they can do as much damage, if not more."

Mace looked at the two women. "Take a pack with some food. And make sure your power-cells are all full."

A comm opened from Jeff. "Keep us in the loop here, Mr. Hardy. Camera feeds and data would be appreciated. We might be able to help with targeting, or at a minimum give an analysis of what we see."

Mace nodded. "I'll ask Jasper to send you the same. Just don't let the fight distract from your work. We need that weapon."

Humphrey said, "I count seven hundred ten Karthian ships, Mr. Hardy. Feeds from the scouts say the bulk of their fleet is still at Nellivue. And the missing ten ships just joined them there."

Hans Mueller frowned. "I can't say I like the sound of that. Ten ships... they must be something unique. Do we have any data on them?"

Humphrey replied, "One moment... cargo transports. Could just be a resupply mission."

Jasper pushed a video feed to the comm display. "Those new ships are moving toward the planet. Trajectories say they are going into high orbit. Hang on. They're releasing something."

Mace stood. "A bio-weapon?"

Jasper shook his head. "Nope. Data says nukes, hundreds of them. If they make it to the surface and detonate, that will be it for the Gorange."

Jasper's comm froze. Several seconds later it returned to having motion. "I just talked with the Gorange commander. He said regardless of what they dropped, his ships will remain here for the fight."

Humphrey said, "Scout data feeds are showing detonations, Mr. Hardy. Multiple detonations. At least two hundred megatons per. Some below the ocean's surface."

Mace reached his fingers inside his helmet and rubbed his temples. "Thank you, Mr. Mallot. I think we return our focus to what's directly in front of us now."

Humphrey added, "Ships are moving. Multiple wormholes opening. Destination is the Tarnuks colony."

"As I feared," said Jasper. "They're splitting us up."

Mace looked over the battle data. "Where's Stark?"

A comm was opened. Stark's silhouette sat in his usual darkened chair.

Mace said, "Why are you still at Earth?"

Stark replied, "A decision was made to make our stand here. I have no doubt the Karthians will defeat Mr. Collins. Rather than asking our people to sacrifice themselves in some other system, they'll be fighting at home instead. I can only conclude it will add to their ferocity in battle."

Mace shook his head. "The whole reason for fighting out here was so we didn't have to fight at Earth. You did just see what they did to Nellivue, right? All it takes is a couple of those bombs to get through your screens and the results would be devastating. I beg you to commit those ships to the fight out here."

Stark sat silent for several seconds before closing the comm.

Johnny huffed. "Guess we know where that coward stands. He's all fight when the odds are greatly in his favor."

The ships of the Dunden Heap opened a wormhole to Earth and began passing through.

Mace opened a comm. "Admiral, what are you doing?"

The Dunden admiral replied, "We pledged our loyalty to King Stark. We will make our fight at Earth alongside him. We owe nothing to the Targarians."

The comm closed. Mace looked around the bridge at the others as he lowered his faceshield.

Johnny nodded. "I'd say that means strap yourselves in. Mr. Crawford, if you'd kindly take over the comms, I'll be heading to the shuttle."

Jordan replied, "I'll be out there with you, Mr. Tretcher, in the second shuttle with two of my men."

Humphrey said, "I can handle the comm station. Transferring controls... and locked in. You are free to go, Mr. Tretcher."

Johnny stopped at the command chair, placing a hand on the shoulder of Mace's battlesuit. "We've come through every time before. This won't be any different."

Mace patted his gloved hand. "Watch out for our ladies out there. I'd like to see the three of you come back alive. I *need* the three of you to come back alive."

Johnny smiled. "Haven't let any of these pukey little aliens kick my ass yet. Not gonna let 'em start now."

Johnny looked over at Fatso Geerok. "No offense intended, Mr. Geerok."

Fatso half bowed. "None taken. I know where your words were directed. And I agree with them."

Johnny chuckled. "You know, for someone I initially despised, you turned out to be OK."

"I'm still learning the ways of the Humans. And I now think more highly of myself as well."

Johnny left the bridge. The Karthian ships moved from a defensive to an offensive formation. Wormholes opened and Jasper Collins' ships streamed through, along with more than a hundred space-based microwave stations.

Mace asked, "Those from Divinia?"

Jasper slowly shook his head. "Tarnuks."

Mace winced. "You abandoning it?"

Jasper slowly nodded. "Sixty-seven million Targarians. I can't protect them. I now wish I had made the effort to move as many as I could. And I've ordered evacs of the Fuham, Chathria and Wallamongus colonies. It was foolish to think I could save them."

Mace sighed. "We can only do what's possible, Mr. Collins. We'll do our best to stop them here."

Humphrey said, "More wormholes opening here. The main Karthian fleet is dividing. I count six hundred ships at Tarnuks. The rest are here. That gives them roughly fifteen hundred ships to our four-fifty."

Jasper said, "We'll have another three hundred sixty microwave stations in a few minutes."

The space surrounding the Dethika colony was filled with stations and ships. A massive fleet, backed by an immense space station, sat in opposition. The minutes before the assault began seemed like hours.

All at once, the Karthian fleet moved forward at a slow pace.

Jasper commanded, "As they come closer, fall back. We need to draw those ships within range of the ground-based stations. I want as much firepower bearing down on them as we can muster."

Johnny came over the comm. "We're all set."

Jordan Crawford added, "Set here as well. We'll move out when the shooting starts."

Mace nodded. "We'll try to offer cover where we can."

As the first of the ground-based microwave cannons chose their targets, the other ships engaged. The heavens above Dethika were soon filled with plasma and laser strikes. The bright flashes from each quickly dissipated as the inertial dampening fields absorbed the energy.

The *Rogers* followed her two shuttles as they moved in on approaching Karthian cruisers. The hull of the *Rogers* rumbled as the first laser strikes were absorbed.

Johnny passed his video feeds through a comm channel. Humphrey pushed them to the main display wall.

Johnny's image shook as the approaching cruisers trained their fire on the small ship. "Wow, this bucket could use some new shocks."

Mace asked, "What's your shield percentage?"

"It's only hitting forty... whoa, I take that back: 73 percent on that one."

Mace fired off his wormhole weapon. "That was a double strike. We're moving between you and one of those cruisers."

Jordan said, "We're taking the other one."

Mace replied, "Backup coming your way. Mr. Mueller, hit that cruiser with everything you have. I'm punching a hole in her aft section. Mr. Crawford, clamp on near the front!"

Johnny said, "We've got a grip. Jane and Jenny are moving over. As soon as they're in I'll follow."

The *Rogers* circled, firing on a third cruiser that had come into her space.

Jane yelled out, "We're in! Room is clear!"

Johnny replied, "On my way!"

Jordan Crawford followed: "We have access. Shuttle is empty. Moving into main hallway. Fire is heavy!"

Mace took a deep breath. "Take your time! We've got a handle on the ships from outside!"

Johnny said, "Resistance is light. Hold on... whoa Nellie! A dozen lasers just hit the wall behind us! Jane! Get them off me! We're blocked up!"

Plasma explosions boomed over the comm, followed by the rapid fire of an AR-15. Screams could be heard as two assault parties charged forward on their respective ships. At almost the same moment, the blockades on both were cleared.

Johnny ran forward on a rampage: "Arrgghh! I'm coming for you fish-faced mutants! Get ready to eat my plasma!"

Jane yelled, "Stop, you idiot! This hall's not clear!"

Johnny raced forward as Jane and Jenny dropped to the floor. Twenty seconds later he sprinted back, laser pulses pounding the walls and floor around him as he dove over the top of the girls and tumbled to a stop.

Jane and Jenny opened up with a barrage of precision shots on the half-dozen Karthians who rounded the far corner in front of them. The defenders down the side hall pulled back.

Jane stood. "Let's move! They're repositioning! Johnny, get your ape-butt off that floor!"

The three turned down the hall to the right, blasting each doorway as they approached. At the end of the hall, Jenny poked her head around for a view of the opposition. She pulled back just as the first laser pulse sizzled past, melting a six centimeter hole in the wall across from them.

"They've got some kind of bigger cannon sitting out in the middle of the hall. It has plating around the front and I'm guessing it might have a dampener field running. The front of that plate has four protrusions that look a lot like our field transducers."

Johnny took several steps back to a door, pumping a plasma round into it and nearly sending Jane into a fit.

"Tell us what you're doing next time, idiot!"

Johnny chuckled. "Sorry, just trying to find an alternate route."

Jenny again stuck out her head, this time Jane pulling her back hard as the laser cannon melted another hole in the hallway wall. "Let's not do that a third time, shall we."

Jenny nodded. "I can live with that."

Johnny poked his head out of the doorway he had just opened. "This way. Follow me."

Mace's eyes were in constant motion as he attempted to follow the two shuttle crews and at the same time fire on the fourth cruiser that had joined in the fight.

Fatso Geerok moved to Johnny's console. "Mr. Mallot, pass me the control of the comms. Your expertise is needed on those sensors."

Mace nodded as control was transferred. "Thank you, Mr. Geerok. Mr. Hobbs, keep us circling that first cruiser!"

"That I can do, sir!"

Johnny sent three heavy plasma pulses into the back wall of the room he had entered. A plasma cutter was then used to quickly cut through the metal wall.

A hard kick with his boot sent a mostly cutout plate buckling to the side. Johnny stepped through to the room on the other side. The feat was repeated on a new wall as Jenny watched the door behind them. A third wall turned out to be a bulkhead.

Johnny turned with a scowl. "How far down that hall was that cannon?"

Jenny said, "Twenty meters?"

Johnny cringed. "We've only moved fifteen."

Jane said, "You hit that wall with a few plasma bolts and start cutting. I'll keep them occupied. At a steep enough angle, I can have bullets bouncing off the walls. If you make your cut you'll at least have an angle on them."

Jenny nodded. "Yeah, I don't think that cannon had much of a swivel on it. It looked to be more of a ground-based weapon than something you'd use on a ship."

Jane said, "Jenny, you cover my back."

Chatter from the AR-15 could be heard between plasma rounds impacting the side wall. Jane would poke the barrel around the corner at the bottom of the wall, fire off a half dozen rounds, pull it back and then move it up high for the same. Following her motions, laser pulses impacted the wall behind her.

Jenny turned to the door on the back wall of the hall. Using Johnny's technique, she blasted and then cut a hole through to the room the laser cannon was impacting.

Jenny opened a comm. "Jane, pull back for a second. Johnny, tell me when you're ready to kick through."

Jane paused as Johnny replied, "I'm ready..."

Jenny said, "When you hear me firing, wait two seconds and kick down that wall!"

The chatter of an AR-15 could again be heard, followed by the loud metal clang of a wall plate coming free. The hallway twenty meters up erupted in laser and blaster fire as Johnny made his presence known.

"Cannon is clear!"

Jane raced around the corner, kneeling and firing three precision shots into Karthian soldiers who were occupied with Johnny. Jenny followed after, sprinting all the way up to the weapon. Hiding behind the shield plate of the cannon, Jenny cut down the four remaining, overwhelmed Karthian soldiers.

Mace let out a deep sigh as he turned to the other video feed.

Chapter 22

Jordan Crawford's crew moved methodically along. Fire then cover, move forward, fire then cover. The constant moves kept the Karthian crew forever regrouping. Fifteen minutes after the engagement began, they reached the reactor room that powered the ship. One by one the four immense Karthian reactors were powered down. The plasma store quickly ran dry and the ship's cannons went silent. A precise shot by Hans Mueller blew the nose of the vessel off. The *Rogers* efforts were quickly turned to a newly arriving ship.

Johnny, Jane, and Jenny continued their movement through the narrow Karthian halls toward the bridge.

Mace asked, "What kind of numbers are we seeing from the larger battle?"

Humphrey replied, "Fifteen ships lost to their forty-eight. But we've also lost eighteen of the microwave stations. Those seem to be a prime target."

Mace shook his head. "We won't survive those numbers."

Johnny yelled over the comm. "Bridge at the end of this next hall!"

Jenny said, "We just passed a bulkhead. What say we cut through walls to there?"

Jane nodded. "Start cutting! Johnny and I will keep them occupied!"

Five room walls took Jenny minutes to blast and cut through. As the last wall cut was complete, Jenny stepped back through the previous cut and used two plasma rounds to blow the wall plate cutout from the center of the wall. The room was quickly filled with laser pulses as the crew and soldiers on the other side defended the bridge.

Johnny took the opportunity to charge. As he reached the end of the hall he dove, sliding on his belly as he sprayed the room with plasma. Jenny followed by kneeling at the hallway corner, handing out her brand of justice for the invaders' prior genocides. In the chaos that ensued, Jane moved forward, delivering justice of her own. Seventeen seconds later, the bridge of the Karthian cruiser was silent.

Johnny said, "We have a cruiser. What should we do with her?"

Mace replied, "We just need it permanently disabled. Crawford and his crew took a different approach. They attacked the reactor room and shut down their systems."

Johnny nodded. "Hmm. We passed that room a while back. Would have been easier than taking this bridge. Good to know for next time."

Jane said, "Move over and cover the door. I'll take this thing offline. Or at least make it dysfunctional. We can hit those reactors on our way back."

Mace replied, "If you do, shut them down first. You don't want one going supercritical and melting down on you before you get out."

Jane nodded. "Got it."

The *Rogers* continued to circle as Jane and Jenny destroyed the bridge stations with countless plasma rounds. A rush back through the hallways was met with disjointed and chaotic attempts to stop their assault.

Once offline, the reactors took repeated plasma strikes before they were inoperative. With a jump across to the shuttle, the grappling clamps were released and the shuttle was on the way toward a new target. The *Rogers'* cannons soon had the two assaulted cruisers exploding and breaking apart.

The shuttle assaults continued with six Karthian cruisers being taken out of the fight over a three hour period. Elsewhere, Jasper's crews in the Collins ships had battled to a two to one kill advantage, while the Karthian focus remained on destroying the microwave stations. The cost in ships was high, but the odds of a victory continued to move in the Karthians' favor.

Fatso Geerok turned to Mace. "Mr. Hardy, I know you didn't ask, but I took the liberty to contact the Mawga. I've managed a conversation directly with the emperor. Would you be willing to offer assistance later should the Mawga want out of the agreement with the United Front?"

Mace fired off a wormhole, just missing an approaching cruiser. "Would I be willing to what?"

Geerok replied, "The emperor will send his fleet in support of our efforts here if you would be willing to assist with the negation of their recently-signed treaty with the UF. They are beginning to see the signs of what it means to be a second class citizen in that empire. He fears they are about to dismantle his armed forces anyway. All he asks is your commitment. He seems desperate."

Mace nodded. "If he's willing to send us help now, I'm willing to do all I can for the Mawga later. I can't promise anything more than my support."

Geerok spoke into the open comm channel, turning back toward Mace when the conversation was complete. "The emperor is sending his entire fleet. He commands two hundred eighty-four cruisers, a Muhatha, and four Dauntless. The Dauntless ships he received in a trade with the Dellus before their demise."

Mace asked, "When can he send them?"

"They are on their way now."

A wormhole opened several minutes away from the battle scene. The Mawga fleet slipped through and formed up for an attack.

Mace opened a comm to the fleet admiral. "This is Mace Hardy. Use your ships to attack the left flank. Those ships are picking off our microwave stations. It's critical that we keep those alive."

The Mawga commander replied, "I've been asked to follow your lead, Mr. Hardy. I'm passing those orders along to our captains. And I will say I've misjudged you Humans from the beginning. When this is over, perhaps our peoples can become true allies."

"Allies are good, Admiral. We, too, need all we can get."

The Mawga cruisers were less than stellar performers when it came to the wide open battlefield, but what they lacked in strategy and tactics they made up for with determination. This was now their war. They were fighting for their emperor and would not be denied victory.

Shortly after the arrival of the Mawga forces, the tide of war began to turn against the Karthians. Their assaults on the microwave stations had claimed more than two hundred forty ships at the expense to the Targarians of one hundred thirty-four stations. For the first time in the fight, the allied fleet showed optimism.

Johnny came over the comm. "You can scratch cruiser number four. And hey, we almost took a critical hit while floating back to the shuttle. See if you can keep those ships off us during that time. I'd rather not get vaporized if possible."

"Noted. Mr. Mueller, pay special attention to those shuttles when their crews are in transition. That's when they are most vulnerable."

Hans nodded as he fired off a burst, ripping apart the cruiser Johnny had just come from. "Will do."

In the next hour that followed, with Mawga help, the Karthian war effort was in peril. Word then came of the annihilation of the Tarnuks colony. The six hundred ships that had sowed the seeds of destruction were now opening wormholes for transit elsewhere.

Humphrey Mallot said, "We have incoming! The fleet from Tarnuks is joining the fight here! They're targeting the Mawga ships!"

Twenty minutes passed before the evidence became clear. The Mawga ships were no match for the Karthians. Fifteen microwave stations had gone offline in the final five minutes of that short span.

Mace growled. "Crap, so much for any advantage. Mr. Collins? Any way to bring forward more of those stations?"

Jasper scowled. "Don't see that we have a choice now. I'll pull them all except those guarding Divinia and Croawla. I'll divert all refugees to those two planets. That'll give us another six hundred stations here."

Mace nodded. "We're gonna need them."

As the new stations moved into the fight, their microwave cannons began to have an impact. The sudden advantage was just as quickly taken away as another five hundred Karthian ships came through the rift and immediately hurried into the fight. The newest microwave stations were caught in the open without any support. Seventy of the Karthian cruisers that attacked were destroyed, but not before the ranks of the stations had been ravaged. The remaining Karthian ships joined in the ongoing fight.

In the span of the hour that followed, the two hundred ninety ship Mawga force had been reduced to forty-three ships. The orbital microwave stations only numbered in the tens.

The Karthians then enacted a new strategy. Transports loaded with soldiers, which had remained in reserve at the back of the Karthian fleet, flanked the battlefield and assaulted the planet directly.

The microwave stations on the ground focused their effort on the invaders, but those efforts were futile. The bulk of the ground-based stations went offline in less than an hour. It was soon apparent that Dethika had fallen.

Jasper came over the comm. "I'm pulling all forces back to Croawla. I advise you do the same."

Mace sighed as he gave the order. "Johnny, leave that ship as it is. We're pulling out. Mr. Crawford, bring the shuttle in. We're done here."

A comm was opened to the Mawga admiral. "Sir, we're falling back to Croawla. I suggest you evac your ships as soon as possible. I'm sending over the coordinates."

The admiral replied, "Horrifying beating we've taken today. I hope you're able to justify this cost with your help for my people."

Mace frowned. "If I remain alive when this is done, rest assured I'll do my best."

The allied ships began to jump from the space surrounding Dethika. The shuttles docked and the *Rogers* quickly followed. As the ships reformed among the microwave stations at Croawla, a count was displayed on the main wall.

Humphrey said, "The Gorange are down to sixty-five ships. The Mawga thirty-eight. The Targarian fleet has one hundred twelve Collins and seventy-six cruisers. That puts us at two hundred ninety-one ships remaining, Mr. Hardy. Croawla has one hundred forty-two orbital stations and eighty-six ground stations."

Mace frowned. "What was your last count for the Karthians?"

"In the neighborhood of fifteen hundred. And that massive station which hasn't been involved in the fight."

A comm opened from the Mawga admiral. "Mr. Hardy, given our losses, the emperor has ordered us home. Our ships will be dismantled and our armed forces civilianized. The emperor is releasing you from your commitment."

Mace nodded. "I can only thank you for your sacrifices here today, Admiral. Tell the emperor I will honor my pledge. I can only hope I'll live to repay my debt."

The Mawga Muhatha opened a wormhole to Rhombia before following the thirty-seven other remaining ships out of Targarian space. Mace looked down at the deck as the wormhole closed behind them.

Johnny walked onto the bridge. "I just saw the totals. We're getting our asses kicked."

Mace shook his head. "We're too outnumbered to be effective. Had Stark committed his ships we might have been able to hold them off with a few hundred of those shuttle assaults. Good job, by the way. You, Jane and Jenny, and Crawford's team took down ten cruisers between you."

Johnny nodded. "I'm sure we have a couple dozen more in us if that's what we're called to do."

Mace asked, "Mr. Collins, what kind of results did you see from your shuttle teams?"

Jasper scowled. "Of the two hundred thirty-six teams we started with, only seventy-seven remain. They took out a couple hundred Karthian ships. But those fights were too long and drawn out. Our remaining crews are pretty shot up as well. Our Collins ships did better. We lost seventy-eight and managed a hundred ninety kills. How'd you fare?"

Mace pushed the data across the comm. "We took down sixteen total. Somehow we managed to only lose two transducers. We're replacing those now. I can't help but think Stark's crews would have had similar numbers. At least their shuttle crews that is."

Jasper returned and angry look. "I just hope I live long enough to punch that coward in the face. He's just itching to see my people dead. The man has no redeeming qualities whatsoever."

Mace propped his elbow on his armrest and his chin on his fist. "He does seem to come and go. Just when you think he's on your side, he flips to the opposition. I can't say I trust him, but if Earth's gonna survive this, we're gonna need him."

Jasper threw up his hands. "No... we don't. It's the people who are fighting. Stark hasn't lifted a finger. And if you think about it, almost every strategy he's masterminded has been a flop. The man is rotten, and will never be anything but rotten."

"I can't really argue with you, but at this point I still think we need him. If anything, he's a unifier."

Jane came onto the bridge limping.

Mace asked, "What happened?"

Jane shook her head and laughed. "The ape ran me over."

Johnny said, "I told you I was coming. Can't help it if you can't get out of the way."

Jane sighed. "I was in a kneeling stance firing when he came ramming around a corner. Knocked me back into some protruding box that grabbed my ankle. Thought the suit was gonna snap off my leg. Anyway, it's just a sprain. Jenny put a wrap on it for me."

"Maybe on this next run we swap places," said Mace.

Jane held up a hand. "Noooo, you need to be sitting in that chair doing exactly what you were just doing. We can handle the assaults. You keep at keeping our shuttle safe."

Jordan Crawford said, "I have a few team members I can swap out."

Jane turned with a scowl. "You mind your own team. We're in good shape and don't need any help."

Mace opened a comm to Malcolm Stark. "We could use your help, you know. Had your teams been there, we'd have still been fighting."

Stark replied, "I did the best I felt I could. Did the Mawga fleet not help?"

"That was your doing?"

Stark's silhouette nodded. "The emperor is frantic to end the protection agreement he so gleefully signed. He now sees his mistake and is trying desperately to wiggle out of it. I had hoped the assistance of his fleet would be enough. Unfortunately, it was not. His withdrawal tells me he is capitulating. I very much doubt his head will still be attached this time next year."

"You never had any intention of offering them your help, did you?"

Stark sat silent for several seconds. "I couldn't foresee a scenario where that help would be available to give, Mr. Hardy. If you lose at Divinia, the Karthians will attack here. If they attack here, and if perchance we somehow manage to survive, I can hardly imagine we would be in the position to offer any assistance to the Mawga. As much as the emperor might demand it from us due to our agreement, we would have no way to fulfill it, and he would have no way to enforce it. Just be happy he was foolish enough to commit the ships when he did."

Mace frowned. "You just have no problem with stabbing people in the back, do you?"

Stark let out a long sigh. "I play to win, Mr. Hardy. The weak will perish and the weaker will be used as tools towards the end-goal I seek. Humans are the only species I care about. We will one day dominate this galaxy. I just have to keep us alive long enough to do so."

Mace rolled his eyes. "Still hooked on the domination schemes. I should have known. One day you'll get your due, Stark, and I hope I'm there to see it."

"I look forward to that day." Stark bowed as the comm closed.

Chapter 23

The damaged Targarian ships were lined up at the repair docks when the Karthians continued their push. The colonies that had been partially abandoned were the first to see action.

The ground-based microwave cannons were quickly overwhelmed. Whole city populations were scorched as the Karthian cruisers paraded along, raining down fire from above. Jasper sat in misery on the bridge of the *Organ Cave*.

Mace opened a comm. "You've done all you can."

Jasper replied, "Have I?"

Mace asked, "What more could you possibly do? The Karthians outnumber us."

"I have to wonder if I committed my shuttles too early. Or should I have moved all the microwave cannons up to Dethika when I had the chance?"

"You can't turn the clock back. Focus your energies on winning this thing. You can cry to yourself later."

Jasper looked at the comm camera. "Hmm, that sounds more like something I would say. You're right. Instead of sulking I should be leading."

Jasper stood from his chair. "Staff! Over here, right now!"

The comm closed.

Johnny raised his eyebrows. "Wow, lit a fire under him."

Mace replied, "Basically the same thing you guys have done for me over and over. You can't change what's already happened, but you can affect the future. Mr. Hobbs, take us to Promexa. I'd like to have a word with Favia."

The *Rogers* was met by two warships as it came through a wormhole. This time, instead of the normal cautious greeting and ship inspection, the Human ship was escorted into orbit around the planet. A Hoorka shuttle landed in the docking bay, and a diplomat emerged and gestured toward the shuttle.

"The queen has requested your presence, Mr. Hardy. And that of Jane Tretcher, if she is aboard."

Jane stepped forward. "Right here."

Mace asked. "Is everything OK? We came to see Favia."

The diplomat bowed and again gestured toward the shuttle. "Please, sir, the queen has personally requested your presence."

Mace waited for Jane and followed her up the ramp. "Wonder what this is about?"

"And why would the Hoorka queen ask for me?" asked Jane.

The ride down to the planet was swift. The shuttle landed on a deck with a long walkway that led directly into the palace. A hovercart, settling on the deck, met the guests as they came down the ramp.

The attendant bowed. "Please watch your step and hold a rail."

The flat craft, not much bigger than a golf cart, lifted and sped toward the palace. As it reached the cover of a massive portico, it again settled on the deck. The attendant bowed as he gestured for the guests to step down. A second attendant escorted them into the palace.

Green marble, lined with thin gold stripes, adorned the walls. A transparent floor covered a rushing stream as they walked from immense room to immense room. The attendant stopped and bowed, gesturing toward a set of large wooden doors, one of which was open. Rising steps on a far wall led to a central throne, where the queen was seated and waiting for them.

Mace walked in first, followed by Jane.

"I like the throne Jasper made for his people, but it's underwhelming as compared to this."

Jane commented: "I wish the diplomat had said something. What's the etiquette for meeting the queen? I could have at least dressed better than this battlesuit. I still have Karthian blood splatter on it."

They walked up the steps toward the queen, who was facing the other way. Two guards stepped forward, stopping the guests before they reached her. The queen stood. Jane's eyes grew wide as a flowing gold lamé gown, dotted with emeralds, splashed from the queen's lap onto the floor. The Hoorka queen stood in all her glory, a heavy green makeup covering her face.

Jane curtsied.

Mace half bowed. "Your Highness… you asked for us?"

The queen said with a grin, "How quickly you have forgotten me."

Jane looked up immediately. "Favia? But how?"

Favia gestured toward the steps. "Please have a seat. I'll explain."

Mace took his place. "I've never been much of a fashion guy, but you are stunning."

Favia smiled as she sat on the step just above them.

Jane said, "Should you be on the floor in that?"

Favia laughed. "They clean these steps at least three times a day. I get dirtier just standing up. How have you been? I'm excited to see you both!"

Jane asked, "They made you queen? How'd that happen?"

"My wealth and generosity brought about the end of the war. The King himself abdicated so that I might rule. It's all happened so fast. I'm still coming to grips with it. The feeling of responsibility is immense."

Mace nodded. "I could see that."

Jane laughed. "I hope you aren't referring to yourself with that comment."

"I was. Just as it applies to you and everyone else on the *Rogers*. We all fight for Earth. The responsibility is immense."

Jane held up her hand. "OK, sorry. Just sounded like something Johnny would say."

Mace looked back at Favia as he took a deep breath. "I'm sorry if I seem abrupt, but we're in the middle of a war we need to get back to. A species called the Karthians have invaded our space. As we speak, they are wiping out the Targarians. They've already annihilated over a dozen other species, and will be heading toward Earth soon. I don't know that we can stop them. We're here to ask for your help."

Favia sat silent for several seconds. "What could I possibly do?"

"We need ships, or weapons, or anything that could turn the tide of this war. We're getting slaughtered because we're outnumbered three or four to one. Is there any help you could possibly provide along those lines?"

Favia slowly shook her head. "I've only just acquired the crown. We've just come out of a long war. The people will not want to get involved in another one, especially one that is of no danger to us. I'm sorry, Mr. Hardy, I don't think I can offer that kind of help. I could send food. Or establish a trade route. Conducting war is not something I have the power to do."

Favia took a deep breath. "I could extend credit. I am currently the wealthiest person in the kingdom. Is there somewhere you could purchase weapons or ships from?"

Mace sighed. "Unfortunately, no. Our one trading partner who might have made that possible is no longer interested in helping us. Another of our species traded their sovereignty and the wormhole technology for protection. That negotiation left us with nothing to barter with. Not that we would have given that technology away anyway. It's too powerful to be in the hands of the untrusted."

Favia nodded. "That is the one technology that saved us. Even now we fear the Volgars are attempting to steal it from us. Should that happen, our truce with them might be forgotten and our colonies crushed with sudden and overwhelming attacks."

Jane asked, "Are there any weapons technologies you could trade? A more powerful cannon or shields? Even hand weapons, if you have them."

Favia lowered her eyes. "As the new queen, I don't even know if I could ask."

Mace stuck his hands inside his visor and began to rub his temples. "If I gave you the design for a weapon, do you think you could mass produce it in an insanely short period of time?"

Favia replied, "I could try. How soon would you need whatever it is built?"

Mace pulled up an image of the orbital microwave stations. "We would need as many as you could produce by tomorrow."

Jane half frowned. "Subtle, Mace."

"I'm just being real."

Jane said, "It took our people a few weeks to set up an assembly line for these, after that another month to really begin cranking them out. The Hoorka won't be able to match that as it's not even their design."

Favia clapped her hands together. An attendant was quickly by her side. "Bring the royal engineer."

The attendant bowed and scurried away.

Mace said, "You seriously have a royal engineer?"

Favia nodded. "The palace provides me with an expert staff that are capable of meeting any of my requests—within reason, of course."

The royal engineer sprinted into the room, bowing and taking a knee four steps below his queen.

Favia said, "My guest has a design I would like you to look over. I would like to know if it is possible for us to build it. And if so, how fast can we produce them and of what quantity? I would like your very best estimates. This is a matter of utmost importance to me. You have one cycle to complete this task."

Mace held up his arm pad for a data transfer.

Favia waved her hand when the transfer was complete. "Go now. Time is of the essence."

Jane asked, "How long is a cycle?"

"Approximately ninety of your minutes. I don't know why, but I prefer your twenty-four hours to our ten cycles. Perhaps it's just the longer day on Earth I prefer."

Jane looked around. "Well, if you're looking to trade, I'd be glad to swap a little piece of property in Norfolk for this place."

Favia smiled. "I do miss the Human humor. Our people are often too serious."

Mace replied, "Well, from what I've seen it hasn't done you wrong."

Favia nodded. "I suppose."

The chat continued until the royal engineer returned. "I have the estimates, Your Majesty."

Favia motioned with her fingers. "Tell us."

The engineer cleared his throat. "A reasonable estimate would be two months for a prototype, with another two months to bring an assembly line up to speed. My staff and I believe each line assembled could produce three units per day. I would assume however, because of your urgent request, you want something more than reasonable.

"With that assumption, we believe a functional prototype could be assembled in ninety cycles. We also estimate an assembly line, if prepared in parallel, could be fully operational in three hundred cycles."

Mace did the math on his arm pad. "Hmm. That's almost three weeks. I don't think we have a week left."

Favia looked at her engineer. "If you had unlimited funds, how long is your absolute best estimate? If the defense of this planet depended on it?"

The royal engineer stared at a far wall for several seconds. "I'm pulling numbers from the air, but I would suppose half the estimate for production. For the prototype, that is already the best we can do, my Queen."

The queen said, "You have the funds, Mr. Cattess. I want two hundred lines operational as soon as physically possible."

The engineer gazed at his queen. "Two hundred?"

Favia waved. "Yes. Make this happen, Mr. Cattess, and your queen will be extremely pleased with your service. Now go. Time is of the essence."

The engineer stood and sprinted as he talked into his comm device.

Jane looked at Mace. "Can't say I would mind having that kind of power."

Favia half smiled. "It is a great burden as well. I spend almost every waking moment in thought about how to better the lives of my people."

Jane said, "You have the makings of a great queen, Favia. I'm sure your people will be thrilled with your leadership."

Mace stood. "I don't mean to be abrupt, but we have a war to get back to."

Favia bowed. "I wish there was more I could do. Your kindness and caring is what brought me to this position."

Jane smiled. "We only brought you home. Your own kindness and caring brought you here."

Favia again bowed. "If only we were all so humble."

Mace extended a hand, helping the Hoorka queen to her feet. A short walk had the Humans on a lift that carried them to the shuttle.

As they walked up the ramp, Jane said, "What a wonderful person she turned out to be."

Mace nodded. "We can only hope we live long enough to visit her again."

The *Rogers* opened a wormhole to Targarian space.

Mace opened a comm. "Mr. Collins, what's our status?"

"They're still digesting those colonies. How'd it go at Promexa?"

"How'd you know we went there?"

Jasper shook his head. "Because you opened a wormhole there. You think everyone looks away when a wormhole is suddenly opened?"

Mace returned a smile. "No, I suppose not. Our trip was both good and bad. Favia has been made queen of the Hoorka. Her throne room puts yours to shame, by the way. Anyway, she couldn't give us ships of Hoorka weapons, so I gave her the plans for the microwave stations. She has her people scrambling to build two hundred assembly lines for us. Unfortunately those are gonna take ten days or so."

Jasper replied, "Hmm. Doubt we have ten days. Are they able to get around producing the... uh... whatchamacallit?"

Mace laughed. "The domain reflector? Yeah, we don't know. At the moment they have the full plans. We'll see if they have the engineering expertise to replicate that. And that's not to take anything away from your engineers or ours, we just don't have the knowledge required to replicate that part. Anyway, if we can hold the Karthians off for a week and a half, we may have some help."

Jasper asked, "How they getting them here?"

Mace stopped in thought for several seconds. "We ran out of there so fast I forgot to ask. I suppose we'll have to keep track and send transports when the time comes."

Jasper scowled. "*If* we have any left. We just lost 20 percent of what we had trying to get my people off those planets."

Mace sighed. "I'm sure we'll figure it out between now and then. It's what we do."

The forces at Croawla were waiting. Ship repairs continued at the repair docks in orbit around Divinia. New Collins ships continued to be floated out of the construction docks. A jump was made back to Earth to check on the families.

Mace stood at the cave entrance with Johnny. "Almost looks like a hotel in there now."

Johnny replied, "Has its own water purification system and sewage processing. The reclaimed water is dumped in a pond about a quarter mile away. The habitat portion can be sealed off with its own oxygen generation as well. We could literally close the door and live in there for a year. We even have a nice maintenance lab with spare parts if needed. In reality, it's no different than living on a ship."

Mace frowned. "And we've done plenty of that. What scares me is if we manage to survive an attack by the Karthians... will we be the only ones left? They seem to be thorough in their genocide. Each of those planets still has a couple ships left behind whose sole purpose is to hunt down and kill any survivors. Would we survive here for a year only to come out and get blasted afterward?"

Johnny chuckled. "Well, if dying sooner or later are our options, I think I'll take later."

Zax and Fina came up the ramp leading out of the cave. "Mr. Johnny, come play with us?"

Johnny looked at Mace with a half smile. "Duty calls."

Mace walked the ramp into the cave. A short walk had him standing in the kitchen area of the dining hall. Jane and Jenny were preparing a lunchtime meal.

Mace asked, "What are you cooking? Smells good."

Jenny replied, "We scored a couple beef roasts at the Ronceverte market. We have green beans, corn, squash, mashed potatoes, biscuits. Jane even managed to find olives. Did I mention I love olives? We're starting to see more of those products since the skybuses went in. Almost like a global economy is emerging again. Nothing like it was, but it's progress, I guess."

"Is this meal for a special occasion?"

Jenny laughed. "No, we just thought it would be nice for a change. And given the fact we may be invaded in the coming days... I guess there is that."

Fatso Geerok walked into the room. "Mmm, the smell of Human cooking... delightful. I should like to give up the nutrient bars for more of this."

Jenny replied, "Well, enjoy it while you can. If the Karthians show we won't be having meals like this."

Fatso turned to Mace. "The holo-image surrounding this compound is impressive. I couldn't detect a transition when I walked through it. The buildings suddenly appearing was eye-opening, but a few steps back and they were again gone."

Mace said, "Yeah, you can only hide so much. Would be nice if we could hide the individual buildings better, but we'll need to walk between them, so we have to blanket the whole area."

Geerok said, "Why not add a holo-projector for each building as well?"

"You can do that?"

Geerok shrugged. "Why not? It's only a holo-projection. Technically, you could nest as many of those as you want."

Mace patted the former Mawga admiral on the back. "I want. Let's go see if we can get that done."

Geerok replied, "I believe the main projector was set up by two of Mr. Montak's men. They should be able to direct us as to what will be required."

Chapter 24

After a long meal with all the trimmings, the dreaded comm came in from Jasper. "They're on the move. Looks like Croawla. I'm moving up half the orbital stations from Divinia."

Mace replied, "We'll be there as soon as I get everyone back aboard the *Rogers*. And I know I've neglected to ask this, but how are our gatrellium stockpiles?"

Jasper slowly shook his head. "Getting low. Another thirty Collins ships and we'll have to stop production. We have enough to fight and move where we need to, but it's a finite amount. I'm in the process of having the storage at Croawla moved to Divinia. Last thing I want is to be giving it over to those fish heads. The way they use that stuff, they must have a huge stockpile of it."

Mace said, "We lost a lot of Collins ships. You don't think they're somehow recycling the skins on those, do you?"

Jasper shrugged. "Couldn't say. I know they've carted parts of them away. I do have scout ships in the systems they took. Let me ask my people."

Jasper came back from a short conversation. "It seems they have ships out there harvesting debris from these battles. Could be they're mining those debris fields for gatrellium."

"Sounds like we might have a few easy targets to pick off."

Jasper grinned, "Or capture. Might be a good source of gatrellium for us."

Mace nodded. "See if you can find one that's been out the longest. Send us the coordinates and we'll go aboard and check it out before heading your way."

"Will have that for you in a few minutes. And if the Karthian move is like previous moves, we should have a few hours before they attack. They haven't opened any wormholes yet."

The crew of the *Rogers* was back aboard. A jump to Antho, a former colony of the Dunden Heap, had a debris collector ship in sight. Before it could flee, Hans Mueller disabled its drives. Johnny, Jane, and Jenny then attached a shuttle and cut through the hull. Resistance was light as only two of the crew of twenty were armed.

Johnny stood over the Karthian captain on the bridge. "I hope you plan to cooperate."

The captain replied, "Please spare us. We are only following orders."

Jane stepped on his three-fingered hand, bringing about a yelp. "You tell us what we want to know and we might even let you go."

The captain nodded. "Whatever you want."

Johnny said, "You're gathering debris for recycling?"

"Yes."

"Do you separate the materials here?"

"Yes."

Is the ultra-heavy element we call gatrellium one of the items you separate and gather?"

The captain was quiet. Added pressure from Jane on his hand brought "Yes" for an answer.

Johnny reached down, pulling the Karthian up to his feet. "Show me where the gatrellium is."

A long walk had the two standing at the end of a processing line. "The finely-ground ores exit here. This vat is used to precipitate certain metals, including gatrellium. Over here, they are further separated according to the desired end-product. And over here we have the storage area. The blue tank is refined gatrellium."

Johnny walked over. "This is our unit of measure. Can you do a quick conversion to how much this tank holds?"

The captain entered the data. "We currently have forty-six hundred kilograms."

"What's that tank hold?"

"The equivalent of almost twelve thousand kilograms."

"How long did it take you to gather that amount?"

"We arrived from a delivery three days ago. This is our third and final sweep of this star system."

"Did you deliver full loads on the two prior runs?"

The captain pulled up the data. "The equivalent of eighty-nine hundred kilograms, followed by seventy-seven hundred. I expect this run, which ends in five days, to yield six thousand kilograms."

Johnny asked, "Have you harvested similar numbers from other battle sites?"

The captain nodded.

Johnny opened a comm. "We need to hit these salvage ships and hit them hard. They're gathering tons of gatrellium from the destroyed ships. Next time we board we need to check their cruisers for gatrellium stores. We might be passing up gold mines of this stuff with each raid."

"Excellent news. Now the question is, how do we take possession of it?"

"You bring us a cargo hauler and we can dump directly into it. And hey, this captain has been fully cooperative, I think we should let him go—after we take his gatrellium stock that is."

Mace arranged for a cargo hauler to come from Divinia. The recovered gatrellium was then sent to the Alpha Centauri site for storage. Six additional debris harvesters were captured and their gatrellium contents confiscated. As Johnny boarded the seventh, Jasper gave the call.

"We have wormholes opening at Croawla."

Mace said, "Johnny, pump that cargo as quickly as you can. The Karthians are moving on Croawla."

Johnny nodded. "Will do. And hey, I just had a thought. These ships, when they're full, they go somewhere to deposit these ores. What if we did a raid there instead? What if we were able to clean out a huge stockpile rather than these small loads?"

Mace replied, "Let me consult. Continue with your mission."

Mace opened a comm to Jasper. "Johnny had a thought."

Jasper shook his head. "Not possible. Apes don't have thoughts."

Mace replied, "Yeah, well, he had the idea of following or finding out where these harvester ships take this stuff. With the right ships, we might be able to hit a stockyard or supply depot loaded with gatrellium. If it's of sufficient size, it might even slow their attacks out here."

Jasper rubbed his chin. "Might not be a bad idea. We might have a moment's respite anyway. The Karthians only sent through three ships. No doubt scouts. We chased them off. If they do come through in force, you'll have an hour or so to get back. They like to get everyone through and take up formations before attacking."

"You think you could spare twenty Collins ships and maybe three dozen cargo haulers?"

Jasper nodded. "Just tell me where you want them."

Mace smiled. "Give us a few minutes. Johnny needs to track that info down."

After investigating a debris harvester's nav logs, arrangements were made to jump directly to a Karthian ore depot. Twenty Collins class cruisers, along with thirty ore haulers, followed the *Rogers* through to the coordinates that had been provided.

Humphrey was the first to speak: "We have five Karthian cruisers heading this way, Mr. Hardy."

Mace nodded. "The Targarians will be taking care of those. Move us in to that transfer station. We're going aboard."

Mace stood. "Johnny, this time I'm coming with you. Mr. Crawford, I'm leaving you in charge."

A shuttle, piloted by Jenny Taub, pulled out of bay one. Less than a minute later it was settling on the deck in the docking bay of the transfer station. Two laser pulses impacted the side of the shuttle as the ramp lowered and Johnny ran down with counter fire. The two low level security guards on duty quickly gave up. The deck and control center were secured, and the crewmen locked away, before the four began working over the control room computer systems.

Johnny said, "We have twenty-six ore bays with material stockpiles. I have iron, cobalt, magnesium, copper, silver, and... here we go... gatrellium, gold, diamond, emerald, uranium... and a slew of others. I think we hit the jackpot."

"Send the gatrellium coordinates to the haulers. Have them start loading immediately. Not sure how long we're gonna have before a storm of Karthian ships come down on us. How much gatrellium are we talking?"

Johnny paused and looked up. "Nineteen thousand tons. No wonder they're being so wasteful. That's more than we've ever had at any one time. And when I say we, I mean the Targarians."

Mace typed away on his arm pad. "Crap, those haulers can only handle about a third of that."

Mace opened a comm to the *Rogers*. "Mr. Geerok, patch me through directly to Jasper at Divinia."

"Connecting."

An image of Jasper floated above Mace's arm. "We hit the mother lode. I need more ore haulers."

Jasper shook his head. "That's all we have. The rest have been converted to transports to move my people. You'll have to make do. If you can't bring it back, then do your best to scatter it."

Mace winced. "OK, we'll deal with it."

The comm closed.

"Johnny, coordinate with the hauler captains, I want them to drop their loads at the Alpha site and come back immediately. And when I say drop, I mean dump 'em and run. We need them back here for a second run."

Jane said, "Ah, I think we have another problem. This is one of four depot sites. I'm showing seventy-eight thousand tons across the other three locations."

"Wow," said Jenny. "They must have some impressive mines somewhere."

Mace pulled up an image of the massive transfer station and its bays. "The gatrellium bay is the second to last on this arm that runs out this way. What if we hit that spine right here, grapple those last couple bays, and fly them into that star. I'd say that makes it unrecoverable."

Mace turned to the others. "Back to the shuttle, now."

Jane said, "I pushed the locations of those other depots back to the *Rogers*."

Mace talked as they ran to the shuttle. "Here's what I think we do. When the Targarians are finished with those cruisers, they jump to the next depot and secure it. The haulers, once they dump at Alpha, can continue to that next site. We're gonna grab that bay and push it into that sun."

Johnny ran up the ramp. "That's an awful waste."

"I'm not willing to risk having them get it back."

A Targarian commander came over the comm. "Mr. Hardy, the last of the ore haulers is away."

Mace asked, "And the Karthian ships?"

The commander smiled. "Dispatched in the first ninety seconds of our engagement. Those were not front-line ships or crews."

Mace nodded. "Excellent. Make your jump to the second depot and secure it. Those haulers should be showing up right after you get there."

The commander nodded as the comm closed.

Hans Mueller fired three bursts at the spine connecting the gatrellium bay to the rest of the transfer station. The structure split and the separated bays floated freely. Liam Hobbs maneuvered the *Rogers*, and the grappling clamps were attached. A slow initial push was followed by a rapid acceleration.

Liam said, "Three minutes and we should be able to release her, Mr. Hardy. No one will be pulling it back from that point."

Humphrey turned. "That will take us remarkably close, will it not?"

Liam nodded. "It will, but as I said, they won't be bringing it back."

A comm came in from the Targarians: "Four cruisers at the second depot, Mr. Hardy. The first of the ore haulers have arrived."

Mace replied, "Keep us posted, Commander. After that, move on to depot three."

Humphrey yelled, "Wormholes opening! I show at least forty Karthian cruisers coming through!"

"Where?"

The hull of the *Rogers* rumbled as the first of the Karthian laser rounds found its mark.

Humphrey glanced over his shoulder. "They're right on us, Mr. Hardy. I recommend we release and jump while we have room."

Mace looked at Liam. "Mr. Hobbs, how long until we reach the point of no return?"

"Another minute at least. They would still have a chance, but not an easy one."

"Take us there. I'll make the call from that point."

The hull again rumbled, followed by a violent jerk. "Double hit, Mr. Hardy. We can't maneuver carrying this big mass."

"Mr. Mueller, tell me you're hitting them back."

Hans replied, "With all we have. They're jinking where we cannot. My shots aren't hitting their targets."

"Time, Mr. Hobbs?"

"Thirty seconds!"

The *Rogers* bucked and shuddered.

Humphrey said, "That cost us one of our aft transducers!"

"Twenty seconds!"

Mace said, "Mr. Hobbs! Release the clamps! But stay with this structure! Use it as a shield! Mr. Mueller, kill anything that tries to get close to us!"

The metallic clangs could be heard as the grappling clamps retracted into the *Rogers*, freeing them from the bay structure it was holding. A closing cruiser moved into the direct fire of Hans Mueller's cannons and paid the price, falling back behind the others.

"Five seconds!"

Mace started counting down from ten as the Karthians attempted to outflank the *Rogers*' protected position.

After reaching a count of one, Mace yelled, "Mr. Hobbs, break away!"

"We're gonna take some heat, Mr. Hardy! And I'm not talking about from those cannons! There's a massive solar flare coming up toward us. I thought if we could direct that structure into it, we'd save some time."

"Tell me the real problem, Mr. Hobbs!"

Liam looked back. "It's a lot hotter out there than I thought. And we can't go back without that swarm being all over us."

Mace stared at the image of the approaching flare. "Tell me your plan, Mr. Hobbs!"

"We have to fly under that plasma, Mr. Hardy, and I can't say for sure that we'll be coming back from it. But it's the only way to shake those ships. The mass of that sun is preventing us from making a jump!"

Mace gripped his armrests as a new set of laser blasts pounded the *Rogers*' hull. "Do what you must, Mr. Hobbs!"

Humphrey said, "Another transducer gone! We have a weak aft shield, Mr. Hardy!"

Liam Hobbs maneuvered the *Rogers* to the port side of the approaching massive flare.

Humphrey yelled, "Hull temps are spiking!"

Liam grunted. "Come on, Missy! I know you have it in you! You have yet to let us down!"

The *Rogers* turned, rolling up under the outstretched arm of the flare. Two of the thirty-nine remaining Karthian cruisers in pursuit began to glow before their dampening fields failed, turning the ships into fireballs that continued to race toward the sun.

Mace said, "Gonna get hot in here! Close your visors!"

The inner hull temperature rose as Liam Hobbs did his best to steer around streams of plasma that moved about under the main flare. The hull of the *Rogers* rocked, laser strikes impacting her dampening field.

Humphrey yelled, "A port transducer just quit on us! Outer hull showing six hundred twelve degrees! Inside air is at one-twenty!"

Liam yelled back, "Thirty seconds! Come on, you Kaachi bucket of bolts! Hang in there!"

Three of the pursuing Karthian ships burst into fireballs, falling back and taking out another four that were following too close behind.

"Ten seconds!" yelled Liam.

Mace continued to grip his armrests, gritting his teeth.

Liam Hobbs yelled, "We're out! Fifty seconds to a wormhole!"

The *Rogers* continued to jink from side to side. Each maneuver allowed the Karthian ships to move ever closer. A violent jerk twisted Mace in his chair, slamming him against an armrest, ripping the leather covering from his hand. A heavy rumble reverberated through the ship.

Humphrey yelled, "Two starboard transducers gone! Hull is reaching critical temperature in that section!"

Liam said, "Twenty seconds!"

Three Karthian cruisers broke apart, shredding into numerous fireballs before flaming out of existence. The remaining ships turned to avoid the debris.

"Wormhole is opening!"

A second later the *Rogers* was through, slowing to a modest speed as the hull began to cool.

"Damage report, Mr. Mallot."

Humphrey replied, "We lost five transducers. And there was a fire in bay three. Extinguished before it caused trouble."

A comm was opened: "Commander? How goes the transfer?"

The Targarian replied, "No sign of Karthians ships, Mr. Hardy. I have the ore haulers coming for a second run. This depot will be empty in three minutes."

"You detect wormholes, you have those haulers break away immediately, and you follow. We're moving ahead to the third depot to scout."

The comm closed. "Mr. Hobbs, take us to the third depot on that list."

Liam said, "Mr. Hardy, we can't fight in this condition. We need to get back to the repair docks."

Mace replied, "We aren't fighting. We'll have a look and pass that info back to the commander. I want to do the same for that fourth depot as well. After that, take us in for repairs."

The *Rogers* made the jumps and was soon back at Divinia. The raid on the third depot went as planned. At the fourth, fifty Karthian cruisers were waiting for them. Jasper countered by sending in his remaining Collins ships. The Karthians were routed and the gatrellium captured before an even larger Karthian force jumped in.

Back at Divinia, the *Rogers* was moved into a repair dock, where her damaged transducers were to be replaced.

Mace clenched and released his fists several times.

"You OK?" asked Johnny.

Mace nodded. "Side hurts a little. Almost tore the arm off this chair. That was pretty intense back there."

Johnny chuckled. "What was intense about it? That was insane."

Mace shook his head. "How'd we end up in this insane business anyway?"

"It was either this or be victims. And I'm not much for being a victim."

Mace nodded. "Me either. I guess that makes us both insane."

Chapter 25

The *Rogers* slowly pulled out of the repair dock.

A jump to the Alpha Centauri site had Mace wondering: "I thought they dumped it all here?"

Johnny laughed as he pushed a button. "They did."

A holo-projector shut down, revealing a vast pile of gatrellium.

Mace said, "Maybe we should just cover the Earth with those projectors. They'd never know we were there."

Johnny replied, "Unfortunately, it would still show on scans. And we have all the RF signals bouncing around from the surface. The projectors are only good for hiding the visual."

Mace stroked his goatee. "I keep forgetting that. Should we be burying this stuff or something?"

Johnny laughed. "You must have missed science class this morning. We could bury that a kilometer down and they would see it the first time they looked for gatrellium."

Mace said, "Well then, why do we have our cave lined with the stuff? Won't that make us sitting ducks?"

Johnny shook his head. "Jeff and Gnaga used some kind of gatrellium copper alloy. Scanner waves are diffused or something, meaning the scanner only sees the surrounding dirt. Jeff said they could dig into the data and find us, but they aren't likely to do that without a reason."

"So we really aren't all that safe hiding in there."

Johnny answered, "Never were. But the alternative is sitting in the open, so I'll take my chances in the cave."

Mace said, "We should cover this pile in the gatrellium copper and then bury it."

"I think that's being discussed. At the moment it's a question of resources."

Mace tapped his gloved fingers on his armrest. "I'm so ready for this to all be over. The constant tension, the death and destruction... enough is enough."

Johnny walked over, placing his hand on Mace's shoulder. "I'm gonna give you the same pick-me-up talk Jane gave me last night."

Mace looked up. "This has to be good. What'd she say?"

Johnny chuckled. "Was short and sweet. She told me to man-up."

Mace half smiled. "That does sound like a Jane solution. Did it work?"

Johnny laughed. "Don't know. I'm still trying."

Jasper came over the comm. "The Karthians have formed up for a jump, but they haven't budged yet."

Mace said, "You think we hit them hard on those gatrellium stockpiles? That was a huge amount we just grabbed."

"Couldn't say. This is the first time they've formed up like that and not made the jump. Maybe they *are* having to evaluate their options since we raided those depots. Scouts aren't reporting any new ships coming through the rift. There's usually a slow trickle before they form up and join the rest of that fleet."

An officer approached Jasper. "Sire, we have wormholes opening."

Jasper pushed the info to his main display. Hundreds of wormholes opened and ships began streaming through.

Jasper scowled. "Well, crap. Here they come."

Mace said, "That looks like all of them. Sure you don't want to pull the rest of those microwave stations forward?"

Jasper sat silent for several seconds before barking out the order: "I want all orbital stations here, now!"

Mace turned to Johnny. "You might want to grab Jane and Jenny and head to your shuttle."

Johnny nodded as he stood. "This time we'll start with taking out their power. Should move things along faster."

The Karthian fleet numbered more than nineteen hundred ships. The massive station sat behind them, acting as a repair dock and a depot for restocking supplies. The assault line stretched out for two hundred kilometers. The battle for Croawla was only moments away.

Johnny opened a comm channel. "We're ready."

Jordan Crawford followed: "Ready here as well."

The Karthian fleet moved forward all at once. The Targarians waited patiently. The microwave stations were the first to fire, poking small holes in the hulls of the approaching ships. Seconds later, laser pulses were traded for plasma bolts. The attacking fleet moved into and through the much smaller Targarian force, targeting the microwave stations.

The *Rogers* moved up to meet four cruisers as they laid siege to a nearby station. The shuttles departed and were soon clamped to Karthian hulls. Hans Mueller worked his magic with the ship's cannons as Mace worked the wormhole and green energy weapons.

An opening in a Karthian hull was followed up by a precision shot from the *Rogers*' cannons. The exploding ship was the first loss of the immense battle. Minutes later, the two assaulted cruisers went offline, but not before the microwave station was destroyed. The Hull of the *Rogers* rumbled as repeated rounds from the cruisers found her dampening field.

The shuttles each moved to new targets as Hans shredded the disabled ships. Four new cruisers joined the remaining Karthian ship as the next microwave station was attacked.

Mace said, "Keep at them people! We need a win here!"

A new ship approached. Twenty shuttles emerged from bays down each of its sides. Hans changed his targeting, destroying half before the first was able to attach to the *Rogers*' hull.

Liam yelled, "They're clamped on, Mr. Hardy! Three so far!"

Mace unbuckled his belt, standing from his chair. "Mr. Geerok, take over for me!"

Humphrey Mallot stood as well. "I'm coming with you, Mr. Hardy."

Mace hesitated before waving him on. "Someone please inform us of any hull breaches!"

As they ran toward the ship's armory, word came from Liam Hobbs on the bridge. "Deck six, section C. Camera showed Karthian soldiers before it was taken out!"

Mace replied as he handed Humphrey Mallot a plasma rifle and an AR-15. "Patch through the hallway feed, Mr. Hobbs. I wanna know when they leave that room."

"They're moving into the hall already. Second breach on deck four, section F. And a third also on deck six."

Mace took a deep breath. "Hope you said your prayers, Mr. Mallot."

Humphrey grabbed Mace by the arm. "Hold up."

"What you got going?"

Humphrey logged into a console. "I suggest you set your gravity on those boots to the highest level."

Mace thought for a moment, before grinning. "I like the way you think, Mr. Mallot. Everyone, this is Hardy. If you aren't strapped in, set your boots to full gravity. We're about to change our environment for those intruders."

Mace gave Humphrey a nod. "Do it."

The ship's gravity was inverted, turned full on, and then flipped back to its original setting, again at full capacity. The invading Karthian soldiers slammed into the ceilings before being thrown hard back against the floors. Mace struggled to maintain his balance as the ship's gravity flipped full-on in one direction and then the other for most of a minute.

Liam came over the comm as the gravity restored to normal. "I show three sets of invaders down. Some are moving, so you might want to get in there and clean up."

Mace yelled into his comm: "Every able-bodied person on deck six report to the affected areas and see to it those soldiers don't regroup. Mr. Mallot, genius move. Let's go clear deck four."

Hans said, "The shuttles are away. Scratch two more cruisers."

Mace jumped down the final four steps in the stairwell before bursting into the hall. Three Karthians were already beginning to stand. Three plasma rounds saw to it they were unsuccessful. The remaining fifteen soldiers were terminated with prejudice, then Mace turned into the room that had been breached. A tube extended from the shuttle into the room.

Mace sprinted for the tunnel, blasting an unsuspecting Karthian crewman standing at the other end before turning to the cockpit. Short work was made of the two pilots before the Army Ranger returned to the *Rogers*.

"You cleaners on deck six, make a run into those shuttles and gut them as well."

Liam said, "We need to be rid of those ships, Mr. Hardy. They're making maneuvering difficult."

Mace nodded, then stopped. "Mr. Hobbs, how many hits have we taken since those shuttles clamped on?"

"None, sir."

Mace tilted his head to one side. "I'm thinking we keep them. Might be we're not being targeted because of those. Try taking us closer to one of those cruisers. If they don't return fire, Mr. Mueller should be able to cut them up."

As Mace hustled onto the bridge, Liam replied, "You were right. That cruiser let us come within a kilometer. Mr. Mueller taught them to fear our weapons. They're limping back toward that station."

"Fly us in as close as you can to every cruiser we encounter."

Johnny came over the comm. "We still need you to run cover for us."

Mace shook his head. "I want you and Crawford to bring those shuttles back. This is our new strategy until they change theirs. We can kill twice the ships this way. Bring 'em back."

The shuttles docked. Mace gave orders for the breach holes to be covered with hull plating and sealed. Charges were added to the breach tubes, so if needed they could be blown away.

Johnny took over the comm station on the bridge. "We could have continued out there."

"We have a free pass with these Karthian shuttles attached. We can't provide you cover and make use of this at the same time. I'd rather have you here safe and sound."

Johnny said, "Those Collins ships all have holo-projectors. Could they broadcast images of the Karthians shuttles being attached?"

"Scans would reveal they weren't there."

Humphrey replied, "I believe Mr. Mueller does his targeting using visual."

Hans nodded as he loosed the next barrage. "Scans are only good for positioning. I select targets based on visuals. I suspect the Karthians do the same."

Mace opened a comm to Jasper. "I'm sending you some images of Karthian shuttles that are attached to our hull. I believe the Karthians have been avoiding taking shots at us for that reason. Try using the holo-projectors on one of your ships. See if the Karthians bite."

Jasper turned to one of his aides before turning back to the comm camera. "We're taking a beating—dishing it out but taking one, too. We've lost a hundred eighteen of our three hundred eighty stations. We're also finding them to be less effective."

The image of Jasper on the *Organ Cave* shook as multiple rounds impacted his ship's dampener fields.

Mace replied, "If you use the projector, you can go right in close on those cruisers. We've managed four kills since discovering it, and they aren't shooting back."

Jasper nodded. "We'll have those images up momentarily. If this works I'll personally come over there and kiss your boots."

Mace laughed. "You don't have to do that, but Johnny might enjoy it."

Jasper scowled. "That overgrown goat-catcher can kiss *my* boots."

Johnny chuckled. "Goat catcher? You're slipping."

Jasper waved a hand as he returned his concentration to the fight. "Meh. I'm in the middle of a war. Best I got. Hang on... projector is coming online."

Jasper Collins barked out several commands.

Mace asked, "Well?"

Jasper slowly shook his head. "Idiots stopped shooting. I'm rolling this out to the fleet."

The comm closed.

Johnny said, "You know what this means, don't you?"

Mace replied, "What?"

Johnny looked over his shoulder. "Only gonna take a few minutes for them to figure out those shuttles aren't real. That's when they'll start shooting again. Including at us."

Mace nodded. "Mr. Mallot, if that happens, blow those breach tubes so we can be rid of those things."

Liam smiled. "Doing that now and initiating holo-projections."

The Targarian fleet had a surge in kills that lasted all of eight minutes. When the Karthian ships began shooting back, a handful of the Collins ships were caught off guard. The Targarians were forced back into their strategy to defend the remaining microwave stations. As the next several hours passed, the Targarian numbers continued to thin.

Humphrey gave status. "Stations are down to eighty orbitals. The fleet has lost sixty-five ships, a third of those Collins class. I count three hundred ninety Karthians destroyed, another hundred eighty-six have left the fight."

Mace sighed. "That's not enough. We need something to give us an edge."

Mace opened a comm to Malcolm Stark. "We need your ships."

Stark replied, "I cannot commit to your fight. We will fight here, for our own space."

"What if I promised you ten thousand tons of gatrellium?"

Stark laughed. "You don't have ten thousand tons of gatrellium."

Mace nodded. "We do. We stole it from four depots back in Karthian space. You commit the Earth fleet and I'll give it to you when we're done."

"And why would I trust you?"

Mace pursed his lips. "Because I have yet to lie to you. We're at war. We need your help, and we need it to stop this war before it makes it to Earth. Croawla may only have a couple hours left. We then fall back to Divinia. Bring your ships and make a stand with us there."

Stark was silent for several seconds. "This gatrellium, you are certain you have it and that you can deliver it when the fighting is over?"

"Even if I have to pack it there myself."

Stark said, "I'll have an answer for you shortly."

The comm closed.

Chapter 26

The orbital microwave station count at Croawla dropped to thirty-five.

A comm came in from Malcolm Stark. "Mr. Hardy, I may have found a mercenary army willing to offer their help in exchange for gatrellium. They will require fifteen hundred tons up front as earnest money."

Mace asked, "Who are they, and how can I be certain they're worth it?"

Stark smiled. "I believe you know Mr. Knuttin?"

An image of Frado Knuttin showed on a split comm display. "Mr. Hardy, it is good to see you. I am sorry for the difficulties my government has caused you. Their decisions went against my wishes."

"What can you offer?"

Frado replied, "As you know, we recently acquired the wormhole technology. Gatrellium is suddenly at a premium. Our supplies are very thin. I've been authorized to sell, or I should say lease, a hundred of the older dreadnoughts that my corporate fleets have been using. You will have to provide your own crews.

"The consoles are configurable, allowing Humans to pilot and operate the ships. They are well automated and can be mastered in a few hours' time. They also offer a low-end military grade microwave cannon. And when I say low-end, I am talking cannons that are still far superior to the commercial grade units you currently possess. Are you interested in a lease?"

Stark said, "I will volunteer the crews to man them."

Mace took in a deep breath as he fired off several rounds from the wormhole weapon. "Any way we could lease five hundred? I can offer more gatrellium."

Frado smiled. "I'm afraid I couldn't arrange that deal. At most, I may be able to provide two hundred, depending on what our military council says. They would be made available for the duration of the Karthian conflict, not to exceed one of your Earth years in term."

Mace nodded. "Make it happen, Mr. Knuttin. And make it happen now."

Stark replied, "There is still the question of the gatrellium."

Mace said, "I'll have deliveries coming your way in a few minutes. Get those ships here as soon as possible."

Mace passed word to the ore-hauling ships, and the first load of gatrellium was on its way.

Johnny said, "You do know Stark is gonna take a big cut of that, right?"

Mace replied, "He set up the deal, he's providing the crews. Frankly, I don't care if he keeps it all. There are three and a half billion Targarians down on that planet. If we don't do something, they will all be dead in a couple days."

Another hour passed and the last of the orbital stations was annihilated. The Targarian fleet dropped back to within the atmosphere of Croawla to fight. The Collins ships had superior handling when in atmosphere. The hundreds of ground stations provided extra firepower.

Johnny said, "You gonna tell Jasper help may be coming?"

Mace slowly shook his head. "Not until it's a certainty. Besides, knowing Stark, he will purposefully delay until the fight has moved to Divinia. I don't think they will make it here before then."

Johnny frowned, "Can't say I like giving the UF all that gatrellium."

"It's all we have for trade. I'm sure we could buy their protection with the rest of that stockpile, but not without selling them Earth and making us all second class citizens like the Mawga. We're already seeing what that's shaping up to mean."

Humphrey said, "Mr. Hardy, those ground stations are taking a pounding. If this pace continues, we'll be done here in an hour."

Mace replied, "Thank you, Mr. Mallot. Not like we have a choice in the matter. The longer we keep them fighting here, the longer we have to get those UF ships in the fight."

Mace opened a comm. "Stark, tell me the good news."

Stark replied, "The first delivery of gatrellium is in transit. Thirty dreadnoughts are parked in Earth orbit. The remainder will be delivered as the gatrellium arrives at Canto."

"At least tell me you have crews aboard getting familiar with those ships."

Stark nodded. "Crews are aboard. I expect we'll be ready to send them to Divinia before the day is out."

Mace asked, "Why the wait? You should have the rest of the gatrellium to Canto in an hour or less."

Stark sighed. "I won't be sending these men and women to their immediate deaths, Mr. Hardy. They will be given at least a minimum amount of time to train before being thrown to the wolves."

Mace returned an irritated stare. "Not one minute longer than is necessary, Stark. And Divinia will be the destination. Croawla won't be with us much longer."

When the ground-based station count had dropped to twenty remaining, a dejected King Jasper Collins made the call. The fleet was to pull back to Divinia. The three and a half billion Targarian citizens on Croawla would now be at the mercy of the Karthians. Aerial bombardments had already begun before the last of the Targarian ships slipped away.

A stern Jasper Collins was on the comm, broadcasting from the throne room on the *Organ* Cave to his people on Divinia. A short and resolute speech was given, encouraging all citizens to not give up hope.

A teary-eyed Jasper Collins switched comms back to the Rogers. "I failed them. I failed my people."

Mace replied, "You did the best with what you had. And I know this news is late, but we should have two hundred UF dreadnoughts joining us at Divinia. They'll be crewed by Humans... Stark's people. I made a deal for some of the captured gatrellium—way more than I would have liked, but worth it, given our situation. I hope to have them at Divinia by the end of the Earth day at the cave."

Jasper looked at his holo-display. "That's seven hours."

Mace replied, "And the crews are green. I don't think those ships have the best of shielding, but they do have a powerful cannon."

Mace stood and paced about his bridge. "I'm considering making an offer for some of those microwave stations he has positioned around Earth. I'm fairly certain he won't go for that, though. He won't move Earth's fleet here. Why would he send the stations?"

Jasper said, "What about the stations at Canto? Would Knuttin be interested in selling them to us? They already have the protection of the UF. They don't need them."

Mace looked over at Johnny. "See if you can open a comm to Mr. Knuttin."

Seconds later, it was passed to Mace. "Mr. Knuttin, I have another proposal for you. The orbital microwave stations we put up at Canto. Would you be willing to sell them to us?"

Frado thought for a moment. "I would of course have to consult with our authorities on that. They are nice to have from a comfort standpoint, but totally unnecessary now. Let me have a conversation and I'll be back in touch."

Mace asked, "You have the coordinates for here?"

Frado nodded. "They are coming through your comm. I assume the need is urgent?"

Mace nodded. "Very."

Frado bowed. "I'll see to it immediately."

Fifteen minutes later a hail came back. "Mr. Hardy, good news. The council has agreed."

"Tell me what you feel is fair."

Frado smiled. "There are two hundred forty stations. I would think one quarter ton per station would be more than fair."

Mace raised his eyebrows. "A quarter ton per? Deal. I was expecting more given our situation."

Frado said, "This is a private sale, Mr. Hardy, directly to the corporation, which you still own 24 percent of. If you would prefer, I could deduct the appropriate amount of credits from your accounts here on Canto."

Mace nodded. "That would save me a lot of effort. Is there enough there?"

Frado nodded. "We are currently offering those stations in our catalog for five million credits each. Our cost is roughly two. With that number of stations, it would appear you have ample credits to cover the transaction without offering gatrellium."

Mace asked, "What do we have in there?"

"Seven hundred eighty million credits or so. Our quarterly dividend will be issued in a few days time. We have had a very profitable quarter, I might add."

"Take the credits as necessary, Mr. Knuttin. I wouldn't suppose you could sell us any from the catalog also?"

Frado smiled. "I happen to have fifty units in inventory."

Mace nodded. "We'll take them. Charge what you feel is fair. When can we take delivery?"

"Immediately if you like. I can have shuttles up to remove the crews in an hour's time."

"I like. Tell me where to open a wormhole and we'll come get them."

Frado said, "If you would be willing to cover our use of gatrellium, I would be happy to have them delivered."

Mace replied, "You tell me how much you used and I'll gladly double it. I'll have it waiting here at Divinia when they get here."

Frado bowed. "Expect the deliveries shortly."

Mace ordered an ore hauler to bring forward five hundred tons of gatrellium. Ninety minutes later, the first of the stations arrived.

Frado came over a comm. "Mr. Hardy, our gatrellium use for this delivery was only three hundred kilograms. This is far too much."

Mace replied, "OK, consider this: would the corporation like to purchase the remainder of the five hundred tons?"

Frado nodded. "Very much so."

"Take what you would consider a fair acquisition cost, deposit that in our account, and the corporation can use the rest or sell it or whatever you like."

Frado grinned. "Mr. Hardy, this will keep our exploration fleet running for some time. You've just made me an extremely happy Kohamian."

Mace said, "When this is all over, if we survive, I may be able to sell you more."

Two hundred ninety space-based microwave stations sat waiting for crews. Shuttles were dispatched and the stations manned. Several hours later, a wormhole opened from Earth and two hundred UF dreadnoughts slipped through to Divinia space.

Jasper said, "I can't thank you enough for pulling this together."

Mace winced. "Sadly, I think it's Stark who deserves the credit. We could have done this ourselves if we'd thought of it, but we didn't."

Jasper scowled. "I won't be praising that lowlife anytime soon. With these new resources, and had he committed the fleet to the defense of Croawla, we might have been able to drive them back. They lost nearly six hundred ships to our hundred thirty-eight, and some of those are in repairs."

"How many do we have left?"

Jasper frowned. "One hundred five Collins and seventy-seven cruisers. And the *Rogers*."

"And they have thirteen hundred?"

Jasper nodded. "Roughly."

"Any progress from Mr. Moskowitz with the wormhole weapons?"

"You'll have to ask him yourself. I pissed him off earlier after yelling at him for them not being done. I was desperate, didn't mean what I said, but he has no further interest in talking to me."

Mace chuckled. "I can't see him getting mad. You must have really wound him up. I'll give him a look-in and let you know where we're at. I wouldn't worry about him getting mad at you. He knows the situation. I'm sure it's already forgotten."

"I hope so. I like the Doc. He didn't deserve what I unleashed on him."

Mace hopped a shuttle down to Yentis. He was soon standing in the lab behind Jeff Moskowitz. "Doc, how we looking?"

Jeff turned. "You come to yell at me, too?"

Mace laughed. "No. And Mr. Collins is sorry for whatever he said. The stress of all this has us all on edge."

"True, but there are some things that can't be unsaid. I'm afraid Mr. Collins burned some bridges."

Mace looked Jeff in the face. "Those bloodshot eyes are telling. When's the last time you slept?"

Jeff frowned. "Thirty-eight hours ago. I had a four hour nap."

Mace put his hand on his shoulder. "Killing yourself with stimulants doesn't help us. You need sleep."

Jeff shook his head. "Not happening for at least a few more hours. Will take the last boost that long to wear off."

Mace looked at the electronics spread across a table. "How's it looking?"

Jeff scowled. "We have an issue in this section that I can't seem to resolve. There's a feedback loop that may be taking multiple paths at different times. Every adjustment I make, it shows up from another circuit. Adjust there and it comes back here."

"Is this the only issue?"

"No. Gnaga and his crew are having fits with the injector mechanism in the other room. And trust me, you don't want to go in there. They haven't bathed in days and are putting off quite a stench. I'm starting to smell a bit ripe myself."

Mace looked over the table. Could your feedback be transmitted over the air?"

Jeff grabbed Mace by the arms. "Great Scott! That's it! You've solved it!"

Mace stepped back with a half grin. "Really?"

Jeff laughed. "I'm sorry, no. I'm just a little punchy. I've checked repeatedly for broadcast interference and there is none."

Mace half smiled. "OK. I'll take that as a 'time to leave' signal. If you need anything, let us know. Oh, and make a few minutes available to think about an evac plan. The fighting here could start any day, and it may only last a day. So the minute they show, you need to be ready to move to Earth. Whatever you can't take with you, make plans to destroy. We don't want to leave them any gifts."

Jeff nodded. "I'll work on that. Thanks."

A second later, Jeff Moskowitz' attention was already focused again on the work at hand. Mace walked back to the shuttle and was soon back on the bridge of the *Rogers*. The defense of Divinia was organized. It was now just a waiting game.

Chapter 27

Jasper came over the comm. "We have everything in place. The stations are all manned. Stark's crews on those dreadnoughts are continuously running through simulations. Thanks for bringing this together. It at least gives us a fighting chance."

Mace said, "We do have one more option."

Jasper asked, "What's that?"

"We could start moving your people to Earth. It's only four billion here. With Earth's current population, it wouldn't even be crowded."

For several seconds, Jasper wasn't sure how to respond. "Would Stark allow it?"

"One way to find out. We have the gatrellium to spare. We could open a wormhole just above the atmosphere on both planets and put every shuttle we have to use moving bodies. Should I give Stark a comm?"

Jasper sighed. "I suppose that would be best. If we fail here, they would all be wiped out. At least back there they have one more shot at survival."

Mace opened a comm. "Stark, I have a new proposal. We'd like to start sending Targarian civilians through to Earth. We'll send enough food to support them and they'll be responsible for building their own housing."

Stark replied, "And what do we get in return?"

Mace pulled back. "In return? These people are fighting for your survival out here. The return is common decency among friendly species."

Stark thought for a moment. "The answer is no. We've set up our defenses. We've partitioned our lands. We don't have the room."

Mace replied angrily, "Don't have the room? All you have is room. I don't care if you turn over the Sahara for their use. Or Antarctica. They are capable of taking care of themselves."

Stark said, "Perhaps they can make use of the Moon or Mars."

Mace growled. "You know full well they don't have time to establish that kind of a colony. And they'd have no protection if the Karthians made it to Earth."

Jasper cut in. "No longer matters. We have wormholes opening. The Karthians are coming through."

Mace stared at the silhouetted image of Stark. "I'll deal with you later."

Stark replied, "I look forward to our exchange."

The comm closed. The Karthian ships numbered thirteen hundred eighty-six, plus the great station. As they began to form up, another set of wormholes opened and four hundred additional ships came through.

Mace's heart sank. He knew full well what was coming. A minute later, word came from Croawla that the extermination there was complete.

Mace opened a comm to Jeff Moskowitz. "Doc, time to go. Start moving everything you can. And don't hesitate. They could be hitting that city at the same time we're fighting them. We need you to get safely back to Earth. Not to add any pressure, but that weapon might be our only hope. The one we have, I can't use with solar flares anymore. They just move out of the way."

"We're packing up. I expect to be on a shuttle within two hours."

Mace frowned. "You may not have two hours, Doc. Just make sure you get all evidence of this experiment moved."

Mace closed the comm. "I'm wondering if we should be down there helping."

Johnny replied, "They aren't attacking yet. We have time."

Moments later, the Karthian fleet charged forward. The UF dreadnoughts, with their longer range weapons, fired first, knocking out six of the invading cruisers. The Karthians countered by focusing half their ships on this new group. The dreadnoughts managed two additional volleys before the Karthians returned fire. Nearly nine hundred cruisers fired at once, ripping into the dreadnoughts and taking nearly a third offline.

Mace said, "Jasper, the armor on those dreadnoughts is crap. They aren't gonna hold up."

Jasper replied, "Not much we can do. We have to protect these stations."

Another strong volley from the Karthians cut the dreadnought fleet in half. The Human commander, provided by Stark, ordered a retreat. The hundred and two remaining ships would sit on the periphery of the battle and attempt to pick away at the ships they could reach. The Karthians quickly refocused efforts on the microwave stations. Targarian attempts were made to use the holo-images of attached Karthian shuttles, but this time the attempts were failures.

The *Rogers* circled a pair of cruisers as Johnny, Jane, and Jenny boarded one shuttle and Jordan Crawford's team another. Mace worked the wormhole weapon as Hans Mueller fired the *Rogers'* cannons. The crew and their ship were effective, but hardly enough to counter the overwhelming numbers the Karthians had once again fielded. Several hundred cruisers broke off from the main fight and began to bombard cities below.

Mace opened a comm. "Doc, tell me you're on your way!"

Jeff was frantically carrying a box of drawings. "We've only managed half of what we need."

Mace sighed. "Crap. Johnny, Mr. Crawford, I need you back aboard when you finish each of your ships."

"Wrapping up now," replied Jordan. "Are we pulling back already?"

Mace shook his head. "No. We have to rescue our scientists. They're still attempting to move. Get back ASAP. We're gonna have to extract them ourselves. This fight is going bad in a hurry."

Johnny replied, "Two minutes and we're on our way!"

The *Rogers* circled and fired as her two shuttles moved back to the docking bays.

Once aboard, Mace gave the next order. "Set us down right beside the lab building, Mr. Hobbs. I want every free crewman down that ramp to help move them out!"

Mace said, "Doc, we'll be down there with help in a minute. Direct us as to what needs moving. This whole defense is about to collapse. A third of those stations are already down."

Jeff replied, "I'll be here. I need help with the prototype and our new build. The equipment and data should be clear by the time you arrive."

Mace stood and hustled toward the ramp. Three Karthian cruisers fired their weapons at once, all impacting the hull in close proximity. A hard jerk of the *Rogers'* hull launched Mace across the bridge and slammed him to the deck. He pulled himself up, shaking off the incident as he proceeded to run toward the main ramp.

The *Rogers* moved through Divinia's atmosphere as a giant ball of flame before quickly slowing as it arrived above the lab. Fifteen volunteers streamed down the ramp and into the lab building.

Jeff gave directions. "I need four of you over here. Pick up this frame. And be careful, the components are not fully fastened down and we need them intact. I need two over here for these barrels, and six at this table. Just carry everything you can. The rest of you, help me with this injection structure. It's heavy. Will take us all to lift it."

The items were moved as plasma blasts impacted the buildings in and around the lab complex. Smoke plumes were rising from the great blue city as many of its inhabitants ran about the streets. Chaos had come to the once peaceful center of the Targarian Empire.

The heavy structure was carried up the ramp and into the waiting *Rogers*. As it was set on the deck, a Karthian plasma round impacted the roof of the lab building, collapsing a large section, shrapnel flying in every direction.

Mace looked around and yelled, "Where's the Doc?"

Jeff stepped from behind the structure. "Here."

"Close up that ramp and let's get out of here."

Jeff stepped forward. "No! The prototype is still in there!"

Mace growled. "Johnny, come with me. Doc, you stay here and secure this stuff. Jenny, bring out a shuttle."

Mace opened a comm to the bridge. "Mr. Hobbs, as soon as my boots hit the ground I want you up and out of here. We'll follow in the shuttle."

Liam replied as a plasma blast rumbled the hull. "Will be my pleasure."

Mace and Johnny jumped from the bottom of the ramp as it began to close. Jenny slipped out of docking bay one, settling on the ground just outside the lab as the leader of the free Humans and his sidekick entered the failing structure.

Mace said, "Grrr. Hallway's blocked. We'll have to go around."

Johnny raised his glove. "No we don't."

The concussion wave from Johnny's glove busted a huge hole in the concrete block wall in front of them.

Johnny smiled as he gestured. "After you."

The wall collapsed in front of them, bringing with it materials from the floors above.

Mace shook his head as he turned back. "As I said... we go around."

Liam came over the comm. We're free of the atmosphere, Mr. Hardy."

Mace said, "We have a few minutes still. Take them to Earth and come back for us. We need them working on that weapon."

Liam asked, "You sure about that?"

Mace stopped, looking down a hall to check for a clear path. "I'm sure. We can keep ourselves alive for that long."

At the end of a short run, they kicked a door down. The lab room was full of dust that had yet to settle, and smoke from a dozen small fires.

"Crap, we'll have to dig for it. It was sitting on the table right there."

The two Humans began throwing aside the debris covering their prize. Johnny hoisted a heavy beam over his head before tossing it to the side.

"I do love these suits."

Mace replied, "Help me with this. I think it's... right there."

Mace grabbed the boxy device, quickly falling forward as he began to lift it. "Whoa. Gah! It's bolted down! We need a wrench!"

Johnny stepped up. "Move."

A concussion wave flew from the top of his glove, angled to only impact an exposed bolt-head. The steel bolt snapped off, shooting across the room, freeing the corner of the device. Two more attempts had all but a single corner free. A powerful plasma blast impacted the side of the lab building, sending debris in their direction. The two Humans were knocked to the floor.

"You still there?" Jenny asked.

Mace slowly pulled himself up. "Mostly."

Johnny rolled over and grunted, pushing himself to his feet. "So much for the proto."

A steel shank was buried in the front section of the device.

Mace said, "We still can't leave it. Hit that other corner."

Johnny stepped up to the table, firing a concussion wave into the bolt. The shaft bent but didn't break. A repeated attempt failed to free the device.

Johnny reached down, firmly gripping both sides of the frame, pulling with a fierce growl. The device lifted only slightly. Mace took hold and the two Humans pulled with all the might their exosuits could muster. The bolt snapped free.

Johnny said, "Lead the way!"

The building rumbled, dust clouds rose. Fires raged as the Karthian bombardment of the capital city increased in intensity. Mace sprinted and Johnny followed behind. The two emerged and immediately ran up the shuttle's ramp as Jenny directed it to close.

As the shuttle lifted, a heavy plasma round impacted its hull, slamming it to the ground and knocking out a third of its transducers. Mace and Johnny flew up against the ceiling and slammed back down to the deck. The device bounced from Johnny's grip, tumbling across the deck. Again the shuttle lifted, this time avoiding another plasma round, before shooting up and across the city center.

Mace slowly pushed himself up as Johnny rolled over. "Not sure how much more of that I can take."

Johnny chuckled and winced. "Yeah, not what I signed up for either. You said there would be cabanas and beaches."

Mace laughed as he stood. "You misheard. I said cannons and breaches."

Johnny took a deep breath. "Well, at least it all makes sense now."

Jenny asked, "You two OK?"

Mace moved up, dropping himself into the copilot's seat and strapping himself in. "How we looking?"

"Yentis is trashed. The microwave stations are almost all gone. Jasper is fighting on, but he has fewer than fifty ships left. This shuttle is damaged. We can't leave the atmosphere."

Johnny stood behind her chair. "We're stuck here?"

"Until the *Rogers* gets back, we are. All we can do is keep flying in the meantime."

Mace opened a comm. "Jasper, you have to leave. This fight is lost. Take what you have left and move back to Earth."

Jasper shook his head. "I won't abandon my people!"

Mace gave an angry reply. "Your people are Humans! We need your help! Don't throw your ships away for nothing! Divinia is gone! You dying won't change that!"

Jasper looked up at the bridge ceiling of the *Organ Cave*, and then around at her crew. "Pull back! All ships! Set a jump for Earth! We'll regroup there!"

Before Jenny could speak, the Targarian ships slipped away.

"Gah! Why didn't you have him swing by to grab us!"

Two Karthian cruisers broke off in pursuit of the shuttle. Jenny flew their vessel down to the deck, jinking, swerving and popping up and down to avoid the constant barrage of laser and plasma blasts.

As they moved up along a group of coastal mountains, Johnny said, "Take us down in the water! Those weapons will lose effectiveness!"

Jenny shook her head. "Can't do it. We aren't airtight anymore. We'd just fill with water and sink."

Mace opened a comm to Earth through one of the remaining orbital comm satellites. "Mr. Hobbs! Tell me you're jumping!"

Liam replied, "Two minutes at least. We're still on the ground."

Mace growled. "Just come back! We can unload later. We're damaged and stuck down by the surface!"

"We're on our way!"

The hull of the shuttle shook violently as a partial plasma round clipped her aft. A hard bank to port sent a laser pulse past her starboard side. Jenny pulled up and began flying straight.

Mace said, "What happened? What are you doing?"

"They all just left," said Jenny.

Mace asked, "Who left?"

Jenny gestured toward the nav display. The Karthians. They're all jumping away."

Johnny cringed as he gripped Mace's shoulder. "They're moving on to Earth."

Jenny shook her head. "No, they're jumping to the rift."

Mace looked over the display. "Why? They have us beat."

Jenny shrugged. "You want me to call them back? We can ask."

Johnny chuckled. "Sick sense of humor on this one. I like her."

Seconds later, a comm hail came in from Malcolm Stark. Jenny accepted.

A silhouetted Stark sat in his usual chair. "Mr. Hardy, glad to see you survived. I'm tempted to light this room just so you can see the grin on my face."

Mace asked, "What happened?"

"I did what I do best. I made a deal."

"What kind of deal? You had nothing to trade."

Stark nodded. "You are correct. But we... had something to trade. A huge stockpile of gatrellium at your Alpha Centauri site. Nicely hidden, by the way. My people almost missed it."

"What did you do with it? I don't understand."

Stark sighed. "I returned it to the rightful owners. With that, and with a forfeiture of all the colonies they had captured, they were appeased enough to leave Earth alone. You really did a number on them with the depot raids. You would have set their other plans back by years."

Mace shook his head. "You're a fool, Stark. You've just doomed us all. I'd be surprised if your little treaty lasts more than a week."

"It will last. I took precautions. I had your friend Mr. Knuttin broker the deal, and since the UF and the Karthians will now be occupying adjoining space, the Karthians will not want to break the agreement. Earth is now safe, Mr. Hardy. We can get on with the business of perfecting the wormhole weapon your ship just brought home, and in rebuilding our world.

"I'm quite proud of myself as I accomplished all this without firing a shot, although I will say I was disappointed in the performance of the UF dreadnoughts. We lost a hundred and eight crews before the retreat, but their sacrifice was needed to buy us time."

The *Rogers* settled into Divinia's atmosphere. The shuttle was brought aboard and they plotted a return trip to Earth. Jasper's ships were still coming through.

Mace opened a comm. "It's bad there. I know."

Jasper stood on a catwalk of the *Organ Cave* as it hovered above a devastated Yentis. "So many lives lost."

Stark joined in on the comm. "You can't be there, Mr. Collins. Those worlds now belong to the Karthians. You're risking breaking the very agreements we just signed."

Jasper said, "There are survivors down there. We have to help them."

Mace backed him up. "He's right. They aren't all dead."

Stark snarled. "And they aren't part of his kingdom anymore. His kingdom is gone, defeated. The survivors are now subjects of the Karthians. You're putting us all at risk by being there!"

Mace replied, "They are our people, Stark. They stood by us in this fight. We have room here on Earth. We need to bring them here. We owe it to them."

Stark stood in anger. "We owe them nothing! You are going to ruin this deal! The Targarians put us in this fight to begin with. I had a treaty all ready to be signed and they dashed in and broke it. Are you so dense you can't see this?"

Mace closed the connection with Stark. "Jasper, he's not gonna allow us to move them here to Earth, but we do have an option. We can take them to Hardy. It's uninhabited, it's unclaimed, and it's habitable. It will allow them a chance to reestablish a life there."

Jasper nodded as he looked over the destruction with a downtrodden face. "I suppose you're correct."

Mace replied, "I'll make a jump out to check its status. If all looks good, we'll assist with moving your people there. I'm thinking we need to do this as fast as possible before the Karthians come back."

The investigation of Hardy came back as expected. It remained unclaimed and was ready for immediate occupation. Targarian ships gathered up able-bodied workers for transport as the others who remained cared for the injured.

Four weeks passed before the last of the Targarians were moved from Divinia. With a population that had numbered close to eight billion, the Collins kingdom now counted only twelve million citizens.

Establishing the Targarian species on Hardy would be a struggle, and that struggle was compounded by the fact that Stark would have nothing to do with it. No help was offered and none would be forthcoming. To Malcolm Stark, they were Karthian subjects running afoul of their empire.

Back on Earth, the wormhole weapon project was taken over by Stark's people. Jeff Moskowitz, Gnaga Klept, and the others on his science team refused to offer assistance. Having the data and the unit that was nearly assembled, Stark made the decision to release the others. They moved back to the cave compound, where their efforts were put to use assisting the Targarians.

A Stark spy was finally outed. He had initially come in with Jordan Crawford's men and had been passing information to Stark since the beginning. He claimed to have mixed feelings about the venture, but had been unable to withdraw once in. From that point on, the otherwise happy community mostly kept to themselves.

From the chaos, a renewed Earth emerged. Trade was again established with Canto, new factories came online, and the fields of Earth were producing a large excess. Trade attempts with the Mawga had been cut off, their worlds placed off-limits to travel. The UF was tightening their grip.

For Humans, a new baby boom was underway. Efforts to repopulate the world with the recovered embryos was in full swing. With food and space being plentiful, the population was once again set to double. King Stark reigned supreme with the people's support. He had spared Earth from the Karthians and the masses were grateful for it.

For whatever reason, he spared Mace and the others, leaving them to govern themselves. Organ Cave had become their home. Earth had again survived.

∾∾∾∾∾

What's Next?

(Preview)
HADRON
(Vol. 7)
Havoc

This Human is asking for your help! In return for that help I have a free science fiction eBook short story, titled "THE SQUAD", waiting for anyone who joins my email list. Also, find out when the next exciting release is available by joining the email list at comments@arsenex.com. If you enjoyed this book, please leave a review on the site where it was purchased. Visit the author's website at www.arsenex.com for links to this series and other works.

The following preview of the next book in the series is provided for your reading pleasure. I hope you enjoy!

Stephen

Chapter 7.1

Five months after the Karthian peace agreement was signed, the *Rogers* settled on a broad tarmac in the city of New Yentis. The Targarians, ever busy, had just completed their first community center. Modeled after those on Earth, eight such centers were planned for the area in and around the new colony. Forests were being cleared and fields readied for planting. The first mine had been established and the first port dug out and readied for a fleet of fishing vessels.

Mace, using funds disbursed from his ownership in the Knuttin Corporation, had been busy acquiring colonization materials. The new colony at Hardy was in desperate need of all things mechanical. Machinery such as tractors or plows, or diggers for mining, were in high demand. Mace used the advice of Frado Knuttin to purchase the items most in need.

He sat in the dining hall on the *Organ Cave* with Jasper. "All things considered, I think you've got a good start on things here."

"Wish we'd had more time to salvage from Divinia."

Mace nodded. "Can't risk it now that the Karthians have moved in. Stark said they're clearing off every bit of your people's existence. They plan on letting the natural growth run wild for the next couple decades. After that, they'll consider it a resource for possibly populating. He says they are already looking to establish a colony on Croawla."

Jasper frowned. "It was a world rich in resources."

Mace said, "Look, I know all this has been extremely hard on you, but life is what it is. We take what we have and do the best we can. I know you're toying with how to get back at the Karthians. I think you need to set your house in order here first. The Karthians will still be out there when you're ready to deal with them. Any effort you put into thinking about it now only detracts from what you're doing here."

Jasper sighed. "I know. It's just some things can't be helped."

Mace said, "Well I know it's not much, but you at least have all the microwave stations here that Favia built for us. She was kind enough to donate nine hundred of them to you. She didn't have to give a single one."

Jasper nodded. "I know. And my people are ever grateful."

A comm came in from Stark. "Mr. Hardy, I don't know why I'm telling you this, but I just ended a long discussion with the Karthians. They wanted to know where their subjects went. They know they didn't kill everyone, and yet there is no one there."

"So what'd you tell them?"

Stark was silent.

Jasper stood. "I will kill you whenever I find out where you are."

Stark replied, "I had no choice, Mr. Collins. As I said before, they consider the Targarians their property. They felt that I aided and abetted in the theft of that property, and told me to my face that if I didn't tell them where you were, they would consider the agreement null and void, making Earth once again a target."

"I told you this would happen," said Mace.

"As I told you it would happen if you meddled in their affairs."

Mace shook his head. "Since you told us this, what would you have us do? Take them back?"

Stark said, "They would not accept that. What I would expect both you and Mr. Collins to do is to leave that planet. If they find Humans there, they will use that as an excuse to break the agreement."

Mace reached into the opening of his faceshield, rubbing his temples. "We're not abandoning the Targarians."

"Then you are dooming all Humans."

Mace stood and began to pace. "I have one alternative."

Stark said, "I'm listening."

Mace stopped. "We bring them home. Take them all to Earth."

Stark shook his head. "A ludicrous proposal."

Mace held up a hand. "Maybe. Can you tell me how many of those microwave stations you have? And how many ships?"

Stark was hesitant before answering. "Four hundred twelve stations, both orbital and ground. Three hundred six cruisers."

Mace nodded. "OK, we can add just over a hundred ships to that total. And about nine hundred microwave stations."

Stark crossed his arms. "What? Where did you get those?"

Mace replied, "Not saying. But I think we can get more. Possibly as many as three or four hundred. You agree to allow the Targarians to come to Earth, at least until they can get reestablished elsewhere, and I'll see to it that you have more than fifteen hundred stations pulling guard duty there at Earth."

Stark stood and began to pace as well. "If we had more ships I might consider this a valid offer, but I must decline. The two of you need to come home. I am certain the Karthians will be coming your way. And as I said, if Humans are found there, the agreement will be broken, exposing us to attack."

Jasper replied, "Listen, you putrid moron. These are my people. If the Karthians are on their way, then I will meet them here with everything I have. You keep acting as though you speak for all Humans, well you don't. Not this one anyway. Let the Karthians come. We'll give them a fight."

Mace looked into the comm camera. "I have to say that I'm with him. They're gonna come for us one way or another. You either fight along with us or you'll be fighting alone. If you send out your fleet, we could transport everyone home in a couple days. All the stations we have in orbit here would be moved, too. So pick your poison. All together or by yourself?"

Stark rubbed the top of his head in frustration. "Bring them. I'll have every transport and warship there for a pick-up within the hour. But we need to make haste. The Karthians may show up in a week, or it could be in an hour. But they will come."

Mace nodded. "Select an area on Earth they can inhabit and make it as ready as you can. We'll get things rolling here."

Over the two days that followed, twelve million Targarians were moved to Earth, along with the nine hundred microwave stations. Favia was contacted and a plea made for more stations. Three hundred eighty were offered and accepted.

As the last of the transports lifted off the planet Hardy, heading for the heavens, Mace ordered the *Rogers* to the ground and the ramp was lowered. He walked down to the end of the ramp and then spiked a metal rod into the ground.

Johnny asked. "What was that for?"

Mace smiled. "It was a leftover claiming tag from our work with Frado Knuttin and the UF. If the Karthians show, which they will, they'll have to think twice before trying to claim it for their own. They try to remove that marker and they risk war with the UF."

Johnny chuckled. "That ain't the UF's marker. They didn't plant it."

Mace nodded. "Technically, no. But the Karthians don't know that. And if I can convince Mr. Knuttin to file the claim, it at least keeps this planet from the Karthians. We'll no longer have it, but neither will they."

Johnny patted Mace on the back as they walked back up the ramp. "You're nothing but a troublemaker. Anybody ever tell you that?"

"My mom used to."

Johnny smiled. "I always liked your mom."

A week of peace passed. The Targarians were busy once again attempting to build up a community. This time they had resources to begin the process, and Humans seemed eager to help where they could.

A scout ship reported the Karthian visit to Hardy. Five hundred ships lingered in orbit, not risking a visit to the ground of a planet owned by another species, a species they had one previous encounter with at Rhombia. The thrashing they had taken there had convinced their admirals that Hardy was now off limits. The following day, the five hundred ships parked in near Earth space.

Stark opened a comm. "As I feared, our days are numbered."

Mace replied, "They were numbered anyway. You were just too pigheaded to see it. Have they made any demands?"

Stark sighed. "They won't return my hails. I believe this to be an attempt to breed fear."

Mace laughed. "Well, it's working. Mr. Knuttin has already canceled his trade shipments. The UF doesn't want to be involved, even if they one day will be."

Stark asked, "How do you mean?"

"The Karthians are now their neighbors. They fought them once at Rhombia and soundly drove them back. If the UF decides they want more space, they will look to expand this way, because they know the threat. Or at least think they do."

Stark rubbed his chin. "Astute thinking, Mr. Hardy. I must give you credit. I didn't think you capable."

Mace smiled. "That's one of your downfalls, Stark. You think you're brilliant and everyone else is an idiot. What you fail to grasp is that even idiots have brilliant thoughts from time to time."

Johnny laughed. "Did you just call yourself an idiot?"

"Don't be helping him."

Humphrey turned. "Multiple wormholes opening, Mr. Hardy. Ships coming through by the hundreds. Looks like they're bringing the fleet."

Mace said, "Johnny, call everyone in. Looks like today is the day we determine Earth's fate."

Johnny turned. "Well, definitely somebody determines Earth's fate."

The comms were made and within minutes the full crew was coming aboard. "Listen up, everyone. This may be our last fight. If we win here, the Karthians may decide we are better left alone. This is our planet, our ground, our home. I expect you'll all give it everything you have and then some. It will probably take that. Our fleet is small, but our determination big. And those microwave stations out there... Favia indicated they made improvements to the initial designs. She couldn't say what, just that they are supposedly better. And this time around we have a lot more of them.

"I've shared our tactics with Stark, so we should see similar shuttle assaults from his Marines. If we can make a heavy enough dent in their force early on, we might just drive them off without having to sacrifice ourselves. We've tried everything we possibly could. Determination is about all we have left.

"I'll add one more thing. If you're the praying type, you'll want to do that now. And if you're not, well, those who are could use your support. I expect the fighting to start in the next hour, so make your peace and prepare for the worst. This fight is not only for our freedom, but for our existence. We've tried about everything we can. This stand has to work. As a final say, as Shakespeare's Caesar said, 'Cry Havoc! And let slip the dogs of war!'"

Johnny chuckled as the comm closed. "Where'd you pull that one from? I never took you for Shakespeare."

"I think I've wanted to use that since the first time I heard it as a teenager."

Liam Hobbs said, "It's a worn-out phrase, Mr. Hardy. Perhaps something more like Churchill: *You can always count on Americans to do the right thing – after they've tried everything else.*"

Johnny laughed. "You trying to create an international incident here? How about something more along the lines of: *Never, never, never give up.*"

Liam nodded. "I suppose that would work too."

Mace turned to Humphrey Mallot. "Everyone aboard?"

Humphrey replied, "All accounted for, Mr. Hardy."

Mace gestured as he sat. "Take us up to the fleet, Mr. Hobbs. We'll wait it out there."

As before, the Karthian ships came all at once. The large number of microwave stations took a heavy first toll before a new weapon was unleashed. Tens of thousands of small missiles filled the space between the attackers and the orbital stations. The Human fleet attempted to destroy as many as they could, but a second wave pushed past into the stations. Three quarters of the Earth defense shield was taken out all at once. A third wave of missiles finished the job.

The Human fleet countered with more than five hundred assault shuttles while her warships moved into the fight. Karthian ships swirled, jinked, and cut back and forth in an attempt to keep the shuttles from attaching. Nearly half were destroyed when a fourth round of the small but powerful missiles were unleashed.

Jasper came over the comm. "We're losing this and losing it bad. Do we pull back to the Alpha site? Do we fight 'til the end right here?"

"I don't have the answer," said Mace. "I'm beginning to think the Alpha site might be the better option, but we'll need to get our people from the cave."

The hull of the *Rogers* rumbled and jerked as a half dozen Karthian cruisers focused their efforts on her.

Humphrey yelled, "We have six ships after us, Mr. Hardy! Those weapons will be doing severe damage if shots get coordinated, which I expect they soon will be."

Johnny said, "I can't get attached! Might be time we make a run to the cave and call this fight over!"

Mace returned the comm to Jasper. "Mr. Collins, we're cutting out. There's nothing more we can do here."

Jasper nodded. "I have my transports loaded with as many people as they can carry. We'll be escorting them out. Mr. Hardy, good luck and be careful. I wanna see you at the Alpha site. I'm thinking it may be time to become pirates in Karthian space. It won't get our worlds back, but I'm certain I can exact some revenge."

The comm closed as the remains of the Targarian fleet turned toward Alpha Centauri. Jordan Crawford's shuttle was soon aboard the *Rogers*, with Johnny, Jane, and Jenny close behind. The door to bay one was opened as they pulled alongside.

Five Karthian laser pulses impacted the bay area all at the same time. The Human ship jerked violently and shuddered as two decks of the port-side of the ship were ripped apart and set afire.

Liam yelled, "Breaking away! Mr. Tretcher, you're on your own!"

Humphrey added, "Two decks afire! We have casualties!"

Mace followed with, "Mr. Hobbs, get us home! Johnny, get to the cave!"

The aft of the *Rogers* took repeated hits as she raced toward the atmosphere. Bulkheads were sealed and the ship became a fireball as it sped down through the air. Two further strikes to the back of the ship shut down one of the gravity drives; the room that held the controls was violated and filled with flames.

Liam yelled, "We're coming in hard! Brace! Brace! Brace!"

The *Rogers* swooped in, slowing with all the power she had left. As Liam pulled back hard on the controls, a move that had no more affect than an soft pull, the *Rogers* leveled off. As she headed into a valley on the opposite side of a mountain from the cave, three additional laser pulses crippled her remaining drive.

The once great ship dropped into the trees, skidding along as it carved a path of destruction into the forest floor. Tree trunks, dirt, and rocks flew as the lower decks were shredded by the impact.

After what seemed like an eternity of skidding, the *Rogers* came to a stop. Flames began to spread as the hydrogen store spewed fuel from a tiny but deep hole in its redundant linings. A hundred meter tall column of fire billowed up from the back of the ship and the cruisers chasing behind turned away in victory to pursue other targets. The *Rogers* had seen its last fight.

∼∼∼∼∼

Once again, this Human is asking for your help! If you enjoyed the book, please leave a review on the site where it was purchased. And by all means, please tell your friends! Any help with spreading the word is highly appreciated!

Also, I have a free science fiction eBook short story, titled "THE SQUAD", waiting for anyone who joins my email list! By joining, also find out when the next exciting release is available. Join at comments@arsenex.com. Visit the author's website at www.arsenex.com for links to this series and other works!

Take care and have a great day!

Stephen

Printed in Great Britain
by Amazon